DEADFALL

Also by Patti Davis
(with Maureen Strange Foster)

HOME FRONT

DEADFALL

A Novel by

PATTI DAVIS

CROWN PUBLISHERS, INC.
NEW YORK

I would like to thank David MacMichael and Eric Hamburg for all their help and patience in answering my endless questions. I would also like to express my gratitude to Mike Farrell, Haskell Wexler, David Seltzer, Betty A. Prashker and David Groff, Larry Thompson, Jack Artenstein, and Dr. Milton Wexler. And, as always, thank you, Paul, for living through another story with me.

CROWN is a trademark of Crown Publishers, Inc.

Manufactured in the United States of America

Library of Congress Cataloging-in-Publication Data

Davis, Patti.
Deadfall / by Patti Davis.
I. Title.
PS3554.A93762D44   1989
813'.54—dc19   89-1249

ISBN 0-517-57405-5

Designed by Shari deMiskey

10 9 8 7 6 5 4 3 2 1

FIRST EDITION

Hunters sometimes
capture their prey by using a
trap with a falling weight,
designed to maim or kill the animal.
This type of trap is called a
deadfall.

PART ONE

1

A LIGHT CAME INTO THE ROOM IN THE LATE AFTERNOON —an autumn light that glinted through the pine trees and drizzled through the lace curtains. It reminded Darren of something—an imprint from another time, another place—but she could never trap the memory long enough to identify it. Always it would flutter away into the soft wash of sunlight.

For most of the afternoon she had tried to capture this light, mixing and remixing her watercolors until she had filled the palette with puddles of color that didn't quite match the deep gold of the November sun. Several pieces of crumpled Strathmore lay at her feet. She closed her eyes and imagined the dull gray of a winter day. Opening her eyes on the paints and ignoring the streams of sunlight, she mixed the colors of a rainy day. On a clean piece of Strathmore, she did a blue-gray wash, studied it for a moment, and waited for a spark to ignite in her imagination. Nothing.

I could always start painting reindeer on black velvet, she thought.

The struggle had gone on for weeks now, and she understood it better than she wanted to. While Darren tried to paint colorful portraits of the seasons, something restless and troubling was trying to bubble to the surface. Its colors were dark and wanted to be painted, but she shied away, frightened by their power.

It was through an artist's eyes that she had first looked at the house. She and Andrew had walked in from the swirl of a windswept day, with yellow leaves blowing across the brick path and the air bristling with the smell of the sea. The house was sixty years old, with french windows and doors and a huge stone fireplace. The paint on the windowsills was blistered and some of the glass panes were cracked. Everywhere she looked she saw age and neglect, but there was an alcove off the dining room just big enough for her art table, where shafts of sunlight streaked the floor. She envisioned herself painting in that small, windowed room, and the picture felt comfortable and right.

They had been renting a house in Venice then, and Darren was forced to work in the garage because she had changed from watercolors to encaustic—a dangerously combustible process of melting down beeswax and adding powdered pigment and resin. The result was a thick, pastelike substance, which she then poured onto a canvas. Because of the consistency of the mixture, she was able to stick bits of paper or tin or even wood onto the canvas.

Working in encaustic had brought Darren her first taste of success. Some local galleries had displayed her work, and she had sold several large pieces. Until one afternoon when something went wrong.

The most dangerous part of the preparation was making the resin. She had to add turpentine to resin crystals and then heat it up, hopefully without it exploding into flames, but never without extremely toxic fumes. Protected by a face mask, she had been heating the resin over a low flame when suddenly one wall of the garage was in flames. She ran outside screaming for Andrew.

After the fire trucks left, Andrew led Darren into the living room and, after several deep breaths, said, "Look, I really don't want to thwart your creativity, but I thought your watercolors were really good. Maybe you could go back to that?"

"No problem," she said. "I regard this as a message from God."

She suspected that Andrew doubted the sincerity of her resolution, however, because during the move from Venice to their new home in Santa Monica Canyon, the hot plate she had used to melt down the resin vanished. She never said anything; she was perfectly content to work with nontoxic, noncombustible materials, even though no galleries seemed to agree with her choice.

It was just before five; the light faded so quickly this time of year. Andrew would be home soon, and Darren walked through the living room turning on lamps. When she started to close the drapes, her eye caught the silver-framed photograph of their wedding that was on the end table by the couch. Picking it up, she studied it with the curiosity of a visitor. The ocean was in the background—it had been her idea to get married on the beach—and they were both barefoot, she in a white cotton Victorian dress ("A slip," her grandmother would have said. "The girl's getting married in her underwear.") and Andrew in white draw-string pants and a white gauze shirt. His hair was long then—chestnut waves that tumbled over his shoulders. She remembered the day he cut it and how startled she had been that she actually liked it better.

Darren stared at her own image. Outwardly, she hadn't changed that much; her blond hair still fell to her waist and her face didn't reveal that she was twenty-seven. But her eyes had changed. The girl in the photograph had a look as wide and untroubled as a summer sky. She knew she would never again look at the world through those eyes.

In the five years they had been married, Andrew had made several highly acclaimed documentaries, putting them in the same tax bracket with people they had, at one time, ridiculed. Gradually, their orange-crate tables and garage-sale pieces had been replaced with antiques. Still, despite his success, Andrew's gift was his ability to make films about oppressed people and unjust situations without seeming to preach.

Darren looked out the window and frowned at the gathering darkness. She had a habit of worrying whenever Andrew was late, and as she watched night drift into the sky, she thought of how they had parted that morning—with a strange, hollow feeling between them. During the night, sometime after a late phone call had crashed into their sleep, silence had settled on them, large as an avalanche. In the morning it was there, filling the house with its cold solidity. They had gone about their morning ritual of making coffee and sharing the paper, but Darren could hear the rush of distance separating them. It was, she knew, one of the inexplicable changes that occur in the seasons of a relationship. As quickly as it had come it would melt away, like a frozen stream thawed by the sun.

She was jarred out of her thoughts by the sound of a fist pounding on the door.

"Hi, Leland," she said as she opened the door.

"Hi. I wanted to ask you something," Leland said, in a loud voice. Darren had watched Leland grow into an eight-year-old inventor of bizarre experiments and elaborate games. His questions were never typical of an eight-year-old. Aside from a rather quirky mind, he also had trouble adjusting the volume of his voice. If he had been a stereo, someone would always have been turning him down.

"Sure, Leland, what is it?"

"Can I borrow your lawn mower?"

"Leland, it's nearly dark out. Besides, I think the lawn mower is a little big for you. Why don't you just wait until the gardener comes next week, and—"

"I don't wanna mow the lawn," he said, his voice growing even louder. "I wanna put it in the swimming pool to see if it'll float. You know, like a motorboat. Y'see, I figure if I can rev it up enough, the motor might make it like a boat. But I guess I'd have to put rudders on it or something, or maybe a sail. . . ."

Although she had known him for two years, Darren still had trouble navigating the hairpin turns of Leland's imagination.

"It won't float, Leland. It will sink."

"How do you know? Did you try it?"

"No, I read it in a magazine. Someone else tried it and the lawn mower sank."

"What magazine?" Leland said.

"*Omni*. I read it in *Omni*. It was a very scientific experiment."

Leland knit his eyebrows as if he were mentally reviewing all the back issues of *Omni*, trying to figure out which one he had missed. "OK," he said finally. "Well, bye."

Andrew pulled into the driveway as Leland was walking back to his house, his blond head bobbing up and down with his determined gait. Darren knew something was going to end up in the pool.

"Hi, Leland," Andrew called out as he walked toward the house. "You look like you're late for an important appointment."

"I am," Leland said without breaking stride.

"I was getting worried," Darren said, standing on her toes to kiss Andrew.

"Darren, I wish you'd stop assuming I've been run over by a semi every time I'm a little bit late. You remember we talked about that suggestion box somewhere out there in the universe? Well, you keep throwing these little suggestions out into the cosmos. It's making me very nervous."

"Sorry. I just . . . Sorry, you're right. So, what was your meeting about?"

Andrew moved away toward the lawn and stood looking up at the sky. Night lay in soft folds on the ground and the yellow porch lamp cast stripes of light on his face.

"Wait, don't tell me," Darren said. "They want you to do a documentary about astronomy."

"No, not quite. I'll tell you about it in a few minutes."

She walked over to Andrew and rested her head against his shoulder. The thin slice of a new moon hung in the sky and the Big Dipper winked down at them. They stood quietly as

7

the wind shivered the trees and a squirrel chirped somewhere above them.

"You know, when I was a kid," Andrew began as if he were talking to the sky, "I used to stand out in the flower bed and wiggle my feet down into the soil. Then I'd take the watering can and pour water around my feet so I'd grow. I thought if I could just grow up and be big, nothing would confuse me."

"Andrew, is this apropos of something?"

"I'm not sure. I think we should open a bottle of wine," he said, turning toward the house.

"This is sounding more ominous every minute," Darren mumbled, following him.

Andrew poured chardonnay into two Waterford goblets.

"And the good crystal, too? You're either having an affair or you've taken up gambling and lost everything we have. Is that what you're about to tell me?"

"Darren, doesn't your imagination ever get tired of working overtime?"

They sat on the couch and Darren waited while Andrew took a long sip of wine and stared out the window.

"What would you say if I told you that nothing changed in Nicaragua after the Iran-contra scandal?" he said finally. "If I said that American arms were still being sent over there?"

"Oh, Jesus. I see where this is going and I don't like it. What would I say? I'd say I'm not terribly shocked."

"But wouldn't you agree that some people might be?"

"Maybe. But I don't think making a film about it is necessarily going to spark nationwide concern. That's what this is about, isn't it? You've been asked to do a film in Nicaragua."

"Yes, and I'm not so ready to write it off as a bad idea. Darren, what were the hearings and the indictments and the outrage all about if nothing has changed? If someone is flying weapons into Nicaragua, the CIA knows they're flying them in. Think about it, think about the implications. It's like the Iran-contra hearings were a joke."

Darren felt her throat tighten and her voice sounded thin

"Are you two brothers?" Andrew asked, thinking Danny might have gotten their last names wrong. They were both dark haired and had the same olive skin. Anthony was a plumper version of George, who, with his high cheekbones and straight nose, looked like a Latin lover straight from central casting.

"No," George said, smiling smoothly, as if he were used to the question. "We've known each other since we were kids, though, so maybe that has something to do with it."

Andrew ordered coffee from the waiter, and Danny leaned forward excitedly, obviously relishing his role as go-between.

"You're really going to like this project, Andrew," he said. "Go on, George, fill him in."

"We've seen some of your work," George began, "and we were very impressed. Then, after we talked to Danny, we were sure you were the right person to direct this project."

"Have you ever been to Nicaragua?" Anthony asked.

"My wife and I were going to take our vacation there last year, but the plane fares to Hawaii were so much more reasonable."

Neither of them cracked even a smile.

"It's a bad situation, Andrew," George said, shaking his head and staring down at the table. "Nothing's changed—that's what we want to show. And where are the contras getting American-made weapons? Because that's what they have. Someone obviously wasn't too intimidated by the Iran-contra indictments. And here's the really alarming thing: we talked to some children in the hospital who had been shot—one kid almost died from his wounds—and they told us that it wasn't only contras who shot at them. There were some Americans in the group of men who attacked their village."

Darren watched Andrew pour some more wine into her glass. "I was really impressed with these guys," he said. "I guess I wasn't expecting to be."

"Let's not forget, Andrew, that many people might look at your parents and assume that you, too, are worth millions. There are only a few of us who know that you were disinherited as

11

soon as you voiced any inkling of social conscience, which was—what? At age seven?"

"Good point." Andrew laughed. "So I guess I shouldn't assume people are selfish just because they're rich."

"Right. Now that we've settled that, let's go get some dinner. Everything in the refrigerator has rigor mortis."

They drove up the hill to Montana Avenue and managed to get a table right away in a small Italian restaurant where the wait was usually at least twenty minutes. Both of them were careful to avoid the subject of the film until, midway through her pasta, Darren put her elbows on the table and stared at Andrew with a determined look on her face.

"Yes?" he said tentatively.

"I've made a decision."

"I can't wait to hear it."

"I'm going with you to Nicaragua."

"Darren, I should have stopped you after one glass of wine. You're speaking in tongues."

"No, I'm not. I'm serious," she said.

"If I remember correctly, you were the one who decided that accompanying me on films wasn't a very good idea. Has time dimmed your memory?"

"No, but I have the right to change my mind."

"It was a mutual decision, which means I have to change mine, too, and so far I don't see that in the forecast," Andrew said.

Darren had acted as Andrew's assistant on two documentaries. One was a short, informational film shot in Tokyo, which was supposed to document the invasion of American influence. Into a tradition-steeped culture of delicate, wispy art and lengthy tea ceremonies had come McDonald's, Levi's, and punk rock. It had meant a lot of filming in the streets. Darren's job was to relay messages from Andrew to the one interpreter working with them. She was also expected to hold back the bystanders who pressed forward with intense curiosity.

The thick summer air simmered with the smells of car exhaust and fish and too many bodies poured into streets too narrow to accommodate them. After a while their language sounded to Darren like the clicking sounds of dolphins. She tried to imagine dolphins swimming in a sparkling sea, arching and diving—anything to take her mind off the heat and the crowd.

"Darren, we can't work with all these people in the way! Get them back!" Andrew shouted. His face was streaked with sweat and his T-shirt clung to his skin.

"I'm trying, goddamn it! No one in this damn country speaks English!"

"We don't need to," said the interpreter. "We live in Japan."

The other film was shot in Mexico. Look how these people live, it was supposed to say. No wonder they crawl through brambles and sewer pipes to cross the border. Look at the poverty they're trying to escape.

And Darren had looked—at women washing their hair with Tide and rinsing it with garden hoses, at two-year-old children sucking on breasts that had probably nursed too many before them. The women looked back at her as if it were a birth defect to have such fair skin and blond hair.

She was sick for a month after they came home. Her body refused to hold on to food for more than an hour. It rejected it violently, one way or another.

"Andrew, I'm not going with you on any more films," she had said in a thin voice while she knelt on the bathroom floor. "We always end up fighting, and I think it's becoming hazardous to my health."

"Darren, you never had to go in the first place," he had said softly, sitting down beside her and pushing her hair back from her face. "I know you want to be supportive, but I don't want you doing things you're not happy doing. Now, would you please go to the doctor—you probably have dysentery."

Andrew tried to eat his dinner, but Darren's determined look tugged at his attention.

"No, Darren. The answer is no. There are risks, as you so eloquently pointed out earlier this evening."

"That's why I want to go with you."

13

"Got a sudden fascination for the hot spots of the world?"

"No, I just don't want you to go without me. If you're going into a dangerous situation, I want to go with you. I'm not kidding about this, Andrew. I'm very serious."

"Makes perfect sense to me. Why put one of us in danger when we can endanger both of us?" He sighed. "Darren, I'd like to finish the rest of my dinner. Can we discuss this later?"

"How much later?" she said, still staring at him.

"At least two hours. I want my food to be completely digested."

They drove home with the windows down and the smell of the sea rushing through the car. Night had washed down from the mountains and gathered in the quiet canyon streets; lights winked through the pine and eucalyptus. Darkness brought a serenity to the canyon, a feeling that the hustle of the city was distant and unimportant.

She didn't mention Nicaragua again until they were lying in bed, cradled in the stillness of the late night.

"So, is Danny going with us to Nicaragua?" she whispered, moving over to Andrew and resting her head on his chest. His heartbeat was steady and strong beneath her cheek.

"With *us?* Darren, your knack for subtlety is astounding. I'm surprised this is so important to you."

"Well, it is. I just want to be with you."

She slid on top of him and kissed his neck and shoulders, working her way down his body.

"I'm almost certain it's illegal to use sex to get your way," he said.

"No, it was legalized last year. Didn't you read about it?" Darren said, sliding her mouth across his stomach.

"OK, I'll make a deal with you," he said, his breath catching as she took him in her mouth. "You can come for a week."

Darren lay awake long after Andrew had fallen asleep. He goes to sleep so easily, she thought as a passing car disturbed the silence. She listened for it to pull into a driveway or turn around in the cul-de-sac and drive past again.

"I love you," she whispered to Andrew's back, curling around him and slipping her arm around his ribs. The mossy, damp-earth smell of their lovemaking came to her from the depths of the bed, and she took deep breaths of it, wanting it to seep into her dreams.

But instead sleep brought with it the image of a silver wolf, his coat gleaming in the moonlight as he ran across dark fields. Suddenly, without breaking stride, he was above the fields—above the earth—racing toward the moon, which grew larger and more luminous as the wolf got closer. For a quick second his silhouette was etched there. Then, just as quickly, he was gone. Only a trail of smoke was left, gray and wispy, across the face of the moon.

2

AS THE PLANE BEGAN ITS DESCENT INTO MANAGUA, DANNY said, "Well, you two, this is the test. Is this plane big enough that the guys in the control tower will spot it? Or is there a control tower at all? Speaking strictly for myself, although I'm sure Darren here shares my sentiments, I was sort of disturbed that we weren't flying on TWA or Delta or something. I mean, Lacsa Airlines? I get nervous if the airline doesn't have a commercial running on national TV."

"How do you know I share your sentiments?" Darren asked, looking across the aisle at Danny's lanky frame folded uncomfortably into his seat.

"Because I know how you love going on location shoots. I'm surprised you came at all. If you think you had trouble finding something you could eat in Japan, wait till you check out the menus in Central America!"

"I did all right in Japan."

"Oh, sure! What about the day we found you running through the streets of Tokyo yelling 'Free the fish! Free the fish!' It was very embarrassing. I don't think they even have a word for 'vegetarian' in Japanese."

"Look down there," Andrew said, pointing to the green, rubble-strewn area in the center of the city, which had been downtown until the 1972 earthquake destroyed it. Somoza had bulldozed the collapsed buildings and left the shells of others standing, and that was how it had remained.

Towering over the expanse of wreckage was the pyramid-shaped Inter-Continental Hotel and the Bank of America, a sky-scraper that looked strangely out of place. To the north Nicaragua's largest volcano, Momotombo, was reflected in the glassy waters of Lake Managua, and to the south the smaller Santiago volcano leaked smoke into the sky.

The sign outside Sandino International Airport read, *Bienvenido a Nicaragua Libre*.

"Welcome to Free Nicaragua," Andrew translated. "I guess whoever wrote that didn't know the 'moral equivalent of our founding fathers' would come along to argue the point."

The air was gritty and thick with volcanic dust. Darren felt it collect in her mouth and crunch between her teeth; her eyes felt like they were encrusted with sand. She started to wish she hadn't insisted on coming. She hated hot, dry weather; it made her feel irritable and queasy. At that moment the fog was probably curling around their house back in California, thick and gray and swollen with moisture. It would be hovering over the canyon and curling through the streets, soft and quiet as a ghost. She tried to sustain the image in her mind as dust blew past her face.

"Andrew, are you sure someone's supposed to meet us?" Darren asked as they waited outside the terminal with their suitcases.

"That's what they said."

"Well, if no one shows we'll just take a cab," Danny said. "What's the name of the place we're staying?"

Andrew stared down at the curb. "Uh . . . it'll come to me in a minute. I know it's right near the airport. The name will come back to me, just give me a minute."

"Hmm . . . this could be a problem," Danny said. "And me without my American Express card."

Just then a Toyota Land Cruiser pulled up to the curb and a short, round-bellied man jumped out. "Hi, one of you Andrew Laverty?"

"Yeah, me," Andrew said. "And this is my wife, Darren, and Danny."

The man nodded in greeting. "Sorry I'm late. I'm Cory Barnet. I'm here to take you to the hotel. It'll be a short drive— see, it's right across the road there."

"Would it be possible to drive around a bit?" Andrew asked. "I mean, if you have time."

"Sure." Cory shrugged. "It's not the most scenic city in the world, but I guess you know that already."

"I was hoping we could stop in at some art museums," Danny said, sounding quite serious.

Cory gave him a puzzled look until Andrew said, "Don't pay any attention to him. He's only serious about one percent of the time, and that wasn't it."

They pulled away from the airport and turned onto the highway, which was potholed and rutted. Cory maneuvered as if he were driving through a mine field. Between the swerving of the car and the smells of diesel and garbage, Darren felt her stomach start to roll with nausea.

Beside Pepsi signs were walls slashed with red-and-black painted revolutionary slogans. *Sandino Vive* was scrawled across the side of a building next to an advertisement for Esso gasoline. They passed small wood shanties where people sat staring at the road with eyes as dry as the wind. Sandinista soldiers in green fatigues carried rifles and looked better fed than the peasants tugging heavy carts along the side of the road. In the dusty afternoon heat women carried babies in netting on their shoulders, walking slowly past the rusted skeletons of abandoned cars.

A little farther along they passed the Camino Real Hotel, its elegance appearing like a mirage in a wasteland of poverty.

"I guess they were all booked there, huh?" Danny said, and by the tone of his voice, Andrew could tell he was almost serious. With accommodations like that, Danny might never want to leave.

"Sorry," Cory said. "That was a little out of the budget."

They passed *La Prensa* and the Coca-Cola factory, which, Andrew reminded them, was once managed by one of the contra leaders, Adolfo Calero.

Around a curve in the highway, the ruins of downtown yawned before them. Cavernous buildings stood blackened and crumbling in the hot, dusty wind. In the doorway of an abandoned factory, a young boy sat drawing pictures in the dust with his toes.

"People live in these buildings?" Andrew said.

"Yep. With no running water or electricity."

"I think we should come back and film some of this," Andrew said to Danny. "Cory, are George and Anthony staying at the same hotel we are?"

"Uh-huh. But they're not there now. They wanted to shoot some nature shots—you know, show what a beautiful country this is—so they're spending the night out tonight. I'll drive you guys up in the morning."

"Out where?" Darren asked, giving Andrew a hard look.

"Oh, it's north a ways," Cory said. "There's no fighting around that area, don't worry. We'll just be there for the day tomorrow. Yeah, I'll tell you, those two are pretty committed. I don't know if I'd spend the night out in the jungle, war or no war."

The Hotel las Mercedes was a one-story, rustic building that reminded Darren of a cheap Los Angeles motel.

"At least we'll all be on the same floor," Danny said as they got out of the car.

"They got a swimming pool here," Cory told them, handing Andrew his suitcase and carrying Darren's for her.

"All right! Just like Club Med!" Danny laughed.

19

Cory waited in line with them, tapping a cigarette against the palm of his hand and glancing quickly around the lobby.

A man checking in ahead of them walked away and retrieved a woman who had squeezed herself into a corner, trying to look inconspicuous and failing miserably.

"Just another no-tell motel," Andrew whispered to Darren. "Doesn't matter what country you're in, there's always someone fucking around on his wife or vice versa."

"Have you made a survey of this, or are you confessing something to me?"

"Survey."

Cory left them after they had checked in and said he'd meet them downstairs at seven in the morning.

Their room had dark walls of cheap paneling and two queen-sized beds. The orange flowers on the bedspread provided the only splash of color.

"I'm glad we're not going to be spending a lot of time in here," Andrew said. "I could become very depressed in this room."

They left their suitcases packed and went to rescue Danny from a room that was identical except that the flowers on his bedspread were blue.

"Come on, let's get some food," Andrew said.

"Should I take the antibiotics before or after we eat?" Danny asked.

"You know, in some ways you and Darren are very similar."

Several minutes later they sat in the hotel restaurant studying the menu, although Andrew was the only one with a reasonable command of the language.

"We'd better order the *plato típico*," he said. "I think it's probably our safest bet."

"Andrew, how do you know?" Darren said. "It could be cows' udders . . . or some other part."

"No, those are out of season," Danny said, looking intently at the menu. "Especially the other parts. Gee, Darren, my Spanish is a little rusty, but it looks to me like you should consider running through the streets of Managua yelling 'Free the horses!' "

Darren leaned toward Andrew. "Maybe we could just ask for a bowl of water on the floor for Danny."

When the waiter came up, they ordered beers and took Andrew's suggestion about the *plato típico*.

The beer was labeled Victoria, and Danny scrutinized the bottle, holding it up to the light and turning it around. "Looking for a worm in the bottom?" Andrew said.

The *plato típico* consisted of shredded beef, a mixture of red beans and rice, a vegetable concoction, and a soft, pale slab of cheese, which Andrew took a courageous bite of only to discover it was so salty that he drained the rest of his beer in less than a second.

Darren pushed the shredded beef into a corner of her plate and searched through the rest for signs of meat. She tentatively ate some of the vegetables and the rice and beans, but decided she wasn't hungry enough to take too much of a risk since the food was floating in some sort of unidentifiable liquid.

Cory was waiting for them at seven the following morning. Darren felt the air swelling with heat; a weak wind stirred the smells of car exhaust and cooking grease.

"How far are we going?" Andrew asked, climbing into the front seat beside Cory. Darren and Danny settled into the back.

"We're going to be heading north for about four hours. It's going to get pretty hot, so I brought along some canteens of water. Help yourselves when you get thirsty."

Andrew picked up a map from the dashboard and saw that if they continued north, they would come to dense woodland close to the Honduran border.

"We staying on the highway?" Andrew asked Cory.

"Until Matagalpa—then it gets a little more adventurous."

After about ten miles the air started to get cleaner; the patches of green dotting the landscape reminded Darren of California's terrain. But her illusion was ruined by small shacks, crudely built from rough, splintery boards, squatting on the dry ground in undisguised poverty. Darren saw someone milking a cow that had its back legs tied together. A young girl was carrying a pail of milk into one of the shacks.

The sun was climbing in the sky. She could feel her sweat mix with the dust and her tongue was getting thick and sticky. She opened the canteen that was beside her on the seat and took a gulp of warm water. It tasted like iodine pills and smelled like a swimming pool. Passing it to Danny, she said, "I'd suggest holding your nose before swallowing any of this."

"Sorry about that," Cory said, glancing at her in the rearview mirror. "But I don't think you'd like the results if the water wasn't treated."

After about ninety minutes they saw a cluster of buildings ahead of them.

"Why don't I stop here and we can grab something to eat. Might just be some candy bars, but I'll take anything at this point," Cory said.

The map told Andrew the town was called Sébaco. It was small and surrounded by patches of farmland. They found a tiny, one-room store and bought Cokes and candy bars and packages of fried banana chips. As they were paying, they heard giggling behind them and turned around to see children huddled around the door.

"*Cebollas! Cebollas!*" they shouted as the four of them passed. They were shoving bunches of onions at them. One little girl touched Darren's hair and giggled again.

Darren realized how unusual she must look in this dusty country. Her blond hair and pale blue eyes spoke of another world, far away from their heat-laden highways and the rasp of dry winds.

Another child was pointing at Danny's head and laughing so hard he dropped the onions on the ground.

"What? What?" Danny said, feeling his hair. "OK, c'mon—do I have a bird sitting on my head or something?"

"I think it's your hair, Danny," Andrew said. "Bend down so they can touch it." Danny's light brown hair resembled an inflated Brillo pad; with the sun behind him, he looked like he was wearing a halo. The children had probably never seen anything like it; maybe they thought he was an angel, or just a strange person dressed up to look like one. They touched his hair and withdrew their hands quickly, as if they thought it would burn them. By now they were all laughing at this new game.

"Hey, we gotta go," Cory said. *"Tengo que ir,"* he said to the children.

Farther north they had to stop several times for herds of long-horned cattle that made their lazy way across the road. Men on small horses coaxed them along, but with no great sense of urgency.

As they passed through Matagalpa, Andrew checked the map again and pointed out a river called Río Grande de Matagalpa. Darren expected to see a wide, deep body of water carving its way across the land, but after a few miles all she noticed alongside them was a narrow, winding creek.

"Cory, where is this river—the Río Grande de Matagalpa?" she asked.

"You're looking at it." Cory laughed. "The saying here is 'Es grande no porque es amplio, porque es largo.' It's big not because it's wide, but because it's long."

"You seem to know a lot about this country," Darren said. "Have you been here many times?"

"A couple," he said in a clipped voice.

"Ever worked on a film before?" Andrew said. Darren could tell from his eyes that he had noticed the change in Cory's tone.

"Nope. My buddy and I thought it sounded like an interesting project, so we volunteered for the job. Don't have to know much about filming to do the driving and grunt work, you know?"

"Uh-huh. George and Anthony had a cameraman they wanted to use. Is he with them?"

"Sure is. He got in yesterday," Cory said.

"And your friend is there, too?"

"Uh-huh."

Silence settled on them as heavy as the sweltering day. The

world was a noiseless swirl of dust and heat, interrupted only by the rumble of the tires on the road and the air rushing by.

At Jinotega the road became steep and winding. Below were basins of lush farmland; it looked like a painter had spilled green paint on the landscape. Darren could see men working in the glossy leaves of the coffee trees.

"Harvest time," Cory said, squinting down at the trees.

When they reached Bocay, the pavement ended and the road from that point on was dirt. Men in rubber boots and straw hats rode past them on horseback. They drove across several shallow streams and Darren thought of asking if they were impassable in the rainy season. But she was too tired from the heat to engage Cory in another conversation. She looked out the window at women washing clothes and laying them on the rocks to dry. It was a different civilization, caught in a different time.

A spotted wildcat bounded across the road. Around some of the bends, they caught glimpses of the blue water of the Bocay River far below.

Cory slowed down and turned sharply to the right. He was heading toward a thick wall of trees.

"I don't want to alarm you guys," Danny whispered loudly, "but I think the heat's gotten to him. He's driving us into the trees."

"Don't worry, there's a way through," Cory said.

The way through was a path just wide enough for one car. Suddenly, there was no sky, only trees—a soft, sun-prismed world where green was the only color. A flapping of wings came from somewhere in the tall trees, but the sound bounced and echoed, as if defying anyone to locate the noisemaker.

They drove deeper into the jungle. As the trees got thicker and long vines slapped the windshield, Darren felt herself losing her sense of direction.

Her watch told her it was eleven-thirty; the light in the jungle told her nothing. She knew that, in this green world, time didn't matter. There was day and night and the buzzing of insects and the light footsteps of unseen animals. And no matter what happened to them, the jungle would not change. It would go on, in complete and calm indifference to the lives and deaths of people. Darren felt a dizzying rush of fear—the fear of being overpowered by elements she didn't understand. They were trespassers in a place that would make no allowances for them. Leaves would fall and rot in the shallow indentations of their footprints and vines would creep across the paths they carved, covering the tracks of all who passed through and all who stayed.

3

A RED JEEP WAS PARKED IN A CLEARING LIKE SOME STRANGE flower blooming in the jungle. Three men stood around it talking. One was a small, wiry man whose body looked like it had stalled at some crucial junction between adolescence and adulthood. His hair was an indecisive blond, tied back in a ponytail, and his jeans hung precariously on his narrow hips.

The other two, she knew, had to be George and Anthony. One was tall and wore designer jeans and a pale blue shirt; the shorter of the two had on white shorts and a white T-shirt.

"Oh, Cory, you sneak," Danny said. "You didn't tell us there was a tennis court nearby. I would have dressed in my country club outfit."

"I told 'em to wear long pants," Cory said as he stopped the jeep. "It's the jungle, for Chrissakes. There're scorpions, snakes—"

Darren stopped midway between the front seat and the back. "Scorpions and snakes?"

"Don't worry about it—you got long pants on, like I told them to wear."

"Well, it's good to know scorpions have an aversion to people wearing long pants," Darren answered, not at all convinced.

George walked over and introduced himself; as she shook his hand, Darren wondered how scorpions and snakes felt about Cartier watches.

"We strung up a hammock over there, Darren," he said, "if you're tired." Lowering his voice, he added, "The latrine's the opposite way, behind that thick cluster of trees."

Darren looked in the direction he was pointing and noticed that another man was leaning against a tree, watching them.

"Who's that?" she said.

"Pete. He and Cory are doing the driving and making sure we have enough gas—things like that."

Andrew was busy talking to the cameraman and looking at the equipment when Darren came up behind him.

"I'm going to lie down in the hammock for a while," she said, feeling suddenly tired. "Don't wander off without me."

She stretched out in the hammock and looked up at the canopy of trees above her. A feather-soft breeze skimmed over her, and she gave in to the heaviness that had seeped into her limbs.

The dense, green world followed Darren into sleep. Sound swelled around her, telling of more life than she could see—hidden creatures that hissed and chirped and skittered away. She had entered a place of secrecy and mystery and, stealing into its boundaries on feet as silent as the grave, the wolf watched her from the shadows of trees, his eyes like still flames.

She sat up, wide awake. Looking around, she was uncertain for a moment if she had been dreaming. Everything looked the same as it had before she had closed her eyes. The trees towered above her, enormous and mute, and no eyes watched her from their shadows.

She lay back again, concentrating on the sound of voices

nearby and the ripples of heat that found their way through the trees. She was afraid to go back to sleep; the dream had seemed so real, she was afraid she would get lost there.

"Darren, you OK?" Andrew asked from somewhere behind her. She hadn't even heard him walk up. "You're not feeling sick, are you?"

"No, I'm fine. What's up?"

"We're going to walk around. Why don't you come with us? I wouldn't want to abandon you to the hordes of scorpions who've probably already targeted you."

For most of the afternoon they wandered through the jungle, speaking in low voices and trying to be as soundless as possible. Even Danny was uncharacteristically quiet. They filmed the tiny monkeys that leaped and cavorted in the trees, oblivious to the strangers who had invaded their lush, green world. The steamy heat made Darren feel sleepy and slow; she watched without fear as a pit viper slithered across the ground a few yards from them, heading in the opposite direction and showing no interest in them.

"I never would have thought there was so much beauty in this country," Darren said, coming up beside George. "All you think about when you think of Nicaragua is war."

"That's why we're filming this."

Darren walked over to a tree and leaned against it; she felt a beam of sunlight on her forehead and tilted her head up so it rested on her closed eyelids.

"Hey, Andrew, look at this!" Danny called out.

Darren looked around and saw Danny about ten yards away, standing over a mound of dirt and kicking it with his foot. By the time she got there, he and Andrew were already pulling some shiny white fabric out of the earth.

"What is it?" Darren asked.

"A parachute, I think," Andrew said, running the thin material through his fingers.

"A lot of training went on in this area around '81, when we started turning the contras into 'freedom fighters,'" George said.

Cory and Pete had stayed so aloof from the others for most

28

of the day that Darren was startled to hear Cory say, "We should be heading back soon if you wanna get in at a decent hour."

They started back to Managua as the day was easing into evening—a slow, unhurried transition of colors. As they passed through Jinotega, the sunset streaked the sky with orange and pink, as if it were putting on a show just for them.

George and Anthony offered to buy everyone dinner at the coffee shop in the Inter-Continental.

"This is your big chance, Darren," Andrew said as they walked into the hotel. "American food."

She ordered an omelette and wondered at the two empty chairs across from her. "Andrew, shouldn't we have waited for Cory and Pete?"

"They said they might go someplace else. I'm not sure they like our company. Maybe we're too young and rowdy for them."

"Maybe they heard some of Danny's jokes."

There were a few other Americans in the coffee shop, but one in particular caught Darren's eye. He was a freckled, red-haired man who, Darren thought, was probably older than he looked. He was sitting alone concentrating on his food, but she could tell he was also concentrating on them. She wasn't surprised when, midway through their meal, he came over and introduced himself.

"Hi, you guys staying at the hotel?" he said, directing his question at no one in particular.

"Uh, no," George said, glancing around the table apologetically. "It was a little out of our budget. We're here doing some filming."

"Of anything in particular?"

"Probably, but we're not sure what yet," Andrew said.

"I'm Sean Trudell. I'm a reporter. If you need any suggestions, I'd be glad to help. I've been here quite a few times. I know my way around pretty well."

Andrew introduced everyone at the table. When he got to the cameraman, whose name was Morrison, Sean said, "Morrison? That's your first name?"

"Yeah, my parents were big fans of Jim Morrison, so they named me after him."

"So, do you have any suggestions for our little project?" Andrew said.

"You might try talking to some people in Bocay. They've been hit pretty hard a few times recently. They have some very interesting stories . . . if you can get them to talk."

"Why wouldn't they talk?" Darren asked.

Sean looked at her with the palest blue eyes she had ever seen.

"Fear, to put it bluntly."

The next day they repeated their journey north. A thin layer of clouds shielded them from the searing sun; the filmy light was a relief from the heat of the previous day, but flies still caked the windshield and dust coated everything.

Darren, Andrew, and George rode with Cory in the Land Cruiser; the others followed in the jeep. They reached Bocay by late morning and stopped in the center of town, where a single-lane street was bordered by hitching rails on both sides. Horses were tied up, swishing flies away with their tails and pawing at the dry ground.

"Let's get out and look around," Andrew said.

He and Darren walked slowly down the street, past door-ways and curious eyes. A few yards past the last storefront, they came to a building made of wood planks and set back from the street. An American woman was sitting on the ground in front, playing with a group of children. When they got closer, they could see she was teaching them tic-tac-toe.

"Hi. Is this a school?" Andrew asked.

"Uh-huh. Did you want to enroll?" the woman said, smiling broadly. She stood up and dusted herself off. "I'm Tica. I'm the teacher."

She was nearly six feet tall, a sun-browned, athletic-looking woman whose shoulder-length hair was pulled back in a single braid.

As Andrew explained what they were doing, Darren noticed

that Tica's eyes were taking in the rest of the group, particularly Cory and Pete, who were, as usual, standing apart from the others.

Tica agreed to let them film her and her students, and in rapid, fluent Spanish she explained to the children that they were going to be in a movie. She clapped her hands and they mimicked her. Darren looked at the children, with their bare feet and wide open faces. Most of them seemed curious and happy, except for one tiny, thin girl who had only one arm.

They set up the equipment outside and let Tica talk about her experiences. She had come to Nicaragua eighteen months ago, she said, planning to stay only a few weeks. But the children had stolen her heart, and now she didn't want to be anywhere else.

"There was another thing that compelled me to stay," she said. "The girl who was teaching here before me was killed, and no one else wanted to take the job. So these kids were going to be deprived of the opportunity to learn. There's enough deprivation in their lives—I figure they should at least be able to learn how to read and write."

"Was the other teacher American?" Andrew asked.

"No, Nicaraguan. She was young, too—probably would have remained illiterate if it hadn't been for the Literacy Crusade. She was killed by the contras right here in the schoolhouse. The bullet holes are still in the wall over there. And then a rumor was started that the killers were actually Sandinistas dressed up as contras, so you see, part of the problem becomes confusion. People don't know who or what to believe. It's crazy, isn't it? Soldiers playing Halloween games and dressing up like their enemies?"

"The children saw this happen?" Darren asked hesitantly.

"Yes, they saw it. But you have to realize, these kids have grown up in a war zone. The majority of them have seen much worse." Tica motioned to the little girl with one arm, and the girl came over and sat in her lap. "Guadalupe lost both her parents. She was running toward them during the shooting and she got hit. Her arm couldn't be saved. There was no reason—it was just

31

terrorist tactics. So her grandmother is raising her. But her grand-mother is old and not very well. I don't know what will happen when she dies."

They moved the equipment inside to the dirt-floored school-room and filmed Tica conducting class. It was a highly unortho-dox class; spelling and arithmetic were interspersed with movie trivia.

"Who's the nicest outer-space creature?" Tica asked.

"E.T.!" one of the children yelled, and everyone clapped.

"Mork!" someone else called out.

Then she started moonwalking.

"Michael Jackson!" everyone shouted in unison.

Darren was fascinated with Tica, with her obvious love for the children, and with the energy she devoted to teaching them not only basic skills, but also the inconsequential facts that made them feel connected to a world beyond the turmoil of their own country. She counted the bullet holes in the wall—fifteen—and wondered if Tica ever allowed herself to be afraid. Somehow she doubted it.

They stayed until it was time for the children to go home. As the equipment was being moved out, Darren approached Tica and said, "I'd like to come back again. Would that be all right? Not to film anything, but . . . I don't know, maybe I could help out or something."

"Sure," Tica said, giving her a wide, dimpled smile. "You want to come tomorrow?"

Darren glanced outside to where Andrew was talking to George. Dust glittered in the sunlight that streamed through the open door. "OK, I think that would work out. Andrew men-tioned coming back and doing some more filming in this area, so they can drop me off."

Later that night, when Darren and Andrew were lying in the dark, Andrew said, "You know, there's something about Cory and Pete that bothers me."

Darren propped herself up on one elbow. "Me, too. But I'm not sure what it is."

"Well, for one thing, they're so damn familiar with this

country. They know the currency, they never get lost driving around, and I hardly ever see them look at a map. And the thing that really bugs me is that nothing seems to affect them. A one-armed child, people starving to death and dressed in rags—it's like they don't even see it."

"Maybe they're not the emotional types."

"Maybe that's why I don't like them. But I have a feeling it's something else, I just don't know what."

Darren arrived at the schoolhouse a little after ten the next morning. As she approached the open door she heard singing and realized that she was listening to an off-key version of "Imagine." She stood in the back until they'd finished.

"Kids, we have a visitor," Tica said in slow, deliberate English.

A roomful of wide, brown eyes turned in Darren's direction.

"She's from California," Tica continued, motioning for Darren to come to the front of the room. "Pedro, do you know a city in California?"

"Hollywood!" the boy said with a big grin. Darren noticed that he was wearing a Disneyland T-shirt.

"Good, Pedro." Then Tica started speaking in Spanish, and Darren could pick out enough to know she was describing the ocean and the palm trees and the mountains.

The children were transfixed; no one talked or fidgeted or took their eyes off her. She spoke nonstop for nearly thirty minutes and then released her audience to play outside.

"I try not to push my luck as far as their attention span goes," she explained to Darren as the children ran out the door. "Did you understand any of what I was saying?"

"A little. I think you were describing the beach and the mountains, right?"

"See how that high school Spanish comes back when you need it?" Tica picked up a straw hat from her desk and led Darren outside.

They sat down on the front step and watched the children squealing and laughing as they played some sort of game of tag. Only Guadalupe wasn't joining in; as soon as she saw Tica, she ran over and climbed into her lap.

"Guadalupe feels self-conscious around the other children," Tica said, wrapping her arms around the child. "Most of these kids would have hard lives even without the war. They don't have toys, and as you can see, most of them don't have shoes. Some of them have one pair that they save for the rainy season. And now, on top of everything else, they have to live in fear. They've seen things that children should never have to see."

"I really admire you, Tica," Darren said. "I don't think I could do what you're doing."

"Well, I've always had this Florence Nightingale streak in me." She pulled the brim of her hat down, shielding her eyes from the weak sunlight. "Maybe I inherited it. My mother was a nurse, and she was the one who treated us when we got sick. I don't remember a doctor ever coming to the house. We lived in Maryland and sometimes the winters were really bad. So it was very reassuring to know that she could handle a lot of things that would force someone else to go to the hospital. I remember one time one of our dogs got hit by a snow plow. His leg was mangled. My mother put him on the kitchen table and sewed him up. She used whatever we had around to numb him and stitch him up, and he was fine. So I've always kind of had this idea that you're supposed to help, however you can and with whatever you have available to you."

"Well, I still think you're pretty amazing, no matter how you try to explain it."

"You know, Darren, I'm glad you came back today, because I wanted to talk to you about something. I debated whether or not to say this, but I think I should. Let me ask you something first, though. How well do you know the guys you're working with on this film?"

"We don't really know them at all. Andrew met the two guys who put it together last month."

"Oh, yeah. Tweedledee and Tweedledum. How do you tell those two apart, anyway?"

Darren laughed. "You probably don't need to. Anyway, as far as the others go, Danny is an old friend, but we just met the cameraman and the two guys who are doing the driving when we got here. Why?"

Tica stroked Guadalupe's hair and stared out at the other children.

"It's those two, your drivers, who I wanted to talk to you about," she said softly. "I've seen them before. They've been around off and on since I came here, maybe longer. They usually stay at the Inter-Continental, and once I saw them with another American who I know is running weapons into the country."

"Are you sure?"

"Darren, I've been here for eighteen months. It's a small country—it's not hard to find out who is doing what. The peace talks never had a chance of succeeding; they were a joke. There are people in this country who are very friendly with the CIA, and this war is their baby. They're not going to let it go until they've gotten the Sandinistas out. There's a guy who owns a coffee plantation in Jinotega. About six months ago, a truckload of coffee pickers got blown up right near his land. The rumor is that he planned it because he found out some of them were sympathetic to the Sandinistas."

"Tica, if this is true, their only reason for working on this film would be to spy on us. I can't believe they'd feel that threatened by what we're doing to waste their time with us."

"Depends on what you end up filming, doesn't it? Think about it, if you manage to immortalize something that you shouldn't have seen in the first place, your film is going to get a lot of attention. Maybe these two want to make sure that doesn't happen. There's a lot of shit going on here, Darren. You don't have to look too hard to find it."

At twelve-thirty Tica let the children go home for lunch.

"Sometimes I bring food for them and we eat here. A lot of times their mothers don't have enough food at home to give them anything," Tica explained. "I wish I could do it every day, but I can't afford it. Are you hungry, Darren? We could get something at the store."

"I don't have an appetite anymore," Darren said. "I'm going

to have to tell Andrew what you said. I don't know what he's going to want to do."

"Well, let's take a walk and maybe we'll figure something out. I have a great thinking spot up the road."

When they walked out into the street, Darren saw Andrew filming something at the other end of the town. They went in the opposite direction, leaving the tiny, splintered buildings behind them. Through the parchment-thin clouds, Darren could feel the sun pressing down. The air smelled like summer—the hot, dry scent of baked earth.

Darren stopped. "Tica, you know what? I should probably run back and tell Andrew where I'm going, just in case he finishes up and comes looking for me."

"No problem. I'll be up here a little ways. It's not much farther. You won't miss me, I'm the only other white girl around."

Darren started jogging back toward town. After a few minutes she heard singing and turned around to see Tica loping away toward the hills, her braid bouncing against her back. She had the easy, graceful stride of a Thoroughbred, and Darren smiled out of appreciation for this unusual person who had happened into her life.

Her song was getting fainter, buried in the waves of heat that moved like a slow tide across the land.

" 'I've looked at life from both sides now,' " Tica sang out in the seconds before the earth exploded under her. The noise was deafening. Suddenly the sky was raining blood and chunks of earth, and Darren saw Tica's body go in one direction and her legs in another.

It seemed like forever before Darren reached her; the burning in her lungs was the only thing that told her she was running fast. She felt instead like she was running underwater. She stumbled over pieces of flesh, red and wet on the broken ground. Tica's eyes were glazed and wide open, and she was still breathing, but life was spurting out of her. Deep streams of blood were soaking into the dirt. Darren put her hands over what was left of

Tica's legs, but the blood pulsed through her fingers with a force she was powerless to stop.

"Oh, God, I don't know what to do," Darren sobbed. "I won't leave you, Tica. I'm right here. I won't leave you."

Two men in rubber boots and straw hats were running up the road toward them.

"Please help her," Darren said in a thick, choked voice. Tica was looking at her, but Darren didn't think her eyes saw anything.

The men stared and mumbled something in Spanish. Darren thought she heard the word *muerta*, and when she turned back to Tica, she saw that the life was gone from her eyes. The men picked her up and started walking back toward town with her legless, broken body, a trail of blood splattered on the road behind them. It was a macabre death march, and Darren wondered how many times they had made this journey. She got up and started following them, vaguely aware that her hands and jeans were covered with blood. It was drying on her skin and giving off a sweet, sickly smell.

She saw the Land Cruiser racing toward her and realized that Andrew must have been terrified, not knowing if she was still alive. It screeched to a stop and Andrew and Danny jumped out. Andrew ran over to her and pulled her against him so hard he almost crushed her.

"God, Darren, are you hurt?"

She pulled back and saw tears in his eyes, then wondered why there were none in hers.

"No." It was her own voice, but it sounded like it belonged to someone else, someone she didn't know. "Tica—"

"I know. I saw. Come and get in the car."

"No . . . I have to tell the children. I have to."

Andrew told Danny to take the car back and get the others.

"Why?" Darren asked.

"Darren, let's take one thing at a time. First we'll go back and tell the children."

They followed the trail of Tica's blood. Darren felt her jeans sticking to her knees, and her footsteps were heavy and slow.

Then she realized that Tica's legs were still lying in the road where they had fallen. She turned and started to run back.

"Darren, wait!" Andrew shouted, catching up with her and holding on to her arm.

"Her legs . . . Andrew, her legs are just lying there. No one took her legs!" Her voice was cracking and her chest felt like it was in a vise.

"Darren, you have to listen to me." He held her by both shoulders, forcing her to look at him. "It'll be taken care of. I don't want you to go back there."

Through the hum of the warm day and the sound of her own breathing, Darren heard cars coming toward them. The Land Cruiser and the jeep passed them as they stood by the side of the road.

"Oh, God, Andrew, you can't."

"It's what we came here for, isn't it—to let people know what's going on, what's still going on. Do you think Tica would have wanted us to ignore something like this?"

"I don't know! It's too bad you didn't think to ask her: 'Tica, if you get blown in half, would you like us to immortalize it on film? And which half of you would you like filmed?'"

"Darren, wait! Listen to me—"

But she broke away and started walking quickly toward the schoolhouse. She knew without turning back that Andrew was following her, but she couldn't think about him now.

Darren had almost reached the schoolhouse when a woman stepped in front of her with a pail of water. She pointed to Darren's hands and then to the pail. Darren plunged her hands into the water and watched as it turned red. She looked up at the woman's face, at eyes that seemed to brim over with fear and dark superstitions. Maybe in her mind having someone's blood on your hands put you in the clutches of evil, hungry spirits.

The children were drifting back in when she got to the school. Guadalupe was the first to see her, and the child stopped as if she had been turned into a pillar of salt. Darren walked up to her slowly, aware of how she must look to this timid child, not wanting to frighten the girl away. She reached out and put her arms around her; the frail, one-armed body felt lopsided and fragile.

"I'm sorry, honey," Darren whispered. "I'm sorry, Tica is gone. I'm so sorry."

Guadalupe pulled away and stared at her with steady dark eyes, eyes that didn't belong to a child. Then she turned and ran down the road, her bare feet raising small dust clouds as she put more and more distance between herself and this blood-soaked woman who had come as a messenger of death.

The other children were hovering around the door watching Darren . . . waiting.

"Tica está muerta," Darren said in halting Spanish. "I'm so sorry. I—there was nothing I could do."

Andrew was standing a few yards away, and the pain she saw on his face unleashed all the emotion she had been holding back. It broke through the walls of her heart with the force of a tidal wave and drove her to the ground, where her tears fell into the dust.

4

*T*HAT NIGHT WHEN THEY GOT BACK TO THE HOTEL, DARREN stood in the shower for almost an hour, trying in vain to feel clean again. When she came out of the bathroom, she found Andrew sitting on the bed crying. They held on to each other and cried until there were no tears left; then they turned off the lights and sat by the open window letting the cool night wind wash over them. A quarter moon hung in the sky, thin and pearl white.

Slowly, in a voice drained of emotion, Darren told Andrew what Tica had said about Cory and Pete.

"I guess that could explain a few things I've been wondering about," Andrew said. "Like why they never eat with us and how they seem to know their way around so well. There's a problem, though—I mean, with confronting this immediately. Cory's going to New York tomorrow with the film we've shot so far. It has to be run through the lab to make sure everything's OK."

"Can't you stop him? Or at least tell George and Anthony about it?"

"I could, but I'd rather wait. I just have reservations about attacking someone on the basis of what one person said."

For the next day and a half, Darren lay on the bed, staring at the dark walls and thinking about death. Her parents had died when she was in college, but somehow their death seemed almost poetic. They'd died together in an automobile crash. After flying back to New England to visit her at college, they had rented a car and planned to take a second honeymoon in the area, staying in small, quaint inns and not worrying about schedules or obligations.

Darren remembered the spring sun crawling over her back as she'd waved good-bye to them. She wondered at times if a cold wind had brushed her face or a black crow had flown across the sun—anything that might have warned her. But she knew that death had swooped down on them in one blinding second, taking them together, just as they had been in life.

Through the pain that had washed over her, Darren knew that, if her parents had been able to choose, they would have wanted to die together. It made her loss a little more bearable.

But Tica . . . Darren could find nothing to dilute the horror of her death.

It was almost noon; the room was hot and muggy, and dust drifted through the open window. Darren felt an emptiness in her stomach that reminded her how long she had been without food. When she heard the knock on the door, she was tempted to ignore it, but then realized it might be Andrew; he had a habit of forgetting his keys.

It was Andrew and Sean Trudell, the reporter they had met at dinner several days earlier.

"I ran into Sean while we were shooting," Andrew explained, barely looking at her. "We brought you some food."

41

"Andrew, is something wrong?"

"Yeah, something is very wrong. Cory came back from New York this morning with the film we shot over the first few days. There's nothing on it."

"What do you mean there's nothing on it?" Darren asked, sitting down on the bed opposite Andrew.

"Just what I said. I called the lab earlier and they said it was blank when he brought it in. I have this terrible feeling that it's not our equipment. I just don't think that's possible. I think Cory exposed it somehow."

Sean was putting sandwiches and beers on the dresser. "Easy to do," he said with his back toward them. "Just put it through the X-ray machine at the airport, probably in El Salvador when he changed planes."

"What are you going to do?" Darren said.

Andrew stood up, took a sandwich, and opened the door. "I'm going to talk to George right now. Darren, please eat something, OK? You're going to waste away. I'd hate to have to pay Sean to force-feed you," he said, winking at her.

Andrew closed the door behind him, and Sean studied Darren.

"Andrew told me what happened," he said softly. "But he's right, you have to eat. And a beer or two wouldn't hurt, either."

He opened a beer and handed her one of the sandwiches. "I had the hotel make them up for me in case you were wondering where they came from."

She took a swallow of the slightly warm beer. "I can't get it out of my head, Sean."

"I know. You probably never will, either, not completely. Anyone who tells you that time will dull the memory is a fucking liar. It will always be there, in vivid color. You'll see it, smell it, reexperience it. . . . It's part of you now. So, that means you have a task ahead of you. How do you live with something like that without letting it devour you? A lot of people face the same challenge. Too many people in this country have seen too many horrible things. Children have seen their parents murdered, or their brothers or sisters, or their friends."

"What about you, Sean? Do you have memories like that?"

"Why do you think I'm saying this to you? I'm not being unsympathetic or callous. I've been in and out of Nicaragua since 1982, and I've seen a lot of shit go down that you wouldn't believe." He unwrapped a sandwich and held it up to her. "First lesson—don't starve or shrivel up. It won't help."

He was quiet for several minutes, traveling backward through his thoughts. "Sometimes I think it's just willpower," he said finally. "You gotta just muscle your way past those images. Put them in a corner of your mind where you won't always be colliding with them."

Once Darren tasted food, she realized she was ravenous. She finished her sandwich and half of Sean's.

"Very good," he told her with a laugh. "You're making progress. Next step is getting the hell out of this depressing room."

They found Andrew and the rest of them in the chaos of the Mercado Oriental. The marketplace was crowded with women carrying baskets of fruits and vegetables on their heads, and with people haggling over prices. It seemed like everyone was yelling—both the vendors and the buyers. Andrew was talking to a thick-necked woman with a basket of onions and peppers balanced on her head. She had deeply lined skin and her eyes were red and watery. As Danny filmed her, she gave a long, angry speech, apparently oblivious to the fact that her listeners probably didn't understand what she was saying.

Sean leaned closer to Darren and spoke into her ear. "She's saying that the Sandinistas won't let her sell her produce without a vendor's license—they make it so she can't make a living. She doesn't think the contras would be any better, though, because they kill babies and sell the blood."

"Sell the blood?" Darren asked, picturing a vendor hawking small bottles of blood.

"Rumors are the backbone of this country."

Darren glanced around and noticed that George, Anthony, and Cory were missing. When Danny turned off the camera, she moved through the crowd toward Andrew.

"Well, I can't believe it," he said, smiling at her. "What did Sean say to you? Never mind, I don't want to know. I'm just glad you got out of the room." He hugged her and his shirt was damp and warm.

"Your crew is short three people," Darren said.

"They're, uh, talking. And you know what? I think we should take the rest of the day off and go swimming."

They went back to the hotel and spent the afternoon acting like kids at a swimming party. When George finally joined them, he said Cory would be leaving that night.

"What about Pete?" Darren asked.

"He didn't do anything wrong," George said.

"But they're together—"

"Darren," Andrew interrupted, "that doesn't make him guilty."

George stared into the swimming pool, following the ripples with his eyes. "I'm not even that sure that Cory was guilty of what we were accusing him of." He shook his head slowly. "I wanted this film to be a joint effort by people who cared about what was going on in this country. I have this sick feeling that it's all unraveling around me, and I don't know what to do about it. Maybe I expected too much."

Andrew put his arm around George's shoulders, and Darren decided to let them talk alone. She walked over to Danny, who was sitting dejectedly by the side of the pool dangling his feet in the water.

"Want to talk about it?" she said, sitting down beside him.

When he looked at her, Darren thought he was going to cry. "The other day Morrison and I buried Tica's legs," he said slowly. "I couldn't just leave them there, and I didn't know where they took the body. So we got a shovel out of the jeep and dug a trench. . . ." His voice trailed off and he squeezed his eyes shut.

"Danny, a lot of people wouldn't have been able to do that much."

"I know, but I've never had to do anything like that before. I've never even seen anything like that before." Tears streamed down his cheeks, and he turned his face away.

44

"Danny, someone just told me that all you can do is push your way past those memories, because they're never going to get out of your way on their own. I guess that's what we both have to do."

"I guess. I'm going to swim underwater for a while. Thanks, Darren," he said, and plunged into the pool.

Later, with the quiet sounds of night falling around them, Darren and Andrew lay in a bright shaft of moonlight, their legs tangled together. Darren had cried when they were making love. That was the way it was with her tears now; they just came sometimes, as if they had a will of their own.

"Andrew, I want to talk about having a baby."

"We just talked about it not that long ago."

"Months ago, and I want to talk about it again."

"Darren, I just don't feel like I'm ready yet. I still have too much confusion about my own childhood. I have no idea what kind of parent I would make. I'd rather talk about Christmas. It's tomorrow, you know?"

"Strange way to spend Christmas, huh?" Darren said.

"Yeah. You know, when I was a kid it was my favorite time of year. I started thinking about it right after Halloween. And you know what the best part was? I saw my parents less at Christmas than any other time of the year. We had this neighbor, Mrs. Dunberry. She was English and she loved to have me come over. So my mother would drop me off while she went shopping and leave me the whole day sometimes. I remember walking through the snow into this warm kitchen that smelled of things baking in the oven. Mrs. Dunberry would putter around while I drew pictures on the windows, which were always steamed over. In the afternoon she'd make me milk-tea—milk, sugar, and a little bit of English tea—and she'd tell me stories about England, about haunted houses and cobblestone streets and fog so thick you couldn't see your hands in front of you. I listened to those stories a thousand times and never got bored.

"The saddest thing about Christmas Day was that, every year, I asked if Mrs. Dunberry could come over. She didn't have anyone. She said all her family was in England, but I suspect she lied about how much family she had. My parents wouldn't hear of it. She didn't fit in with their rich friends. No one gave a damn that this sweet old lady was sitting in her house all alone on Christmas Day."

Darren shifted in the bed and felt the warm night pressing down on her.

"Andrew, I think I'd like to leave tomorrow."

"OK, but I have to stay and do some more filming. You understand that, don't you? It should only be another week."

"I know. Maybe the time alone will be good for me."

5

*F*OG ROLLED OVER THE HOOD OF THE CAR, SWIRLING against the windshield in ghostly patterns. On the opposite side of the road, the oncoming headlights looked watery and faint. Darren had been home for three days, and for most of that time fog had clung to the city like a shroud.

Her uncle lived on a palatial estate on Mulholland Drive, high above the clutter of Los Angeles. Usually at night the city blinked and glittered below like a bowl of diamonds, but tonight Darren looked down on a rolling white sea.

She was visiting Lawson for the first time since she had come home from Nicaragua, although she had talked to him on the phone, telling him about Tica and the two men she suspected of sabotaging the film.

Lawson had always occupied a special place in her life. He was the one person who had never talked down to her, even

47

when she was a child. She remembered sitting in his lap while he showed her scrapbooks from his college years and his time in the military. He told her about the horrors of war and planted in her the first seeds of political consciousness. Years later, when she protested the Vietnam War, it was Lawson who applauded her stand and defended her in front of her parents, who only saw that she was arguing with her own country's policy. Since her parents' death they had grown even closer; his role in her life had expanded, filling the empty space her parents left behind.

She pulled up to the electric gates that protected Lawson's house from an unpredictable world.

"Are you trying to keep others out or yourself in?" she had once asked him.

"Both," he answered.

She pushed the button and announced herself to the intercom. The heavy gates grated open—a rude disturbance in the still night.

When Darren was younger her parents had taken her to Lawson's house often, sometimes leaving her there for the day. She was sure that behind the gates lay a magical kingdom where anything she imagined could come true. The trees were full of the symphonies of birds and the chattering of squirrels. Occasionally deer wandered calmly through the grounds. In those years his estate had seemed enormous; she thought Lawson was lord of his own country. But as with all things, as she got older it began to seem smaller. It made her sad to lose some of the enchantment; it made her even sadder to see how time was playing with Lawson, whittling him into its own crooked image. Sometimes when she hugged him now, she could feel the frailty of his bones, the disintegration of his muscles.

When she pulled up he was standing in the doorway. He watched her take the flagstone steps two at a time.

"Hello, my dear," he said, holding out his arms to hug her. "I've missed you. Eerie-looking weather, isn't it?"

He was wearing a beige cable-knit sweater, but Darren could see him shiver with the dampness.

"Let's go into the study. I have a fire going in there."

There were rooms in Lawson's house that were like sanctuaries, and Darren had, at one time, named each of them after a season. His study was the winter room because, even on a summer day, it felt like a refuge from a stormy night. On every wall there were shelves filled with books, and the leaded windows looked out on thick trees so that only green, filtered light found its way into the room. On this night the fire cast an orange glow on the oak floor and fog licked the glass.

Darren curled up in one of the overstuffed chairs that was angled toward the fireplace. "This is the perfect type of night for this room," she said as the heat from the fire washed over her.

"I opened a nice bottle of cabernet. Would you like some?"

"Half a glass. I still have to drive home through the fog."

Lawson handed her a glass of the deep red wine; she took a sip and felt it slide across her tongue like warm velvet. As Lawson lowered himself into the opposite chair, Darren noticed that his movements were slow and careful.

"So how are you holding up?" he asked. "Any more nightmares?"

She had told him two days earlier that sleep had propelled her back to the road where Tica was killed; she saw everything again, reexperienced the blood and the horror, and it was just as bad as the first time.

"No, only that one. And Andrew should be home in a few days. I think I'll feel better then."

Lawson swirled the wine in his glass and stared into the fire. "This world has become something that I can't understand anymore," he said softly. His words floated into the still air and hung there. Darren wondered what it would be like to have known the world in slower, simpler times, when the earth was still ripe and the seas were still wild and clean.

"When I fought in World War II, there was no doubt that we were fighting an honorable war. But you can't say that about every battle America decides to engage in. In some ways I think it's unfortunate that we have an example like World War II to justify our promilitary mentality."

"I have a strong suspicion that the two drivers I told you

about were not down there on their own. So, it does get hard to trust your own government."

"Has Andrew told you about any other incidents?" Lawson asked.

"No."

Darren stayed and had an early dinner with Lawson, and then left before the fog got any worse. As she drove home she thought about the strange pull that death has on the living. The loss of her parents had brought her closer to Lawson; it had also turned her in Andrew's direction.

She had known Andrew before, but only casually. On their small college campus they had mutual friends and were in a few classes together. But there remained a distance between them, one that they both enforced. They were like timid animals, circling but afraid to get too close.

Then, suddenly, Darren needed to fill her nights with something other than her parents' ghosts. Andrew became her friend, but she quickly realized that was not where the relationship would end.

When he was there the shadows became just shadows again, the darkness just darkness. The night didn't ripple with strange echoes and ribbons of light that were surely, Darren thought, the restless spirits of her parents.

Sometimes, even with Andrew there, she would listen to the sound of his breathing and hear, mingled in it, so faint that only she could hear, the low whistle of their breath. Before the shadows could come alive again, she would slide over his body and the fury of their lovemaking would make the night quiet again.

Darren spent the next couple of days alone, watching the sky as it changed moods. The heavy film of morning mist melted into blue afternoons that settled quickly into the early dark of winter. At night she sat outside wondering how men could have deciphered winged horses and hunters from the tumult of stars.

Solitude was like a tonic to her, healing the jagged wound of Tica's death. She could hear Leland next door, and she found herself sneaking around the garden so he wouldn't know she was back. Unless she heard Andrew's voice on the phone machine, she let the recorded message tell all callers that she wasn't home.

The year changed under a clear midnight sky. In the distance Darren heard the sound of celebrations, but she treated the moment as if it had no more significance than any other.

On the first day of 1989, she left the sprawl of the city and hiked into the Santa Monica Mountains. The trail sliced through the hills, up to windy ridges where the air was cold and the sea, far below, was a sheet of blue satin. After more than an hour she came to a steel-reinforced wooden bridge that connected two mountains. She leaned on the railing and looked down at a pocket of dark trees, and her memory returned to the jungle, where trees had formed a skyless, green world.

That evening she was fixing dinner when she heard a familiar knock on the door. Leland was standing on the front steps with a baseball bat.

"Hi Leland. Going out for a night game?"

"No. I didn't know you were home. I thought maybe someone had broken in, so I was coming over to check it out," he said in an authoritative voice.

"Oh, well, I hate to dampen your enthusiasm, but knocking on the door is probably not a good idea if you think there might be a burglar inside."

"It's a good idea if you have a baseball bat."

"Right. Silly of me not to think of that. Listen, I'm sort of in the middle of something. Andrew will be home tomorrow—why don't you come over and play then?"

"Okay," Leland said, dragging his baseball bat down the path. "Glad everything's OK!"

Andrew's plane landed under a deep blue sky—the kind of sky that made people remember why they had chosen to live in Los Angeles in the first place. As Darren drove him home, white clouds were chasing down the sun; pushed by a crisp wind, they threw shadows on the ground. Darren could tell that Andrew was tired and anxious to escape into sleep, so they rode in silence.

When they got home he went immediately into the bedroom and collapsed on the bed.

"I'm sorry," he said. "I know I'm not being very romantic, but I'm so damn tired. I'd like it if you would lie down with me, though."

She took off her shoes and then pulled Andrew's off. There was a gentle, blue-gray light in the room. The clouds had dulled the edges of the day. Darren lay beside Andrew as easily as a shadow and ran her hand across his chest, reading the braille of his muscles. Soon his breathing grew deep and heavy. She watched his chest rise and fall, saw his eyelids flutter, and wondered if he was dreaming. Carefully, she slid off the bed and tiptoed out of the room. As she walked through the darkening house, she thought how different it felt when Andrew was there, as if something stolen had been returned.

After staying in bed for most of the following day, they finally moved out to the yard so Darren could do some gardening. As he watched her transplanting a potted fern, Andrew said, as if he had been turning the thought over in his mind, "Darren, you don't need a baby. You have five hundred plants that are depending on you for their survival."

There was a scratching sound at the gate.

"Do you think that's Leland?" Darren said.

"No, he's not that subtle. If he wanted to come in, he'd either yell or break down the gate."

Darren unlatched the gate and was greeted by a buttery brown dog who hadn't yet grown into her tail or her ears.

"Hi, are you lost? Oh, look how sweet you are," she said as the dog licked her hand.

"Darren, who the hell are you talking to?"

"The mailman," she joked. Then she went on in a coaxing tone, "Come on, girl, you can come in."

The dog trotted over to Andrew and, in less than a minute, had him down on the grass with her paw on his chest and her tongue all over his face.

"Darren!"

"She just wants love. Look how skinny she is. Someone probably abandoned her."

Andrew managed to sit up. "I know what you're thinking, but we can't keep a dog without looking for its owner. We'll put up signs and run an ad in the paper. Then, if nothing happens, we'll talk about it. . . . Although I don't really know why we need a dog when we have Leland. He'd probably let you walk him on a leash if you made it sound like a scientific experiment."

A week passed with no answer to their signs or their ads.

"Can we name her Commando?" Leland asked when he was told she would be staying.

"No," Andrew said emphatically. "And I'd appreciate it if you didn't dress her up in fatigues and strap a machine gun to her chest, either."

"I thought of a name," Darren said. "Peanut. She's the color of peanut butter, and it's her favorite food. All I have to do is open the jar and she races into the kitchen."

"I wondered where all the peanut butter was going," Andrew said.

"Peanit—that's a neat name!" Leland shouted, ecstatic at being able to call her something besides dog.

Andrew looked at Darren and rolled his eyes. "Leland, it's Pea-*nut*, like the butter. Say that for me. Pea-*nut*."

"Peanit. That's what I said!" Leland said as he raced around the yard with Peanut close at his heels. Leland had adopted their yard as his playground because it had trellises and bushes where pirates or Indians or monsters could be lurking and, in Leland's mind, usually were. In a single afternoon he could wipe out a battalion of enemy soldiers, a herd of wild boar, three monsters, and Bigfoot, and still make it home for dinner.

"Darren, don't they teach him how to speak in school?"

"He's only eight. He just has some pronunciation problems," Darren said.

Leland was tossing a tennis ball in the air and yelling, "Come on, Peanit, get it before it bounces! Peanit!"

Andrew shook his head. "Now he's dropping the *t* off the end. He sounds like he's running around yelling at his penis."

"No, he doesn't," Darren said, laughing. "I can hear the *t* on the end."

"I'll bet the people five blocks away can't."

Sometime after midnight, with Peanut curled up between them on the bed, Darren and Andrew were woken up by the phone.

"Can't you get Danny to quit doing that?" Darren mumbled as Andrew reached for the receiver.

"Yes, Danny . . ."

It was George's voice that answered him.

"Oh, sorry," Andrew said, sitting up. "This is Danny's usual phone hour."

"The film's gone," George said. His voice sounded tense and brittle.

"What do you mean it's gone?"

"My house was broken into tonight. As far as I know nothing was taken except the film."

"Jesus!" Andrew was supposed to start editing it in two days, and he and George had talked several times about their hopes for the final product.

"I don't know what to tell you, Andrew," George said. "I'm going to report it to the police, but frankly I don't have much hope of recovering it. This was a pretty professional job. I guess we should have fired Pete, too, huh?"

"I don't know if it would have made any difference," Andrew said. "Let me give you a call tomorrow, OK. There's nothing we can do tonight."

Andrew hung up the phone and told Darren what had happened.

"So Tica was right. Who else would break in and just steal some film?" Darren said, staring at Andrew through the darkness.

Darren lay awake for hours, sifting through all the recent events that had changed her perception of the world. It seemed that there were hidden, treacherous things lying in wait for her—things coiled and venomous that were waiting for her to stumble upon them.

She thought about the wolf who still prowled through her sleep. She hadn't told Andrew about him; for some reason she didn't fully understand, she wanted him to remain her secret. Sometimes she thought the wolf was a messenger of death, sent from the gloom of a distant continent. His steady yellow eyes told of things beyond her reach, beyond her control. Other times, she thought he was her protector, hovering nearby to devour anything that might threaten her.

6

FTER A FEW DAYS THEY REALIZED THE FILM WOULD NEVER
be recovered. The most constructive suggestion the
police made was "Ask your friends. Maybe someone is playing a
practical joke on you." It was obvious there were more serious
crimes on their agenda.

George started showing up at Darren and Andrew's house in
the evening, usually just in time for dinner. But nothing they did
or said seemed to lighten his mood. It was almost, Darren thought,
as if he had lost a child; that was the extent of his depression,
black and unyielding.

Andrew dealt with it the way he usually dealt with problems: he worked out at the gym for hours a day until his muscles
were so sore he could think of nothing else. He went to sleep at
nine and got out of bed each morning as the room was just
starting to get light. In the gray dawn he rummaged through his

drawers for sweat clothes and socks, slid open the closet drawers to search for his shoes. Darren knew he thought he was being quiet, but the noise he made would probably have roused someone from a coma.

A few hours later he would come back, flushed and dripping with sweat. He would shower, dress, and fix himself a breakfast that a linebacker would be proud of.

Darren had watched Andrew go through this frequently, and she was getting curious about the strange world he disappeared to each morning. He came back talking about split routines and how his arms were starting to get really cut, and Darren had absolutely no idea what he was talking about. He started cooking pasta several nights a week, claiming he needed the carbs, or he would bring back fresh loaves of bread from the bakery and eat them with cottage cheese instead of butter. He separated eggs, eating only the whites, and made thick concoctions of protein powder and juice. Every day he looked leaner and more muscular.

Darren wasn't sure if she was motivated by curiosity or the desire not to be left out, but she decided to start going with him. Without announcing her decision ahead of time, she got up with Andrew one morning and started getting dressed.

"Darren, what are you doing?" he said, one sock partially on his foot and the other slung over his shoulder.

"I'm going with you. I'm going to start lifting weights," Darren answered, lacing up her Reeboks.

"Whoa, wait a minute. I don't know if you'll like it there. It's pretty hard-core. We're not talking about your basic aerobics class here."

"I know. I can handle it. They do allow women in there, don't they?"

"Yeah, sure. OK, well, if that's what you want, go ahead. Where's my other sock?"

"On your shoulder."

Some of Darren's confidence was deflated when they walked into the gym. She was confronted with a roomful of equipment she didn't know anything about and too many people who looked like they knew everything about it.

"Andrew, you're going to help me, aren't you?" she said in a meek voice.

He smiled at her. "I thought you could handle it."

"I can—I mean, I will . . . as soon as you show me what to do."

"OK, we'll do your arms, your stomach, and your legs. That should be enough for your first time."

Her arms were fairly strong from all the gardening she did, but when he had her work her abdominals, she thought she was going to break in two.

"You're doing real good, Darren. How do you feel?" Andrew asked as he led her over to the leg-extension machine.

"OK, I guess. Actually, I feel a little light-headed."

"That's normal. You'll get into it. Pretty soon you'll be coming home bragging about your lat spread."

"My what?"

"Never mind. OK, sit down and hook your feet under here. You're going to lift up; it will strengthen your quadriceps."

After her second set, a striking, black-haired woman with the high, sharp cheekbones of an Indian and a body that seemed like it had been sculpted by an artist walked up and asked if she could work in.

Darren looked at Andrew with uncomprehending eyes.

"Sure," Andrew said to the woman. "She wants to trade off sets with you, Darren. While you're resting, she'll do a set."

The woman moved the weight up to sixty pounds and Darren watched the muscles in her thighs bulge and tighten with each extension. Her eyes were squeezed shut, as if there were nothing else in the world at that moment except the movement of her legs.

When Darren started to do her set, the woman said, "Don't kick your legs up like that; bring the weight up by tightening your quads. This isn't an exercise in momentum."

"Thanks for your help," Darren said when she was finished and had climbed off the machine to discover her legs felt like molten lava.

"Sure. My name's Cassie."

"Darren. Nice to meet you."

On the way home Darren said, "She's really amazing looking, isn't she, Andrew?"

"She's pretty amazing period. I've seen her in there squatting two hundred pounds. Too bad Geronimo didn't have her muscles; Arizona would still belong to the Indians."

Over the next week Darren got a little bit bolder, letting Andrew go off and do his own workout while she stuck to the machines she was familiar with. She saw Cassie watching her sometimes and instantly thought she was doing something wrong.

One morning she was sitting on a bench doing biceps curls and Cassie appeared in the mirror behind her. She was wearing black tights and a black T-shirt tied above her waist to reveal an abdomen of rippling muscles.

"Just use your arms," Cassie said, "not your back. You should adjust the back of this bench so that it supports you better and doesn't allow you to push with your back."

"Thanks," Darren said self-consciously. She felt like a school kid who had been reprimanded.

"Listen, would you like a workout partner?" Cassie asked. "We both come in at the same time, and it helps to work out with someone. I think you have a lot of potential, but it would help if you had some guidance, and if you'll excuse my bluntness, I don't think you're going to get it from your husband."

Darren looked over at Andrew; he was doing squats as an enormous man spotted him.

At first Darren didn't know if she could survive this new venture. Training with Cassie was like auditioning for the marines. Her muscles burned and throbbed as if they were being shredded at a very slow pace. Several times Darren felt like she would black out, or cry, or both. Of the two choices, she decided blacking out was preferable; she could never live down the humiliation of weeping in front of people who probably moved pianos around just for kicks.

She learned, though, to challenge her limitations—or what

she thought were her limitations. She learned that *can't* was a relative term; when she would moan that she couldn't do another rep, Cassie would say, "Yes you can. One more." And somehow, from a place inside her that she was just beginning to discover, she would summon the strength.

Into the gray, sullen days of February, Darren accepted Cassie's relentless instruction and endured the painful protests of her own body. Gradually, her muscles started to respond. She stood in front of the mirror when she got out of the shower and saw that her legs were developing a sinewy, sculpted look of strength. Her arms had always been strong, but they were smooth; feminine looking, her mother would have said. Now she could trace the definition of her muscles as they moved beneath her skin. She knew Andrew liked it; she could tell by the way he ran his hands over her body when they made love and the way he watched her when she dressed.

Her new strength was not all physical, however. The fears that had followed her out of Nicaragua started to look small and inconsequential. It was as if, by sheer power, she had driven back the shadows that had fallen across her path. Now, when she thought of Tica, she could see her smile rather than the image of her death.

Darren started to feel that a new phase of her life was beginning. She planned to start painting again, and would let her new strength guide her hand. Then one morning all of her fears rumbled in again. . . .

Darren and Andrew had walked down to the beach as an orange dawn was fading in the sky. The minute they hit the sand, Peanut took off at lightning speed in a single-minded effort to rid the beach of any sea gull who had the audacity to alight there.

She could tell by the frown on Andrew's face that he was embroiled in thoughts that were not exactly uplifting.

"What are you thinking about?" she said.

"The film—how heartbreaking this has been. I don't know if I mentioned this to you, but we were planning on approaching Senator Janes about doing some sort of introduction to it. Just a two-minute thing, you know."

"He probably would have. He's been pretty outspoken about opposing aid to the contras."

Andrew stopped and faced Darren. Their footsteps dotted the sand behind them, preserved for the moment by an unambitious tide.

"I've been trying to think how to tell you this . . ." he said.

"Uh-oh. This sounds like something I'm not going to like. You're going to leave me for a redhead with a Mercedes and a trust fund."

"No, not quite." He laughed, then paused and looked out at the ocean. "I'm going to go back to Nicaragua, just for a couple of weeks. Sean is still there."

"Then I'll go with you," Darren said, trying to shrug off the fear that tugged at her.

"No. Not this time. If I can get some pictures of some of the things that are going on there, maybe I can get a studio to back a documentary. I don't know, it's not like there haven't been films about Nicaragua, but the fact is that even now, after the election, when people assumed things would change, innocent people are getting blown up and maimed. . . . Maybe I can get pictures that other people can't. I can be pretty inconspicuous when I want to be. It's something I have to do, Darren, and there is no way in hell I would let you go with me. I can't put you in that kind of situation."

"You're not even going to discuss this, are you?" Darren said.

"No. No compromises on this one."

PART TWO

7

KENT JANES WALKED QUIETLY UP THE STAIRS, HOPING NOT to wake Cecilia until he had set the breakfast tray on the bed and kissed her. Mornings were important; they could determine the tone for the whole day.

Sometimes Kent would watch her sleeping, as still as a painting, her hair spread across the pillow. He would remember how she used to look: her hair sun-bleached and short and her cheeks flushed and healthy looking. Now her hair was a mouse-brown color; much of it had fallen out and what was left fell long and straight over her shoulders. In some ways, though, she was prettier now. There was a serenity to her face and her skin was smooth as a snowdrift. But it was her eyes that fascinated Kent. They seemed to go on forever—tunnels to a place deep inside her that he was forbidden to enter.

He opened the shades and let in the filmy light of an overcast day. It was late February and winter had a firm grip on Washington.

"Cecilia," he whispered, "I brought your breakfast." He kissed her mouth and saw her eyelids flutter, faint and quick as an insect's wings. He knew she was awake. Cecilia remained behind her closed lids until she'd braced herself for daylight on the other side. She didn't sleep like other people; her face never got scrunched into awkward expressions and her breath never turned sour. She almost seemed ageless, while Kent felt that he aged years with each day that passed. He never believed the people who told him how good he looked. He knew his body was still lean and athletic looking; his five-mile run every morning guaranteed that. And his light brown hair had no gray in it. But couldn't people see the sadness that tugged at the corners of his eyes, the tension that had turned his mouth into a thin, straight line?

Finally Cecilia opened her eyes. "Good morning," she said, brushing a strand of hair from her cheek.

"How do you feel, darling?" Kent asked. It was always his first question of the morning.

"All right, I guess. Could you close the drapes a bit, please?"

Obediently, he pulled the heavy fabric across the window, shutting out the day. He had given up arguing with her about it; daylight was her enemy and nothing he said could change that.

Sitting down on the edge of the bed, Kent poured coffee into the delicately flowered cup. "Jessica's not here yet," he said, "so I made your breakfast. I hope it's edible."

Cecilia smiled thinly, and Kent knew this would not be one of the rare days when her old cheerfulness returned.

Kent and Cecilia Janes had been married for nine years. They met while working at the same California law firm. Cecilia was the youngest lawyer at the firm and, at that time, the only female lawyer. Kent observed the discriminatory attitude of his colleagues and made a point of going out of his way to support and encourage her. He sought her opinion when the others wouldn't have bothered to ask for it.

66

When Kent realized that his feelings for Cecilia were becoming more than just professional, he kept it to himself because, among other things, he could get no reading on how she felt. Several times they had gone out for a drink after work, and Kent had deliberately kept their conversation confined to legal matters and office talk. He was afraid to even ask where she lived; she might think he was making a pass at her.

Then, on a crisp April evening, he stopped by her office and said, "If you're about through, would you like to join me for a glass of wine?" She was wearing a blue silk blouse that matched her eyes and a black skirt that made Kent notice for the first time that, aside from the other qualities that attracted him to her, her body was slender and perfectly proportioned.

"I hope I'm not out of line," he said later in the subdued light of a Beverly Hills cocktail lounge, "but would you like to extend this into dinner?"

The glow of a single candle shone through the pale wine. Cecilia leaned back in the booth and studied Kent's face.

"Is this invitation personal or professional?" she asked.

"Which would you like it to be?"

"Personal. I can get professional invitations anywhere, except perhaps from some of the stuffy old codgers in our prestigious law firm."

Over dinner Cecilia seemed to relax and become more at ease talking about herself. Kent hoped it was his company, but he suspected part of it was the wine.

"It seems that, in order to be successful, you have to put your personal life on hold," she said. "But I guess I asked for it. I came from a very traditional family. My mother cooked, cleaned, raised the kids, and never asked about business or money. She didn't even know how much money they had—my father never let her see a bankbook. So, I decided I was going to be different. I was never going to get sucked into a situation like that. I would not only be as smart as my father, I'd be smarter. I'd be more successful than he could ever be."

"And have you been?"

"Yes."

"It's funny how archaic his attitudes sound now," Kent said, pouring more wine into their glasses.

"But they're not. Look at the men we work with. They're irritated as hell that a woman is doing the same job they're doing and doing it well. It kills them."

Kent laughed. "I guess you're right, especially when she does the job better."

They walked out of the restaurant into a night that was ripe with the aromas of spring.

"Can I drive you home?" Kent said.

"My car's at the office, although the garage is probably locked by now. So I guess the answer is yes."

Cecilia lived on the outskirts of Beverly Hills, on a street lined with jacaranda trees. Her third-floor apartment was sparsely decorated with a few antiques and some framed Picasso prints. It had the immaculate look of a home rarely occupied. Kent wandered around the living room, looking for personal touches, knickknacks that might be clues into her life. There was a small crystal bowl filled with marble eggs; he thought of asking her if each egg had a special meaning.

"If you're trying to glean insight into my personality from the decor of my apartment, don't waste your time," Cecilia said, startling him with the closeness of her voice. "I barely have time to buy food, much less find creative expression through interior decorating."

"You like Picasso," Kent said, turning around to face her.

She didn't back up. Her eyes seemed to challenge him, and for a moment he felt thrown off balance, almost dizzy. "Yes," she said, "I like the confusion of his work. I always feel like my life's too organized, like it could use some confusion."

Her look was calm and unwavering, but it was as devoid of revelations as her home. Kent put a tentative hand on the small of her back and felt her move into him. His fingers traveled across the slippery silk of her blouse to the curve of her hips, and he felt her mouth move onto his and her arms tighten around his neck. He felt himself getting hard against her, and he knew she could feel it too.

"Come on," Cecilia whispered, leading him into the bedroom. Naked, they lay on top of the covers. A cool wind drifted through the open window and fluttered across them. Kent knelt over her, pushing her thighs apart. She reached around his neck and pulled herself up, sliding her tongue down his neck, across his chest. She fell back against the pillows, took him in her hands, and guided him inside her. Kent was vaguely aware of the wind getting colder, of the night outside getting quieter. Cecilia's hunger exhausted him; the moon had climbed to its midnight height by the time he fell asleep.

Six months later they were married, and they moved into a small house tucked away in Benedict Canyon. Gradually, and with Cecilia's encouragement, Kent found himself taking a more active role in political issues, which had always interested him but never with any thought of making his future there. Cecilia was relentless in her belief that he should consider running for political office, and thus the groundwork was laid for a senatorial campaign.

He turned out to be one of the most charismatic figures to enter the political scene in years, and with little real opposition, Kent Janes was elected senator in 1982. He was cheered on election night by a large crowd of supporters as Cecilia stood by his side, smiling and eight-months pregnant.

After their daughter was born, Kent flew to Washington and found a house in Georgetown he thought would be perfect for them. He came back with pictures of a large brick house with leaded windows and a driveway, which, in Georgetown, was a rarity. Most houses had no accommodations for a car.

"We'll move when Laura's a little older," Cecilia said.

"I'm sorry, we can't afford to keep both houses."

"We can for a little while."

A little while became two years. Cecilia and Laura visited Kent in Washington occasionally, but it was clear that Cecilia was not ready to move from California. For Kent it meant long nights missing his wife and daughter and mornings heavy with their absence. But he would have endured a lifetime of that over the event that brought Cecilia to Washington permanently.

The phone call was from their neighbor in California. Kent would never forget her voice—the dull monotone of someone buffeted by the shock of seeing tragedy scrape by her, inches from her own life, warning that it could just as easily have been her.

Kent caught the next plane to California. He found Cecilia in bed, sedated, and several neighbors keeping watch over her.

Earlier that day she had been on the phone, believing that Laura was in her room playing. Kent imagined his wife's terror as she went through the house calling Laura's name, and the awful silence bouncing back at her. Her search ended in the yard when she saw that the gate leading to the pool was open—the gate that was always supposed to be locked. Laura's lifeless body was floating in the deep end.

In the months that followed Kent watched his wife slip away, retreating to a world of darkness and shadow where guilt was as essential to its structure as steel girders are to a bridge.

The front door closed downstairs and Kent heard Jessica's soft footsteps heading into the kitchen. She always walked as though Cecilia was sleeping; more often than not, she was right.

"Jessica's here now," he said, leaning over and kissing her forehead. "I've got to get going. Try to eat some breakfast, OK?"

Cecilia pushed the scrambled eggs with her fork. "I'll try," she said.

Kent walked out the door into a stiff, bitter wind. He forced his mind away from his wife and onto the day's schedule. He had a meeting with his administrative assistant at ten, although Phillip had been slightly mysterious about his reason for needing to meet with Kent. He had called him at home last night and said he'd received an anonymous letter that they should discuss.

Phillip Payne had gotten in touch with Kent shortly before the '82 election. It was, by that point, obvious that Kent would win, and it was obvious to Phillip that he should go to work for the newly elected senator.

"I just got back from a fact-finding trip to Central America," he told Kent, "and I know your views on U.S. involvement there. To be perfectly frank, Mr. Janes, I think you need someone like me. I think my experiences there could be very helpful to you. I went all over El Salvador and Nicaragua."

There was something about Phillip's confidence that made Kent like him immediately. He didn't perceive him as arrogant, just sure of himself and his capabilities.

Phillip was waiting for him when he got to the office; he had a habit of showing up early for appointments, but it wasn't a habit that Kent discouraged.

"So what is this mysterious letter?" Kent said, leading Phillip into his private office.

"It's from Miami, and like I told you, whoever wrote it didn't sign their name. But, according to them, there is a group of men in Miami who are taking weapons into Nicaragua to arm the contras. Not that this is completely surprising, but the thing that caught my attention was that this person says they're first flying them into El Salvador—landing at Ilopango. Senator, you can't fly into Ilopango without the U.S. military knowing about it."

"I realize that, Phillip, but if I don't know who is telling us this, how can I do anything about it?"

"I don't know. It's a bitch, isn't it? All the good information seems to come without a return address."

8

ANDREW LEFT FOR NICARAGUA ON THE FIRST DAY OF March. Darren watched as the plane disappeared into the sky; she said a silent prayer and willed it up into the blue heights to follow the vapor trails.

The night before they had gone to dinner in Malibu, to a restaurant that jutted out over the sand. The light from a full moon floated on the sea like liquid silver, and breakers crashed lazily on the shore below them. Neither of them mentioned Nicaragua. Darren didn't need to put her fears into words; they were there, hovering like dark ships on the horizon.

They drove home along the Coast Highway, the white orb of the moon hanging large and ripe in the sky, and she thought it was one of the most perfect nights she had ever known . . . except for the fact that, by tomorrow night, Andrew would be gone.

Their lovemaking was a slow dance, lulled and lazy from the expensive wine and rich food. When Andrew rolled to his side of the bed, Darren turned toward the window and felt moonlight bathe her face. Its soft light spilled across the walls and made the air shimmer.

On the outskirts of sleep, the wolf was waiting for her. He raced into her dreams, his eyes yellow as lanterns and his body lengthening into a streak of silver against an ink-black sky.

Sean picked Andrew up at Sandino Airport in a jeep that looked like it had been rescued from a salvage yard.

"This yours?" Andrew said, throwing his suitcase in the back and climbing into the torn front seat.

"Yep. Bought it from some guy for a hundred bucks. He couldn't afford the upkeep anymore."

"Upkeep?" Andrew laughed as Sean maneuvered around the potholes in the road. "You expect me to believe this piece of shit has been kept up? I've heard tractors that are quieter than this."

"By Nicaraguan standards this is in good shape. Note the existence of four tires and an engine that does turn over, regardless of how it sounds to your sensitive ears."

Andrew checked into the Inter-Continental and called Darren to say he'd arrived safely. His room was clean and modern; inside those walls he could imagine he was anywhere—San Diego, Baltimore, you name it. It was one of those hotels that refused to let its decor give away what city it was in. "You're in America," it said the moment you entered the lobby.

Andrew and Sean had dinner at Los Antojos, across the street from the hotel. They sat near a patio where brightly colored parrots were flapping and circling in the air.

"They're why I like to come here," Sean said, pointing to the parrots. "The food's pretty good, but these fellows fascinate me."

When Andrew told Sean about the theft of the film, he heard in his own voice the somber note of defeat. He knew it would never be returned; any hope he had tried to hang on to was gone.

"So that's why you're back, huh?" Sean said. "And I thought you just wanted to hang out with me for a while."

"Well, I do. But I probably wouldn't be here if everything had gone as planned."

"Darren didn't want to come?"

"She did want to, but I said no. Actually, I'm sort of surprised she didn't stow away in the baggage compartment." Then he turned serious again. "What I'm hoping, Sean, is that I can get enough interesting shots that I can get backing for another film—maybe even from a studio. You have a pretty good idea of what's going on here, and I thought if I tagged along with you I might get what I'm after."

They spent the next few days in Managua. Andrew took his video camera everywhere, shooting many of the same things he'd filmed before: the emblems of poverty that were everywhere and the faces of people who had resigned themselves to a life that would never be kind.

They went to San Vicente Hospital in Matagalpa, where the moans and cries of pain were audible proof that pain medication and anesthetics were almost nonexistent. As Sean and Andrew moved silently among the beds, children watched them with eyes that pleaded for relief. Some of them had bandaged stumps where an arm or a leg should have been; some had been riddled with shrapnel or torn apart by bullets.

"Most of them will never get artificial limbs," they were told by a young doctor whose face was sagging with exhaustion. "We can't even relieve their pain."

Andrew thought of the tiny, one-armed girl in Tica's schoolhouse and of Darren kneeling down in the dirt hugging her, trying to take away the pain of another death.

"It makes it hard to believe there's a God, doesn't it?" Andrew asked as they walked out of the hospital into the blaze of sunlight.

"I've wondered about it frequently," Sean said.

Sean told Andrew about a small hotel in Estelí that would be a good change from the Inter-Continental. On a cloudy afternoon, they left Managua and drove north to Estelí.

The rooms at El Nicarao encircled a courtyard where they

ate dinner at a rough-hewn table adorned with a single candle that flickered and danced in the wind. A new moon shone thin blades of light on the ground, and the night was quiet and black around them. To Andrew the courtyard felt like a fragile circle of warmth—a pool of firelight in a wide, dark night. In that ring of light, laughing and drinking with Sean, Andrew felt that nothing could harm them. They were safe from danger, but if he looked out beyond those thin boundaries, he felt the cold pull of fear.

The next morning, as a light mist drifted through the window, Andrew woke up and blinked his eyes at the thin gray light. He wasn't sure at first what had woken him up, just that something had. Then he heard the voices outside, voices he had thought were only in his dream. People were shouting, obviously upset, but they were speaking too fast and he couldn't make out what they were saying through the walls.

There was a knock on the door and Sean's voice asked him if he was awake.

"What's going on out there?" Andrew asked, opening the door.

"Some people got killed near here. I thought I heard gunshots last night, but then I thought it might be my brain cells exploding from all those beers. Come on, get dressed. I want to see what happened."

As Andrew pulled on his clothes, he heard, above the tangle of voices, a woman's sad, high wail. In any language that sound meant the same thing. He grabbed the video camera and ran out to the jeep, where Sean was already waiting with the engine running.

They drove up to the group of people, who were still talking in loud voices, and Sean jumped out and spoke to one of the men. Sean pointed to the jeep, and the man followed and jumped in the back. The man indicated a small cluster of shacks about two miles away; through the mist they looked like dark smudges on a white background.

Sean was driving so fast that Andrew almost fell out of the car. They screeched to a stop at the houses; Andrew counted five of them. Several men were already there and were walking away, their faces grim and bitter, when Sean pulled up. The man who had ridden with them got out to speak to the others while Sean and Andrew moved slowly toward the first house.

A woman's body was sprawled in the doorway, her blood like a dried river running from the steps to the dusty ground. Her face was frozen in a last desperate scream, and her arm reached out for help that never came.

They looked past the woman into the house. A man was lying facedown in a pool of blood; a tiny leg stuck out from beneath his body. Andrew fought past his nausea and turned the man over. It took all his strength, as if death converted the years of a lifetime into pounds of lead. The bullet had gone through his body into the child's; the shield of her father's body had been useless.

Andrew kept the camera running, although he felt like he should apologize to the souls of these dead people for immortalizing the ugliness of their deaths. When he noticed Sean kneeling down beside a man's body for what seemed like a long time, he put the camera down and came over to him.

"What is it, Sean?"

"Look what he's got in his hand. It's incredible—he picked his killer's pocket even as he was dying. We should get this on tape, Andrew. I'm sorry, I know it seems ghoulish, but—"

"I know," Andrew said as he picked up the camera. "It's what I came back for, isn't it?"

Sean uncurled the man's fingers and removed a silver money clip with an American eagle engraved on it. Between the folds of money, stained with blood, were some identification cards.

"Well, what do you know," Sean said. "Someone named Emerson Kyle has a security pass for Ilopango Airport. I think we'll just hang on to this."

He put the cards in his pocket and went into another house, Andrew following behind him with the camera. Everywhere it was the same—bodies twisted into grotesque shapes, testaments to their final seconds of terror.

As they were walking out of one house where a woman and a baby lay on the floor, emptied of blood, Andrew thought he heard a scraping sound on the floor behind him.

76

"Did you hear that, Sean?"

He turned off the camera and walked slowly back across the rough planks of the floor, stepping around the streams of blood and swallowing hard against the sickness rising in his throat. He knelt down and looked under the bed; a pair of frightened brown eyes stared back at him.

"Jesus Christ. Sean, come here. It's all right," he said to the child. "It's all right, we're not going to hurt you."

The boy couldn't have been more than six years old. He was trembling, crouched against the wall, staring at the two strangers who had discovered his hiding place.

"*Estás herido?*" Sean asked.

He shook his head and pointed a small hand toward the woman and the baby sprawled on the floor a few feet from the bed.

"*No te vamos lastimar,*" Sean said softly, and reached his hand under the bed toward the boy. The boy slid away, whimpering.

"Wait here with him, Andrew."

Sean ran out and came back moments later with the man who had ridden over with them in the jeep. Andrew and Sean moved away from the bed while the man knelt down and spoke gently to the boy in Spanish. Finally, they heard the boy slide across the floor and then he crawled out from the hiding place that had saved his life.

The man who had coaxed him out left, and Andrew approached the boy hesitantly. He reached out and brushed some hair from his forehead, and the child seemed to know that he wasn't the enemy. "Come on," Andrew said, "let's get out of here." The smell of death was heavy in the room and was getting worse as the sun melted the mist outside and warmed the air.

Andrew picked up the boy and carried him outside. As they approached the jeep their passenger ran up and motioned for them to follow him. Andrew thought about putting the boy in the jeep, but his arms were locked around Andrew's neck and his body felt limp and drained of energy. So he carried the boy and he and Sean followed as the man led them to a small, open area between two of the houses. Four stakes had been pounded into the ground and on each one a torn, bloodied body was hung. Andrew looked at the child in his arms, not wanting him to see any more horror than he already had, but the boy was asleep.

"Sweet dreams," Andrew whispered, burying his face in the boy's neck and breathing in the light, sweet smell that he hadn't yet outgrown. "I hope you can still have sweet dreams."

He forced himself to look up again at the grisly scene in front of him. He felt Sean taking the camera from his shoulder and realized that they were witnessing something even more horrible than death. Apparently death wasn't enough; the bodies had also been decapitated and the heads switched. The women's torsos wore men's heads and the men's wore women's. He walked over to Sean as slowly as he could, trying not to wake the sleeping boy in his arms.

"Sean, take him please." As soon as the child was in Sean's arms, Andrew ran behind one of the houses and vomited. He was shaky and sweat was running down his face. He heard the sound of a man sobbing, and for a minute he was so disoriented he thought it was his own voice, his own sobs. But as he walked back he saw that it was the man who had been their guide for this journey into terror.

The boy was awake now, but Sean had his face turned away from the bodies. "Andrew, give me your camera and take him back to the jeep, OK?" he said. He seemed to be the only one who was still holding himself together.

Andrew took the boy into his arms again, feeling a shiver pass through him as the small, warm body sank into his chest. He walked out to where he could face open land, and as he stood there with the child in his arms and the litter of dead bodies behind him, he noticed a thin ray of sunlight piercing the layers of mist. He remembered that when he was a child, not much older than the boy he was holding, he would imagine that God sometimes parted the clouds to get a telescopic view of His creation. But now, in these sun-split moments with so much death around him, God had never seemed so far away.

They drove back to the hotel in silence, the boy sitting on

Andrew's lap and the weeping man in the backseat. The sun was rising in the sky as they watched the man walk away from them without looking back, his shoulders still shaking and his head bowed toward the ground.

"What are we going to do about him?" Andrew said, nodding toward the boy.

"I'm not sure. Let's talk to the woman who runs the hotel; maybe she knows someone. But first let's spend some time with him. He might have seen who did it."

The child's name was Antonio, but it took a while before he would say any more than that. They sat in the courtyard where, the night before, moonlight had encircled them with bands of light. They bought Antonio some beans and tortillas and sat patiently as he picked at the food. Andrew felt the heat of the day rush over him, but nonetheless he had the sense that there was a cold wind rising up from the earth, just beneath his feet.

Sean kept talking to Antonio in Spanish, asking slow, gentle questions, and finally he began to answer. Andrew understood most of what he said, but he let Sean translate, hoping he was wrong about what he thought he had heard.

"Americans," Sean said with a blank, glazed look on his face. "He said the men who killed his mother and sister were Americans. He hid under the bed and he heard his mother scream, and then he heard their voices. They talked like us—Americans."

Andrew stared back at Sean. "I guess that doesn't come as too much of a shock. We even know one of their names."

Sean talked to Antonio for a few more minutes and then asked Andrew to stay with him while he went to find the woman who ran the hotel.

Andrew looked across the table at Antonio's hands, so tiny and smooth and perfect.

"Maybe people don't really die," he said, knowing Antonio didn't understand what he was saying but continuing anyway. "Maybe they become stars in the heaven, constellations. They turn into points of light that form beautiful patterns in the sky. So whenever you look up, you can feel close to the people you lost. They're always there, bending over you in the dark."

Antonio watched him with steady eyes. It didn't seem to matter that Andrew was speaking a language he didn't understand; the sound of his voice was enough.

They drove back to Managua without Antonio. The woman at the hotel said she knew a family who had lost a child, and they would take him in.

"Are you going to write about it?" Andrew asked Sean.

"That's what I'm here for."

"But I mean, everything? Everything we saw?"

Sean nodded. "I don't know if it will all end up in the paper, but I'm sure as hell gonna tell it as we saw it."

Andrew looked up at a plane flying above them. Sunlight bounced off the wing, and the plane looked like a tiny shard of silver in the vastness of the sky. Andrew wished he could lift himself to those heights and leave behind what he had seen, but he knew he would carry those pictures with him forever, just as Darren would always remember her last image of Tica.

9

ITH THE HOUSE TO HERSELF AND NO ONE ELSE'S SCHE-
dule or wishes to consider, Darren had started to
get up at five o'clock each morning so she could be at the gym by
five-thirty. In the time that Andrew had been away, she had
fallen in love with that time of day, when dawn was just a thin
whisper at the edge of the sky. In the stillness of that world, silent
and stitched with stars, she could almost hear people breathing
the steady, deep rhythms of sleep in the dark houses she passed.
It was as if everyone were being rocked by the same lullaby. It
felt like her secret, as though she alone were awake, watching
over the city as it slept.

Walking into the fluorescent light of the gym was like a
splash of cold water, but she even liked that part of it. By the
time other people shook dreams from their heads, she would be
feeling blood pump into her muscles and her breathing would be

quick and deep. And for that hour she could forget that Andrew was somewhere in a country where those quiet blue hours just before dawn often carried the smell of death.

The day before Andrew was due to arrive home, Darren and Cassie were sitting in the yard having a glass of wine. Evening was pulling light from the sky, painting it deep shades of lavender and blue. Leland and Peanut were racing around playing some incomprehensible game that Darren had warned Cassie not to try to decipher.

Suddenly, Peanut came to a dead stop, tilted her head, and ran toward the house. Darren turned around to see Andrew stepping out the back door.

"Andrew, why didn't you let me know? I would have picked you up at the airport," she said, running over to him.

"I know, but it was sort of a spontaneous thing. I didn't want to screw up your day. Hi, Cassie."

Cassie finished the last of her wine and stood up. "Good to see you, Andrew. I think I'll leave you two alone now."

Leland was yelling for Peanut, who was ignoring him and devoting all her attention to Andrew.

"You know, I was wondering for a minute if you'd let Leland get a little too creative with your dog's name," Cassie said. "I could have sworn he'd renamed her after his own genitals."

"It's a common misconception," Andrew said, glancing at Darren. "We were thinking of getting a cat and naming it Breast just to add to the confusion."

Darren studied Andrew's face. Even in the soft, purple light, he looked pale and tired. There were dark circles under his eyes, and his smile seemed to be fighting through a thick layer of sadness.

"Leland, I think play hour is over for today," she said.

"OK, but I hope you're through kissing and stuff by tomorrow."

"We'll try," Andrew said, tousling Leland's hair as the boy walked reluctantly toward the gate.

"When Cassie left Darren poured Andrew a glass of wine

and led him into the living room. The house was quiet and growing dark; she turned on a single lamp, liking the sleepy feel of the shadows.

"I read Sean's article in the paper," she said. "Unfortunately, I read the other pieces, too. The ones that explained what 'really' happened."

"I know. It's almost funny, in a sick sort of way. Sandinistas dressing up as contras and even managing to pass themselves off as Americans. You'd think they could come up with something better."

"Andrew, did something else happen? You sound worse than you did on the phone."

He took a deep breath and let it out slowly. "I don't know if I'm imagining things, but last night Sean and I were in the bar at the hotel and there were a few guys—Americans—at a table near us. It sounded like they were from Texas. I picked up snatches of their conversation, and I couldn't shake the feeling that they were talking about those people in Estelí. I had the feeling they were the ones who did it."

"What were they saying?"

"Things like 'We taught 'em a fucking lesson' and that someone will 'get an eyeful.' Just pieces of the conversation. That's why I don't know if I'm reacting out of paranoia. It was just . . . I never thought I would see something like that. And that little boy I told you about—I think it helped me to hold on to him as much as it probably helped him."

Darren wondered if carrying that child around had made him think differently about having children of his own, but it was the wrong time to ask.

"You know what I'm going to do tomorrow?" Andrew said. "I'm going to call Senator Janes's office and try to work my way through the chain of command and get in touch with him. I have a feeling if I describe enough of what I saw, I might just be able to reach him."

"Are you still going to try to get backing for a film?" Darren asked, almost hoping the answer would be no. She had a sense that things were spinning out of control, moving at jaguar speed toward an end they weren't prepared to handle.

"Absolutely. I'm going to make it as hard as I possibly can for them to bury this."

Darren left Andrew sitting in the living room staring out the window. She took the clothes out of his suitcase and put them into the washing machine, and when she came back he was asleep on the couch. He was half sitting, half lying down, with his arm dangling over the side as if sleep had crept up from behind and hit him over the head. His face was drawn into a frown and his jaw was clenched.

"Wouldn't you be more comfortable in bed?" she whispered, bending down and kissing his forehead.

"Uh-huh," he mumbled, pulling himself up.

"Andrew, were you having a bad dream?"

"Probably. It seems to be a common occurrence these days."

The next day Darren heard Andrew on the phone talking to someone in Kent Janes's Los Angeles office. He was saying just enough to work his way up the chain of command, and after fifteen minutes he yelled out to her, "I got the name of Janes's assistant in Washington!"

"Great," she said, wondering if it was.

He was on the phone for nearly an hour, talking to someone named Phillip Payne. Darren heard him explaining about the film that had been stolen, about the two men who had volunteered to be on the crew, and about his second trip. She walked outside as he was starting to describe the scene in the village; she had heard about it enough.

The day was changing colors. Fog was rolling across the sky, and Darren sat in the yard watching its soft, white conquest. When she heard Andrew in the kitchen, she went back inside.

"Are you through with your phone calls?" she said, coming up behind him and wrapping her arms around his waist.

"Yeah, why?"

Darren kissed the back of his neck. "Because I don't think we've made love enough since you got home."

She could feel something different in Andrew's lovemaking—something about the way he moved inside her—but she wasn't sure what it was. For a moment she thought he was crying, and when she pulled back to look at his face, she saw that his eyes were wet and shiny.

"What is it?" she said softly.

"You still want to have a baby?"

"Yes."

"OK."

They were quiet for a long time. The world outside the windows was damp and white, and the trees looked like dark statues.

"I don't know. Being with that little boy, Antonio, was probably a big factor. I ended up feeling that maybe I was being selfish, that I was hanging on to the pain of my own childhood as an excuse. When I was holding him in my arms and talking to him, even though he didn't understand what I was saying, I had the sense that I could be a good father, that it was something I shouldn't stop myself from doing."

Darren said nothing; she didn't want to break the spell. It was as if Andrew's decision were so new that a single wrong word could splinter it.

10

KENT JANES CLOSED THE DOOR SOFTLY BEHIND HIM AND walked down the front steps. The sky was just getting light; the pink dawn made the brick houses look rose-colored, as if they'd been painted during the night. As he started running he could hear his footsteps echo in the still morning air. Lights were coming on in a few of the houses, and he knew that by the time he finished his run, the morning aromas of bacon and freshly brewed coffee would be wafting up from a dozen different kitchens.

His morning runs were something he rarely missed; even on rainy days he would see neighbors peer out their windows to watch him slog through sheets of rain in the darkness of a winter morning, putting in his five miles.

This morning, though, every muscle in his body seemed to rebel. Maybe I just have too much on my mind, he thought, increasing his pace as if he were waging a war with his own body. He felt his lungs burn with the increased effort, and he picked up the pace even more.

As the sky paled and the morning stars faded, he calculated that he had probably slept no more than three hours the night before. It was almost two before Cecilia had finally quieted down. He had thought, at first, that the lithium, which the doctor had hoped would work for her, had failed, but he discovered a nearly full bottle and realized that she hadn't been taking any for weeks.

"Manic-depressive psychosis is a cyclical thing," the doctor had explained to him. "There are periods of extreme withdrawal and depression, and then episodes of agitation, even aggression. We've had a lot of success with lithium. In most cases it evens out these phases, so the changes are no more dramatic than you or I having good and bad days."

But Cecilia had not been taking her medication, and Kent had come home the previous evening to find her storming through the house, tearing clothes out of closets, books from shelves, complaining there was just too much clutter around, too many useless things. When he tried to calm her down, she yelled at him to get out of her way. Couldn't he see she was busy?

"Who the hell else is going to weed out all this stuff?" she screamed. "No one else lifts a damn finger around here!"

When Kent came back downstairs with the full bottle of lithium, he said, "Cecilia, there's a reason the doctor wanted you to take this."

"I don't need any goddamn pills!" she yelled. "If I'm so hard to live with that you have to tranquilize me, why don't you just put me away somewhere? That's what they did with my grandfather. Out of sight, out of mind."

"Cecilia, what are you talking about?" Kent asked gently, not sure that she was really talking about anything.

She grew calm for a moment, but it was an icy calm, thin and sharp as the slice of a knife. "They decided he was crazy," she said, "so they locked him up somewhere and let him die."

Then it started again. She ran to the kitchen and started pulling pots out of the cabinets, crashing them on the floor.

"Cecilia, please listen to me," he pleaded. "You have to take your medication. Please just try to understand what I'm saying. Try to calm down and listen to what I'm telling you."

"Fine, I'll calm down. What should I do? Count to ten? Isn't that supposed to work?"

She began counting, but with each number her hysteria grew until "ten" was an earsplitting scream that Kent was sure would bring neighbors and police to their door. She collapsed onto the floor, shaken and breathless, and sat in the middle of pots and broken dishes, crying like an injured child. Kent finally persuaded her to take the lithium, but hours went by before either of them got to sleep.

Kent started walking a block before his house, letting his breathing return to normal. The days were getting warmer; in a month the pear trees that lined the Georgetown streets would be exploding with blossoms, making him feel like he was running through a Monet painting. But this morning, there was a cold, bitter feeling in his stomach that even the thought of spring couldn't melt.

Kent showered and dressed, moving as quietly as a thief so that he wouldn't wake Cecilia. He poured himself a bowl of corn flakes and swallowed two cups of strong coffee, hoping it would make him a little more alert.

At eight o'clock he walked through the glass doors of the Hart Senate Office Building. He passed the white, plant-filled tubs, strategically placed to block car bombs, and crossed the marble floor of the atrium. He knew his secretary wouldn't arrive for another hour, and he welcomed the time alone to sort out his thoughts. But when he walked through the door of the outer office, Phillip was waiting for him.

"Good morning," Kent said. "You're in awfully early, aren't you?"

"I thought it would be the best time to catch you. I need to talk to you about a phone call I got yesterday."

They went into Kent's office, a tastefully decorated sanctuary that looked more like a living room. It reflected Cecilia's touch—the rich blue Chinese rug and the antique mahogany desk were her additions. It made Kent sad sometimes that there was so much of her in that room, but he would never consider changing the decor just to spare himself the pain.

"I'm all ears," Kent said, motioning Phillip toward the leather chair that faced the desk.

"I got a call from someone named Andrew Laverty," Phillip said. "He makes documentaries, and he made one in Nicaragua, only it sounds like it was sabotaged. I talked to him for a long time, Senator, and I don't think he's inventing things. I think it would be worth it to have a conversation with him. He just got back from a second trip there, and he and a reporter friend of his were among the first people to find those villagers that were killed."

"You mean the ones who were murdered by the Sandinistas-in-disguise?" Kent asked.

"The very ones," Phillip said. "I hope you won't mind, but I practically promised Mr. Laverty that you'd be calling him."

"OK. . . . Was there something else, Phillip? You look like you're not finished yet."

"Actually, there was. I've been going through some back issues of *Soldier of Fortune* magazine—"

"Phillip, I'm shocked. I always had you pegged for a *Time* and *Newsweek* guy."

"Research, Senator. I don't exactly have a subscription to *Soldier of Fortune*. Anyway, that letter from Miami kept nagging at me, so I took a shot in the dark and I found something that may or may not be significant. Apparently there's a retired colonel named Hadley who lives in Miami and is fairly vocal about what he thinks should be done in Central America, particularly Nicaragua. He's mentioned in several issues. Seems to be on the magazine's 'Most Admired' list. He also gave an interview in one issue and was pretty open about his weapons collection."

"Well, I don't know what I can do with that information except just hang on to it, which I will. Thanks, Phillip. I have some work to do, so I'd better get to it."

As Phillip closed the door behind him, Kent went to the window and looked down at Saint Joseph's Church. Staring at the brownstone building, he found himself wishing that some sort of divine message would drift through the roof into his office, telling him how to prove what his instincts already knew.

Kent arrived home shortly after six. He had been on the Senate floor for most of the day, and he was tired and edgy. He knew Cecilia's doctor was already waiting for him; he had called that morning and asked Dr. Easton to stop by.

He found him sitting in the living room with a cup of tea.

"Dr. Easton, I hope you weren't waiting long. I had trouble getting away. Can I exchange your tea for a drink?"

"No, thank you. It's still working hours for me."

Garrett Easton was, by Kent's calculations, at least ten years younger than he looked. Somewhere along the line his body had lost its battle with gravity, and everything from his eyelids to his belly was starting to drop. He favored three-piece suits and a neatly trimmed mustache, and his hands were soft and manicured. His hair was still dark, but at least half of it had also given up the fight; Garrett attempted to conceal his baldness by parting his hair just above his left ear and combing it across the top of his head, plastering it down with something that never dried. He was, however, a highly qualified professional who seemed to genuinely care for his patients.

Kent had noticed that the doctor seemed more comfortable around Cecilia than around him, leading him to believe that he was more at ease in the company of people who were in emotional tatters.

"If you don't mind, I'm going to have a drink," Kent said, going to the sideboard, where crystal decanters reflected the lamplight.

The living room, like Kent's office, was filled with antiques. Cecilia had coordinated the room into a soothing array of beige and green; even the oil paintings on the walls blended into that color scheme.

Kent sat down in the forest green armchair that faced the couch.

"So, did Cecilia give you any reason for not taking her medication?" he asked.

"Not really. You know, I should tell you that there is a possibility that lithium won't help. It doesn't help everyone. I want you to know that, although I obviously can't make that diagnosis unless she takes it regularly. I'm hesitant to suggest that you make her take it because I know what a strain that might put on your relationship."

"Our relationship is already strained, Doctor," Kent said, regretting the sharpness of his tone but too tired to do anything about it. "I don't know my wife anymore. She's a stranger to me. Laura was my child, too—I feel the loss, too. But now I feel the loss of my wife as well. Cecilia just retreated. She's gone into a different world, and I'm not allowed entrance there. I know this is going to sound horrible"—Kent took a deep breath and let it out slowly—"but I resent her for leaving me to suffer on my own, for not allowing us to go through this together."

Dr. Easton let him finish. He paused for a moment before he leaned forward and looked intently at Kent. "Senator Janes, I'm well aware that it's hard on you. And the resentment that you feel is not horrible, it's natural. Something like this is often harder on the family members than it is on the patient. I think it would help if you had someone to talk things out with on a regular basis. It doesn't have to be me, but it certainly can be."

Kent felt tears pressing against the back of his eyes. "You're probably right," he said. "Let me give you a call sometime tomorrow and we'll set something up. And please, you don't have to call me Senator Janes. Kent will do fine."

"All right. I prefer being addressed by my first name also." With that Dr. Easton stood up to leave and held out his hand to Kent.

"By the way," Kent said, "something Cecilia said last night made me curious. She said her grandfather was institutionalized for some sort of mental disorder. Could something like this be hereditary?"

"There does seem to be some sort of genetic predisposition to forms of psychosis, yes."

Kent watched Garrett Easton walk down the steps and get into his car. He almost dreaded going back into the house, into the oppressive silence that seemed, now, like the razor-sharp stillness that forecasts a storm. He poured himself another scotch, turned off all the lamps, and sat on the couch. The night wove a dark web around him and he felt the liquor travel warmly through his veins. Hidden by the moonless night, Kent Janes gave in to his tears and cried as freely as a child.

He sat alone in the dark for almost an hour, and when the flood of emotion had ebbed, he walked slowly upstairs. He could tell by the shallowness of Cecilia's breathing that she was still awake. He took off his clothes, threw them on the chair, and slid into bed beside her.

Kent slipped his arms around Cecilia and pulled her on top of him. She was so light it was as if the breeze had moved her. The memory of how she used to straddle him, peeling off her nightgown and lowering herself onto him, made the sadness well up in him again. Now she just lay there, weightless as a cinder. He rolled over so that she was underneath him and made love to her gently, as if she would shatter like crystal.

"I love you," he said, hearing in his own voice a note of helplessness.

"I love you too," she answered, but her words skimmed over him and fluttered through the open window on a gust of night wind.

11

*A*S APRIL SLID INTO MAY AND THE DAYS GREW WARMER and longer, infused with the scent of jasmine blooming in the garden, Darren was left with more time to herself than she wanted. She did a few watercolors of the dawn light washing the garden in pink and gold, and one of Peanut stretched out on the grass—an image of the total relaxation that only animals seem capable of—but the paintings ended up in the closet with the others that she didn't think were good enough.

Andrew, meanwhile, was trying every avenue he knew to get financing for his documentary on Nicaragua, but no one was interested. He checked his phone messages several times a day, hoping for word from Kent Janes.

"That's last year's cause," one studio executive said, and, despite his anger, Andrew knew the man was voicing a sentiment that others felt but were afraid to say.

He felt himself being driven by an energy that seemed raw and almost frantic. It was as if he wanted to make up for lost time, to explore new feelings while he was still running away from old ones. It was a race for a destination he felt he should have reached years before.

The faces of the dead in Nicaragua floated through his nightmares, reminding him that there were more whose faces he would never see. And it wasn't only Nicaragua. The death squads in El Salvador were filling their quotas every week, but no one wanted to talk about that either. Andrew started to attend meetings of a group called Safe Haven, which was dedicated to providing refuge for people from El Salvador who had managed to escape. There was a part of him, though, that felt the futility of their efforts.

Darren tried to watch impassively, fearing that if she pointed out Andrew's feverish pace she would only make it worse. But it was starting to grate on her. She decided that she would make plans for them to go away for a few days and present it to him as a surprise. Andrew never objected to surprises; it was a part of childhood that he hadn't known until he reached adulthood. She made reservations at the San Ysidro Ranch outside of Santa Barbara—a rustic, but expensive retreat where the costliest cabins had Jacuzzis on private decks that faced woods of evergreens and ferns.

When Andrew was reading the paper one morning, she slipped the brochure from the ranch in front of his face.

"Oh, yeah, nice place," Andrew said, glancing at it. "We should go there sometime."

"We certainly should. How about tomorrow? They're expecting us."

For a minute she thought he was going to tell her about some meeting he couldn't change, but instead he smiled as if it were Christmas morning and he'd gotten everything he'd asked for.

The next afternoon they threw some clothes and cans of dog food into Andrew's car, put Peanut in the backseat, and drove up the coast.

Peanut's first adventure when they unlocked the door to their cabin was to run out to the deck and fall in the Jacuzzi. After they dried her off, they walked up the road into the hills.

It was so still that when they talked they almost whispered, as if they were trespassing on a place where they didn't belong. Above them the evening sky was shifting into a perfect shade of blue for the exchange of the moon for the sun.

"I guess I've been sort of hard to get along with lately, haven't I?" Andrew said.

"Well . . . I might have put it less politely."

"Have you ever felt so angry that you think if the right circumstance came along, you could just lose it completely?"

"Yes. I don't think that's an unusual feeling."

"But I've had that feeling almost all the time lately," Andrew said, his voice rising in the shadowy air. "I know that what that kid told me was true. Shit, we found evidence of it. There are Americans going into another country and killing people. It's like finding out your neighbor is in the Ku Klux Klan, but nobody wants to hear about it or do anything about it."

"You are trying to do something about it, Andrew. Don't be so hard on yourself. You're doing everything you can. But you know, maybe for a couple of days you need to let it go. That's why I thought this would be good. You've been going like you're on fire. You need to just take a few days to cool off and relax," she said as the dark drifted in around them and their feet stirred up dust on the narrow path.

They ordered dinner in their cabin, and while they waited they sat in the Jacuzzi, the moon casting filigreed light through the trees. There was no city glow to interfere with the design of stars. Bundled in thick terry-cloth robes, they sat out on the deck and had dinner by candlelight, with the night sounds of owls and crickets serenading them from secret hiding places in the undisturbed woods.

"Wait here for a minute," Andrew said after he poured more wine into Darren's glass. He disappeared into the cabin and came back with the blanket from the bed. He laid it out on the deck and took off his robe. Moonlight played across his body.

With the wind whispering over them, they made love in the silvery light, the wine heavy as syrup in their veins and their bodies still warm from the Jacuzzi.

When Andrew slid out of her, leaving a sweet pain behind, Darren curled up next to him and pulled the edges of the blanket around them. Andrew's breathing was getting slower; she fell into its rhythm and felt her eyelids getting heavier. A flurry of wind shook the branches above them and lifted the smell of damp soil from the woods, spinning it through the air. She could smell their own scents—heavier, like something plucked from the sea.

When the night got colder they took the blanket back inside and fell asleep on the bed, tangled together, with the wind blowing through the open door.

In her sleep Darren was aware of Andrew changing positions, moving toward the other side of the bed. The night air rushed in to the places where his body had been. With the same hazy awareness, she saw the wolf's yellow eyes and the perfect precision of his movements. For weeks he had been absent from her dreams, but he crept toward her with the familiarity of one whose return should never have been doubted.

In her dream she mirrored his movements, floating toward him, matching the steady gaze of his eyes. She stroked the velvet of his coat and felt the coldness of his nose as he sniffed her hand. And then, as always, he sped into the night, a ribbon of mercury against the sky.

Andrew tried to hang on to the relaxation that had finally seeped into him during their few days in Santa Barbara. But he returned home to find a phone message from Senator Janes's office and two from a member of Safe Haven in an urgent-sounding voice that scraped out of the phone machine. Andrew felt a strange surge of anxiety sneaking up on him again, pressing on his temples and shivering up his spine.

He managed to reach Senator Janes on the first try, and their lengthy conversation left him feeling better, but he would have preferred it if Janes had offered to jump on a plane the next day and meet with him.

"You have to realize," the senator said, his words sounding cautious and measured, "that information has to be absolutely incontrovertible for it to be of value. You've given me the account of a child, and while I might believe you, a child's testimony is not always highly regarded by many people."

"Well, I couldn't exactly go in and fingerprint the place," Andrew said, instantly regretting his sarcasm.

"I realize that; I'm just telling you what the problems are here. I understand that you don't want to tell me everything on the phone, and I will get in touch with you when I'm in California next time and we can set up a meeting."

The next evening Andrew left the sea breeze of Santa Monica Canyon and headed toward the San Fernando Valley. He had agreed to meet some members of Safe Haven at a church where a family of Salvadoran refugees had been staying. The church had agreed to harbor them, but now they were frightened and reluctant to continue the arrangement. Another refuge had to be found.

It was just getting dark as Andrew turned onto the San Diego Freeway. He switched on the radio and thought of Darren's expression when he told her where he was going and why.

"Please don't tell me you're going to bring them here," she said.

"Darren, I wasn't considering that. We're just going to examine the options and try to figure out what to do."

A piano instrumental was playing on the radio, and sweet chords filled the car. The sky was deepening to purple and a mild spring breeze ruffled his hair. It was one of those nights when the city felt slow and gentle; even the passing headlights looked friendly.

The church was just off Ventura Boulevard. There was a parking lot in front and, as he pulled in, Andrew noticed several familiar cars.

Inside, two men and one woman he knew from previous meetings were involved in a heated discussion with the priest. Huddled at the end of one of the pews were two poorly dressed

97

men whose dark eyes peered out from their dark faces and a woman with a newborn baby nursing at her breast. Andrew knew they probably understood none of what was being said, only that they were the ones under discussion.

He sat down behind the three people he knew and realized as he did that he had inadvertently reinforced the battle line between the two sides.

"It's been more than two weeks now," the young priest was saying. "I agreed to help, and I am certainly sympathetic, but I was under the impression that my help was needed for only a short time. I'm just not willing to take this kind of risk indefinitely. And now with the baby . . ."

"How old is the baby?" Andrew asked.

"A week," the woman said. Andrew tried to remember her name. She was one of the founders of Safe Haven and he had seen her frequently, but she had a brusque, authoritative manner that made him shy away from any in-depth conversation. It was probably indicative of his feelings that he had forgotten her name.

"She was born here in the church," the priest said. "Fortunately we had already alerted a nurse who is a church member and she helped with the delivery. I don't know what we would have done if there had been complications. So you see, the child just makes it even more impossible to keep them here."

Andrew looked around at the people he was sitting with. "I have this uncomfortable feeling," he said, "that we're talking about this family as if they were bags of grain or something. Look at them. They're crouched over there like frightened animals. They know we're talking about them, but they have no idea what we're saying. It just seems as if we could be a little more humane in our approach to this problem."

"Being humane is what this whole thing is about," the woman whose name escaped him answered. "If they get caught and sent back to El Salvador, they'll be killed. We're trying to keep them safe."

"I understand that, but someone should talk to them. Doesn't anyone here speak Spanish?"

98

All four of them shook their heads.

"Well, I speak a little," Andrew said, getting up and walking to the back pew where the family was sitting, motionless. Outside, the wind had picked up; he could hear it raking the sky and scraping across the roof. He wondered if it was the start of a Santa Ana—the hot, dry winds that blew in from the desert and pushed all the smog out to sea, where it would lie like a wet, brown blanket on the horizon. Andrew regarded Santa Anas as a bad omen; things happened during Santa Anas—bad things like fires, shootings, earthquakes.

He stood in front of the mother and held his hand out to touch the baby's head. The woman smiled at him and held the child out, like an offering. He saw the fear in her eyes turn to cautious trust, and he was still holding her gaze when the walls blew apart. He was being catapulted through a world of smoke and thick ribbons of fire that tore into him. There was no sound anymore, just a horrible, dead silence. He felt his body being ripped apart, but there was no pain, just the black smoke choking him and searing his lungs and his flesh. And then darkness crept into the edges of his vision. . . .

12

*D*ARREN GOT HOME AROUND EIGHT-THIRTY, EXPECTING to find Andrew already there. She had gone to Lawson's for dinner, not wanting to spend the evening by herself. As she pulled up to the house, she saw that the windows were dark and Andrew's car wasn't in the driveway, which was the only place it would be since there was no room for cars in their garage. The garage had become a storage area for extra furniture, camera equipment, and boxes of things that they kept meaning to go through but never did.

When they first moved in, Andrew had insisted that Darren park in the driveway; he would find a spot on the street. But one night Darren woke up, looked out the window, and saw two boys trying to break into Andrew's black Toyota Supra. She ran to the front door and shouted, "Get away from that car or I'll shoot your balls off!" From that point on Andrew had parked in the driveway.

She turned on a few lights, gave Peanut some dog biscuits, and had just settled down with a book when the phone rang.

"Hi, where are you?" she said, certain it was Andrew.

"Darren, it's Lawson."

"Oh, Lawson, is something wrong? You sound funny."

"Dear, what was the name of the church where Andrew was going tonight?" Lawson said.

"Um . . . the Church of Saint Mary, I think. Why?"

She listened as Lawson tried to explain what he had heard on the news, choosing his words carefully. But only one word mattered—*explosion*. People didn't live through explosions. Lawson said he would be right over, and she heard the click of the phone when he hung up. A wire was tightening inside her; she sank to the floor of the kitchen, with no strength left in her legs or in her hands. The receiver was in her lap. She could hear the buzz of the dial tone, steady and constant and normal, a sound she heard every day. But now that hum of wires had transported words that had the power to hurl her into an abyss of fear.

It seemed like no time had passed when she heard the doorbell. Lawson . . . Darren managed to get up and open the door, and when she saw him, she fell against him and felt the first wave of tears push its way through the numbness.

"Darren, we don't know anything yet. He could be on his way home, or at a hospital, or anywhere. We can't jump to conclusions. Now, leave a note for him and get your shoes on, all right?"

Darren felt as if she were walking through a dream; any minute she expected to wake up. She found a piece of paper and a pen, but she didn't know what to write. "Please don't be dead" was all that came to her.

"Just tell him we've driven out to the church," Lawson said gently.

"Ok." She left the note on the dining room table and put on her shoes. "Come on, Peanut."

"Wait, dear. I really don't think we should take her."

Another wave of tears crested and broke. "We have to," she said, choking on her own voice. "She knows something's going on. Please don't make me leave her. I can't leave her."

"All right, we'll take her."

They drove along Sunset to the San Diego Freeway, a journey that seemed endless although traffic was light and Darren knew they were making good time. She kept her eyes on the other side of the road, hoping she would see Andrew behind the wheel of his black Toyota, on his way home. He could have left before the explosion; it wasn't an impossibility. The more Darren thought about it, the more she was sure that's what had happened. Or maybe he had heard about it on the car radio and gone back to help.

"He's all right, Lawson," she said emphatically as cars sped past them. "I know he is."

Lawson reached across the seat and squeezed her hand.

As soon as they came off the ramp and turned onto Ventura Boulevard, they saw the smoke up ahead. Darren felt her stomach churn and she struggled to force air into her lungs. As they got closer she saw that an entire block was barricaded by police and fire trucks. They parked a block away and left Peanut in the car. Lawson held tightly to Darren's arm as if he expected her, at any moment, to run toward the smoke looking for Andrew.

A crowd of spectators stood across the street, staring at the smoldering wreckage. She followed their stares and saw that what had once been a building was now a blackened, gaping mouth, frozen into a hideous grin. The wind whipped the smoke into funnels, which rose up toward the stars.

Darren noticed a television news crew; one man was walking around with a microphone talking to different people, and the cameraman was taking in everything. A movie, she thought, it was just a movie! Someone would yell "Cut!" in a minute and everything would go back to normal.

Lawson was saying something to one of the policemen who was standing at the barricade, but Darren couldn't make out anyone's words. Everything had become a swirl of noise and lights. She thought she saw Andrew walking out of the rubble, covered with soot and ashes but unharmed . . . and then the image vanished. The strength left her muscles and Lawson's grip on her arm was the only thing holding her up. He led her over to where a fireman was talking to a man in slacks and a nylon windbreaker. Seeing them, the man interrupted his conversation and came over to them.

"My husband—" Darren blurted out when he got to them, but her voice crumbled. She could taste the smoke in the back of her throat.

"Her husband was meeting someone here tonight," Lawson explained.

The man looked over his shoulder and then turned back to them slowly.

"I'm the arson investigator," he said, directing his words to Lawson. "We haven't found any survivors yet. It would probably be best to take her home and leave me a number where I can reach you."

Lawson gave the man his number and gently started to lead Darren away. "Let's go, dear. I want you to stay at my house tonight."

"But what if Andrew comes home? He won't know where I am," she said in a voice that didn't sound like her own.

Out of the corner of her eye, Darren could see the news reporter and the cameraman coming toward her. Everything seemed to be moving in slow motion except them; suddenly they were on top of her. A light assaulted her eyes and the reporter seemed to lunge at her, pelting her with rapid-fire questions.

She turned and started running, thinking she was running in the direction of the car, but after a few seconds she realized she was going the wrong way. She was in the parking lot that separated the church from the street, and before she could turn around she saw something in front of her that froze her to that spot. She knew a scream must have been what sliced through her throat like a dull blade, but she heard nothing. She felt Lawson near her, and she pointed to a corner of the lot. Andrew's car was there, the front half blown away, but the rear half and the license plate were still intact.

The cameraman and the reporter descended on her again, dissecting her with lights and questions.

"Did you have a relative here tonight?" The microphone was being pushed into her face and she tried to turn away.

"Can you tell us how you feel?"

She wheeled around to face them, slapping the microphone away. "How the fuck do you think I feel?" she screamed.

"Get away! Leave her alone. Go on, get out of here!" Lawson's voice roared through her head. He pulled her in the other direction, away from the brutal, blinding light and back into the smoke.

The drive back to Lawson's was a blur of headlights and windy darkness; Darren stared out at the passing night with wide, unblinking eyes. She was vaguely aware of Lawson's hand touching her shoulder and of Peanut nuzzling her, but she felt removed, as if she were a spectator watching someone else's life unfold.

When they reached Lawson's house he helped her out of the car and up the stairs. He put her to bed the way he had when she was a child.

"I'm going to give you a Valium, dear," he said, "and I want you to take it. It will help you sleep."

"No, I don't want it—just some water," she said in a thin voice. "Can Peanut sleep on the bed with me?"

Darren swallowed the water and pictured it falling into a hollow black tunnel. Drops plinked and rattled against her body like tiny pebbles tossed into a dry well.

When she finally surrendered to her exhaustion, sleep crashed down on her like a wall. She dreamed she was running through a cemetery full of open, upturned graves, looking desperately for Andrew. Finally she came to a large pit full of dismembered limbs. She climbed in and started tossing hands, legs, and heads aside, all the while screaming Andrew's name, screaming, "Where are you?" Soon she was knee-deep in the horrible chaos of limbs and blood, and she didn't know if she could climb out. The sides of the pit seemed to have grown higher, trapping her there, and above her black crows made wide patterns in the blue sky as they looked down at her and laughed.

Morning's first gray light forced her eyes open, but the dream was still heavy and thick in her brain. Her thoughts moved slowly, stumbling over the memory that something terrible had happened, but she couldn't remember what it was.

She sat up in bed and looked around the room, and then it came back to her: the bombed-out church, the man's face as he told them that no survivors had been found. If Andrew were alive, he'd be there by now; he would have gotten her message and come to Lawson's. She fell back on the pillows and looked up at the ceiling, white and smooth. But nothing in her life would be white again. She forced her thoughts into the future and saw a land of arctic temperatures and deep black rivers. She should have gone with him, died with him.

Sunlight was curling around the edges of the shade like a cruel spotlight. She could hear birds singing into the morning, but to her they sounded like the crows in her dream, laughing at her for being alive while Andrew was dead. She was alone; there were galaxies between her and Andrew now, miles of black space. There was only one splinter of light—the tiny, almost imperceptible fluttering in her womb.

13

*I*T WAS WELL PAST MIDNIGHT AND KENT STILL COULDN'T sleep. He had stopped by the Senate gym earlier that evening with the intention of taking a sauna to relax him before going home. From that point on, nothing had gone quite the way he'd planned.

Stephen Betts, the Republican senator from Alabama, was already in the sauna room when Kent walked in. The sauna room was small, with several armchairs covered in white sheets. Kent sat as far away from Senator Betts as he could, although it still wasn't far enough.

"Still going to oppose military aid for the contras when it comes up again, Kent?" Betts asked the moment Kent was settled in his chair. It was an issue they had clashed over many times before.

"What do you think?"

"You just refuse to face the facts, don't you?" Betts said. "Where do you plan to finally dig in your heels and take a stand against Communism—in San Francisco?"

Kent felt sweat running into his eyes, stinging them with salt. He squinted at Stephen Betts, a man no older than himself, but someone whom Washington had aged considerably.

"I don't know about you, Stephen, but I came in here to relax, not talk politics." But the damage was already done; he was far from relaxed.

When he got home he found Cecilia sitting in the living room, a room she had probably not entered in months. She was wearing white cotton slacks and a pale pink blouse, which now hung loosely on her frame. She looked like she had borrowed clothes from someone two sizes larger.

"Cecilia, you must be feeling better," he said, sitting down beside her tentatively, as if she were an illusion that would evaporate if he got too close. The whole house had fallen under Cecilia's spell: Jessica tiptoed around and spoke in a soft, whispery voice, and Kent saw his own movements as those of a wary trespasser, afraid to make too much noise.

"I'm feeling fine," she said, looking at him with eyes that didn't really see him. They were fixed on some distant mirage that only she could see; he just happened to be in her line of vision. "I told Jessica to serve us dinner in the dining room." Kent was surprised that she even remembered they had a dining room.

Jessica arrived five days a week at eight in the morning, stayed to fix dinner and clean up, and then left the house to Kent and Cecilia. It had been a good arrangement at one time, offering the convenience of having a maid and privacy as well. But now Kent sometimes wished she lived in. He liked the sound of movement in the house, the sound of someone other than himself. At night he felt like he was living in a house of shadows where nothing stirred but the wind as it rustled through the empty rooms.

They ate dinner in awkward silence, with the chandelier throwing velvet light around them and the clinking of silverware sounding like loud chimes, punctuating the distance between them. It was obvious to Kent that Jessica was uncomfortable serving them dinner; it had been so long since she had been asked to do anything like that. He wondered why she even bothered to stay with them. The house must seem like a morgue to her.

Kent glanced at the clock and saw that it was almost two; he had to get some sleep or he would be useless the next day. Cecilia turned over in her sleep, but she was so thin now that the movement was almost imperceptible. It still surprised him how tiny and drawn she had become. The memories of how she used to look whirled through his mind in a tarantella of bright images—the athletic strength of her body, ripe and open to him. He remembered the feel of her thighs wrapped around him, the way they used to look in the closet mirror when they made love. But he looked over at Cecilia sleeping next to him and was once again faced with the loneliness of lying in bed with someone who didn't care if he was there or not.

He finally fell asleep, telling himself that he would sleep in rather than go for his usual run. But a few minutes past six the phone rang.

"Senator, I'm sorry if I woke you," Phillip said, "but I thought you'd want to know about this. I heard on the late news last night that a church was bombed in L.A. There was a meeting going on with members of Safe Haven. I made some phone calls to a couple of reporters I know in California, and one of them just called me back. The guy you talked to on the phone about Nicaragua? The filmmaker? Looks like he was one of the victims."

Kent felt his stomach churn; there was no way he could accept that this was a coincidence, but he was afraid it would be presented as exactly that.

He could feel Cecilia's eyes on him as he hung up the phone.

"A man I spoke to last week on the phone has just been killed," he said.

"How?" she asked, her voice flat and dull in the early light.

"An explosion—a bomb. Jesus, I can hear his voice as clearly as if I just talked to him. . . . It's so hard to believe."

*   *   *

Cecilia let her thoughts toy with the image of an explosion; she wondered if there would be time for pain. Probably not. Probably death would be a quick, blinding flash of light. And then the blackness. Cool, deep blackness, a final escape from these days that droned by endlessly, with people chattering at her, opening shades and letting light in. No one understood that all she wanted was darkness. She envied the man Kent had told her about; he was free. He was floating weightlessly in space, where no one could find him or call him back.

Kent was surprised that he was able to get an appointment with CIA Director Braden that same day. He had asked Phillip to try to set it up, but he had not expected to be walking up the steps of the Old Executive Office Building at two o'clock that afternoon. It was one of his favorite buildings in Washington. The architecture spoke to him of another era, of history preserved in discolored stone and fragile parchment. He was glad that Braden had followed in Casey's footsteps and requested an office there; otherwise he would have had to drive to Langley, Virginia.

Passing the stone planters at the entrance, Kent remembered hearing that the architect who designed the building had committed suicide because the United States Government wouldn't pay him for his work.

Announcing himself to the thin, birdlike woman whose job it was to guard Braden's inner office, Kent watched as she buzzed the director and told him Senator Janes was there for his appointment, all without the slightest hint of a smile. After several minutes she stood up and motioned for Kent to follow her. Braden's office had faded green carpet and grass-weave wallpaper. The furniture was plain and functional, completely lacking in artistic flourishes or style. It was, Kent realized, a fitting environment for Braden, who appeared to be the epitome of ordinariness, a man bland as rice. He was short, with gray, thinning hair and black-framed glasses. His voice had been stripped clean of any emotion or inflection; what was left was a thin monotone that was as dull as the dial tone on a phone.

"Please sit down, Senator Janes," he said, indicating a brown leather chair on the opposite side of the desk. "What can I do for you?"

"Well, I'm not exactly sure, but there is something I felt I should bring to your attention. I had a phone conversation with a young man from California recently. He'd just returned from Nicaragua—his second trip there—and he told me some very disturbing things. He seemed sure, on the basis of what he saw, that there are CIA agents in that country facilitating the import of weapons to the contras. He also talked to a little boy who witnessed the murder of his family, and according to the child some of the killers were American."

Braden looked at him with no expression on his face. The walls around them were marked with the ghosts of pictures that had hung there, and suddenly the air felt warm and stifling, as though oxygen were being siphoned out.

"Senator," Braden began, pushing some papers aside and resting his elbows on the desk, "your assistant said that it was urgent that you speak with me. That's why I agreed to see you today. And now you bring me the fantasies of someone you don't even know and the testimony of a child who probably was too shocked to know what he was witnessing."

"There is another aspect to this, sir. The man I spoke with was killed last night. Maybe you heard about it? A church was bombed in Los Angeles. He and some other people were holding a meeting to try to help some Salvadoran refugees."

Kent was waiting for Braden's expression to change, but it might as well have been carved in stone.

"I just have trouble believing this was a coincidence, sir," he added.

"The world is full of coincidences, Senator Janes, whether you choose to acknowledge them or not. Now, if this is all you came to discuss with me, I do have a busy schedule. If you had some sort of proof I could go on, I might be willing to investigate this man's allegations, but as it is . . ."

"I might have had proof if he hadn't been murdered."

14

*D*ARREN HADN'T GONE HOME YET. IT HAD BEEN TWO days, and she knew that soon she would have to face the emptiness of her own house, but for now Lawson's house was her refuge.

She drifted through the days and tried to endure nighttime's long journey; she got little rest from the hot flow of tears that would come suddenly, as if there were some hidden schedule she didn't know about. Mornings didn't dawn, they pressed down on her with a weight that made her heart feel like it was being crushed.

Lawson was her guardian from the outside world. He had made the call to Andrew's parents, and he had told the police that Darren was in no condition to talk to them yet.

But she knew they had to talk to her. She supposed that she would tell them everything—about the film, about his second trip to Nicaragua, about his suspicions. But the thought of wading through the last months of Andrew's life inevitably brought on another wave of tears.

It was ten in the morning when the two detectives arrived at Lawson's house. Lawson let them in and Darren could hear, from down the hall, the low hum of voices. She knew, even though she couldn't make out his words, that Lawson was asking them to be as brief as possible, to please be sensitive to her grief. As she walked down the hall, her footsteps echoing on the oak floor, she started shivering. The tremors came from deep in her body, as though her bones were chilled.

They were sitting on the couch—two men in dark suits and ties, with small notepads resting on their laps. Lawson was in an armchair facing them; she knew he wouldn't leave until the questioning was over. Darren sat down stiffly in a wood-framed chair that was probably designed by some interior decorator who never expected anyone actually to sit in it. Outside the plate-glass window the sky was a perfect blue—a spring sky—but she avoided looking at the sky these days. It made her think of heaven. She could see, though, out of the corner of her eye, the leaves on the trees moving.

Last night she had listened for hours as the wind pushed a branch against the window in her room; it sounded like huge wings scraping across the glass. A coyote howled from somewhere deep in the hills. At first, when she woke up with the night thick and silent around her, she had thought it was a dream and the wolf was calling her. But she was awake, and, besides, the wolf didn't visit her dreams anymore. She understood now why he had come, what he had been trying to tell her. She lay still as ice while the dark spun its web around her and the coyote sent his cries into the moon-edged night.

"Mrs. Laverty, I'm Detective Riley," one of them said. He was heavyset, with a stomach that folded over the waistband of his pants. Darren wondered briefly if detectives were just cops who couldn't run after criminals anymore. "We feel terrible about having to bother you at a time like this, but it would help us in our investigation if we could ask you some questions."

"OK," Darren said. She heard her own voice, but her mind was miles away. She looked at the detective and imagined that, instead of words, puffs of smoke were coming out of his mouth— the smoke of the bombed-out church, smoke that was black as death.

She was trying to pull herself back into the room, to these men who had come to talk to her, but she was floating high above them, where the air was soft as silk and there was no smoke anywhere.

"Had your husband received any threats of any kind?" the other detective asked.

"No, nothing."

"What about explosives?"

"What about them?"

Suddenly she was right there. She was snapped back across the blue expanse into the room, into the wedge of time that was insisting on her presence.

"Did your husband have any explosives that you know of?"

"What the hell are you suggesting? That Andrew arranged to blow up a building where he knew he'd be?"

"We're not suggesting anything," the heavy one said. "We have to consider every possibility."

"Well, you can stop considering that one. Andrew wouldn't even light a firecracker on the Fourth of July. Look, he didn't get any threats, but he did have a film stolen, footage that he shot in Nicaragua. Someone didn't want that film to be seen. And the same sort of people, I would assume, would be angered by the fact that he and some others were trying to help Salvadoran refugees. So why don't you find out who those people are, and you might find out who set off that bomb."

Darren was surprised at the strength of her own voice. The coldness in her bones was gone, and her blood felt charged with electricity. She was angry at these men who had invaded her sorrow with their stupid questions, and she was angry at Andrew for leaving her alone. She felt a tightening in her stomach. She would have to go to the doctor soon, but she already knew. Her period was more than a week late, but she dreaded hearing the doctor tell her. As soon as it was put into words, it would become real.

When she finally went home there were so many messages on her phone machine that the tape had run out, but the only one she really paid attention to was Sean's. He'd called from Managua to say he was on his way back and he would call her as soon as he got in. Maybe he would have an idea who was behind the bombing. . . . But then, maybe it wouldn't make any difference.

She planned a small memorial service at a church in West Los Angeles. She had forgotten until Andrew died that they had made out wills, and in his Andrew spelled out his preference for an intimate, unpretentious service. He had also asked to be cremated. There wasn't much left of him to cremate—Darren knew that—but she just told them to do it. It was such a small amount of ashes, though, a breath of wind could easily have scattered them.

Andrew's parents flew out for the service. It was the first time Darren had ever met them. They sat behind her in the church: a white-haired, diminutive man who looked like he had spent a lifetime saying "Yes, dear" and then shutting his mouth, and a woman who looked like an over-the-hill showgirl. She had large breasts and hips, her hair was dyed black, and her fingernails were red and so long it must have been difficult to wash her face without stabbing herself. Darren wondered what quirk of fate had put Andrew's soul into her womb. A cosmic mistake, she decided; the angels must have been sleeping.

Danny gave the eulogy; he told funny stories about some of his and Andrew's adventures, and he made Darren laugh away some of the pain, if even for only a few minutes. At the end of the eulogy, she heard, so clearly that it was unmistakable, Andrew's laughter. She whipped her head around, half expecting to see him standing in the aisle grinning at her. But the aisle was empty and all that was behind her was a group of somber faces and Mrs. Laverty looking into the mirror of a gold compact, dabbing at tears that weren't there. The sound stayed with her for the rest of the day. She wouldn't tell anyone; they'd think she was crazy. But she knew he had been there.

Everyone went to Lawson's house after the service, and Darren felt like she was treading water. She started to reach for a glass of wine and then remembered she was pregnant.

Jesus, she thought, this baby is going to have to fight its way past Andrew's death just to get some attention.

She noticed Andrew's parents standing off to the side and knew she had to go over and talk to them.

"I'm sorry this is the first time we've met," she said, more to Mr. Laverty than to his wife. "I mean, under these circumstances. . . ."

Mrs. Laverty took a sip of her drink and the ice cubes clinked against the glass. Darren could smell that it was gin.

"I suppose none of us should be surprised," she said. "Our son was always tempting fate, always getting involved when he shouldn't. And when you go outside the law . . . well, now we see what can happen."

"I wouldn't exactly characterize Andrew as a criminal, Mrs. Laverty," said Darren, trying to suppress her anger. "He was trying to help people—people who have been oppressed and tortured. And he was trying to draw attention to an unjust policy in Nicaragua. It's a pretty sad statement on the condition of this country if that automatically puts you in danger."

"Nonetheless, he was breaking the law," this steely woman answered.

Darren bluntly excused herself and went to find someone else to talk to, although what she really wanted was to talk to no one.

Sean was standing near the doorway that led to the hall looking nervous and uncomfortable.

"Trying to sneak out without talking to me, Trudell?" Darren asked as she walked up to him.

"No. I swear I was going to talk to you before I snuck out. I just . . . I have a lot of trouble at gatherings like this, you know?" In his dark suit, with his hair neatly combed, Sean looked even younger than he usually did. He was also more fidgety than a kid who had been forced to dress up for church.

"I know exactly what you mean," Darren said. "I wish I

could escape with you." It seemed strange to her, but Sean was the only person she felt drawn to right then—maybe because he was the only one who understood exactly why Andrew had been murdered. It was an unspoken understanding between them. "Sean, I know this isn't the appropriate setting, but can we get together sometime? I need to talk to you."

"How about if I come to your house tomorrow morning for breakfast? I'll bring you some of my homemade bread."

"You bake bread?" Somehow it was hard to imagine.

"Took me years to admit it, but yes, I do. I stop short of wearing an apron, though. It might take some more therapy to get over that hurdle."

The next morning Darren sat out in the garden watching the thick fog drift by in billows. She had woken up feeling nauseated and was trying to settle her stomach with peppermint tea. The steam from the mug curled up and mingled with the fog.

"Nausea is a good sign," the doctor had assured her. "It means everything is working the way it should. If it gets too bad, though, you should let me know."

Darren took deep breaths in between sips of tea and wondered exactly how bad "too bad" was. She had never done well with sickness.

Everything in the garden was blooming—the fuchsias were like red-and-purple emblems against the dull day, the azaleas were snowy with white flowers, even the yellow rosebush that had been sickly and infested with bugs the year before was exploding with blossoms. It seemed to her like a betrayal, this burst of color.

She didn't hear the doorbell, but Peanut's barking let her know someone was there.

Sean was holding a bottle of orange juice and two loaves of bread wrapped in plastic bags.

"You can put one in the freezer for later," he said as he followed her into the house. "This is a great place, Darren. Andrew told me what a labor of love it was."

Sean hoisted himself onto the kitchen counter as Darren

filled the tea kettle with water. "I'm having herb tea, but I'll be happy to make you some coffee. I might even have some real coffee beans left in the freezer."

"That would be great," Sean said, glancing out the window at the white sky. "You quitting coffee or something?"

"I had to, Sean. I'm pregnant."

He looked at her with an expression that reflected all his colliding emotions. She knew the look by now; her doctor had looked at her the same way.

"Did Andrew know?"

"No. Funny thing is, I was going to tell him that night. I hadn't been to the doctor yet, but I was sure I was pregnant and I couldn't keep it to myself any longer. I was waiting for him to get home so I could tell him."

She poured hot water over the coffee grounds and waited as it dripped into the glass pot. "Please don't look at me like that, Sean," she said without looking at him. She could feel his eyes on her, and it almost seemed like she could feel his thoughts. "It's just the way things happened."

They carried a tray of bread and jam and two steaming mugs out to the deck, where the light was soft and pearly. Darren let the silence drift between them long enough for her to organize her thoughts. It seemed so long since she'd had a real conversation with anyone.

"Sean, I have this feeling I'm being lied to. I don't know why, but every time I get a call from the detective who questioned me, I get this uneasy feeling. He's told me that they're following everything that looks like it might be a lead, but they're coming up empty. Apparently no one received any threats, but . . . I don't know. I keep thinking he's lying or holding back something."

"He is."

"What do you mean? How do you know?"

"I talked to the widow of one of the men who was killed. Her husband was threatened, and she told that to the police."

"Well, why haven't you printed that? You're a reporter, isn't that your job?" Darren heard the accusation in her voice.

117

"Darren, I'm not the enemy here. If I thought it would help, I would print it, but at this point I'm just a little bit curious about why the police are holding back information. If I blaze away now with a full round of ammunition, we might never know the answer to that."

"OK, I'm sorry. I shouldn't have come down on you so fast. So what do we do?"

"Maybe you should talk to this woman, and to the other families. They might open up to you more than me. Although you can skip Gretchen Wright's family. Only her father is alive, and even if you're lucky enough to catch him sober, he doesn't make much sense."

She tried Marion Nolan first, assuming that, because they were both young widows, talking to her would be easy. She knew almost immediately that she was wrong. Mrs. Nolan's voice was strained and taut as a wire when she answered Darren's introduction with "What do you want?"

"Well, I understand that you told the police there had been some threats against your husband," Darren said, not willing to be put off by this woman's reluctance to talk to her.

"I told the police, I told a reporter. Why do I have to tell you too?"

"Because the police told me they got no information about any threats."

"Look, it doesn't matter now. What does matter is that I have a two-year-old son and I'm not as willing to put him in danger as my husband was. I begged him to get out of that group. As soon as we got the first phone call, I pleaded with him, but he wouldn't stop. Now I have a responsibility to protect my son, and that's exactly what I'm going to do. I would appreciate it if you did not call here again, Mrs. Laverty."

The next day Darren drove down to Pico Boulevard and turned left. She was headed east, toward the worst section of Santa Monica, the section Andrew called "the senseless murder district." As she passed Twentieth Street, she locked the doors and rolled up her window so that only a slender stream of air blew through the car. It felt good to be doing something; she had spent so much time alone lately that it seemed like she had *heard* the garden blooming—the petals unfolding in the early mist, the blossoms struggling to be born.

The Watsons lived in a small yellow house just below Pico. She had spoken with Mr. Watson on the phone, and he seemed to have no idea what his son had been up to, but Darren thought that if she visited him something might come back to him.

She stopped at the curb and looked at the house, at the bars on the windows and the dead flowers in the window boxes. A cat was curled up in front of the door and the morning paper was still on the front lawn. She picked up the paper and maneuvered her way past the cat to ring the bell. A stooped man in brown polyester slacks and a dull red cardigan answered the door.

"Mr. Watson? I'm Darren Laverty. We spoke on the phone?"

"Yes, yes. Come in," he said, and unlocked the screen.

He led her into a dark living room where the television was turned to a soap opera and the drapes were pulled halfway to block out the daylight. Darren remembered an elderly lady who had lived on her street when she was a child; she never opened the drapes all the way, as if she feared the sunlight would steal her soul. Going into her house was like venturing into the shadows of someone else's nightmares.

A plump woman with gray hair was sitting on the couch staring at the television. She was wearing a green housedress and clutched a handkerchief in her hand. Darren suspected it was probably the first thing she reached for in the morning, the way some people reach for their glasses.

"This is Mrs. Watson," Mr. Watson said in a loud voice. The woman turned to Darren and gave her a thin smile, and Darren noticed that her eyes seemed unfocused, as though she wasn't really seeing anything at all.

Mr. Watson sat down beside his wife and motioned Darren toward a worn armchair.

"She's come to talk to us about Sam, dear," Mr. Watson said, raising his voice again.

119

His wife nodded and returned to the television, although Darren suspected she wasn't really watching that either.

"What I wanted to ask you about," Darren began, "is whether your son ever got threats because of the work he was doing with Safe Haven?"

"Safe what?" Mr. Watson said.

"Safe Haven. The group your son was working with. They were helping Salvadoran refugees. One of the other members got some threats . . . before that night. Did Sam ever mention anything like that?"

"Oh, Sam doesn't tell us much of anything that he's up to. He has his own life, you know. He comes by on Sundays sometimes and has lunch with us, but he never talks about himself much. Mostly he tries to get us to go out more. But, you know, this city just isn't what it used to be. Used to be a nice neighborhood here where you could sit outside in the evenings, chat with your neighbors. Didn't have any fireflies, though, like they did where I came from."

Darren decided that Mr. Watson was so entrenched in his denial of his son's death that it would take more courage than she had to confront him with reality. "Does Sam ever talk about doing something illegal?"

"No, no, I think I'd remember that. I taught the boy to obey the law. No, like I said, he's just always after us to go out, go to a movie. But the wife here likes to watch her TV shows—knows every one of the stories—and I like to putter around in the garden. Had a great batch of strawberries this year. We have a good life here, I suppose. No need to go out, really, what with all the things going on nowadays. We had to put these bars up and all. I don't drive anymore, but I keep the old car out back in the garage. Sometimes I go back there and shine her up. . . ."

Darren let him ramble on and glanced around the room. There were a few pictures of Sam when he was a child and a teenager, but none of him as an adult. She knew from the papers that he was thirty-five when he died, but in this house he was still fifteen. Time had stopped here, leaving the Watsons with memories that were easier to live with than the world outside their barred windows. She refused to be the one to try to inch them forward into the present.

The fog had burned off; through the half-opened drapes a slat of sunlight shone into the room. Darren refused the iced tea that Mr. Watson offered her, but she accepted some strawberries from his garden that he had washed and put in a plastic bag.

As she drove home, the air shimmered with heat and she could smell the asphalt as it softened in the hot sun.

Peanut jumped on her when she walked through the door, clinging to Darren's waist with her paws and refusing to let go. Since Andrew's death she panicked every time Darren left.

"It's OK, Peanut, it's OK. I'm home, I'm not going to leave you," Darren said, trying to calm her.

She ran cold water in the bathtub and soaked her feet; lately they felt like she'd been walking on hot coals. The bathroom was dim and cool and she felt like she could have stayed there for the rest of the day.

"I'm trying, Andrew," she said softly. Her voice bounced off the tiles and returned to her. "I promise I won't give up. I'll find out who did it, even if everyone else gives up."

PART THREE

15

*D*ARREN, I THINK THIS IS A VERY BAD IDEA," LAWSON
said. "You can't just fly to Washington, walk into a
senator's office, and expect to meet with him."

They were sitting in the shade on Lawson's patio, but even
the shade brought little relief from the heat. The foggy mornings had evaporated in a white-hot blaze of summer, and now
there was so little moisture in the air that everything seemed to
crackle. It was brushfire weather, and Darren swore she could
smell a tree smoldering somewhere in the dry hills.

"I don't understand why you're fighting me on this, Lawson.
I'm trying to find out who killed Andrew, and the more help I
can get, particularly from someone as influential as Senator Janes,
the closer I'll be to an answer."

"Doesn't that job belong to the police?" Lawson asked.

"Yes, it does—or rather, it *should*. But the last time that detective phoned me, he said they were coming to the conclusion that it was just a random act of violence, sort of a variation on the drive-by shooting that seems to be in vogue."

Lawson looked at her, and his face was tired and troubled.

"Maybe he's right, my dear," he said softly. "I just don't want to see you get hurt. You've been hurt enough already, and now it appears that you might be banging your head against a wall that's not going to crumble under your efforts. What did your friend Sean say about you marching into Senator Janes's office like this?"

"He said maybe I should call first."

Lawson looked puzzled. "Was that a joke?" he said.

"I don't know, probably."

The hot, swollen air was pressing down on her. Darren didn't know which was making her feel worse, the heat or Lawson's attitude. She felt a wave roll through her stomach and imagined that it was the child growing. Tiny and frail as a curled leaf, it was sprouting limbs and organs; veins were lengthening and drawing their map across the small landscape of a new life. And each time something else grew, it would send a ripple through her body, and she would feel it rock her stomach, like a wave on the ocean.

"I just feel like you're not being very supportive," Darren said, hearing in her voice the sulking sound of a child who was not getting what she wanted.

"I can't be supportive of actions I don't agree with, my dear."

"So does that mean you won't let Peanut stay here for the day and a half that I'll be gone?"

"Don't be ridiculous," Lawson answered. "I'm not going to punish your dog because I disagree with what you're doing. I assume that means you've made up your mind, then?"

"I have to do this, Lawson," Darren said. "If Andrew had enough trust in Kent Janes to call him and tell him everything that he told him, I'm going to trust that he'll help me . . . somehow."

"I hope you're right," Lawson said. "While you're here, may

I ask you something else?" He paused and then plunged ahead. "Are you doing all right for money? I don't know how you and Andrew had handled your finances. . . ."

"I'm fine, Lawson. We had a lot of money saved up and there was also a life insurance policy. Money is one thing I don't have to worry about for a while."

"If you need help—"

"I know. Thanks." And she knew he would have written her a check on the spot for whatever she needed.

Darren left Lawson's as an afternoon wind was starting to brush through the trees. She hated leaving with a disagreement lingering between them, but she was tired and irritable and she wanted to go home, where at least she could smell the ocean. At Lawson's the dust rose from the surrounding hills and lingered in the air; just the scent of it made her thirsty.

As she got closer to Santa Monica, she felt the change in the temperature, and it seemed easier to breathe. Darren imagined Andrew sitting next to her in the car telling her that she was doing the right thing, telling her to follow her instincts. That was the rule he lived by. "You get into trouble whenever you don't follow your instincts," he'd say. She wondered why his instincts hadn't made him turn the car around that night and come home instead of going to the church.

Kent pulled his black BMW into the driveway, turned off the ignition, and stared at his house. The car felt like a cocoon, and he wasn't ready to leave its protection and walk through the front door into a house where nothing was predictable or safe. He leaned his head back against the seat and thought of the woman who had been waiting in his office that morning, determined to see him.

He had noticed her the minute he walked in; he knew she must be waiting for him. He wasn't even surprised when his secretary introduced her as Darren Laverty. It was almost as if he had known that too. Maybe it was that she looked like she was from California—her long blond hair and loose cotton dress looked out of place in Washington, which was on the conservative end of the fashion scale.

127

When she stood up to shake his hand, she had looked directly at him, her blue eyes burning into his. If he'd had an appointment, he decided, he probably would have canceled it, her determination was so obvious.

"I won't take up much of your time, Senator," she said, "but I flew out from California to talk to you, so I'd appreciate a few minutes."

"Of course," he said, ushering her into his office.

"How long was she waiting here?" Kent whispered to his secretary as he passed her desk.

"About forty minutes, Senator."

He knew she would have waited all day if that's what it had taken.

She sat across from his desk and fixed him with that same look, a look that demanded his full attention.

"You spoke with my husband shortly before he was killed," she said.

"Yes, I remember our conversation. I was very sorry when I heard—"

"I know. Everyone is sorry. But no one seems really dedicated to finding out who planted that bomb. That's why I'm here, Senator. To be honest, I don't know what exactly I expect you to do, but I think pressure has to come from somewhere, and I'm certainly not important enough to exert that kind of pressure."

"Tell me the problem," Kent had said.

"The police are saying that there's no evidence that the people in the church were the targets. But there is evidence. The widow of one of the men told me—and the police—that her husband had received threats because of his work with Safe Haven. According to the police, however, she never said anything of the kind. They're going to close the book on it, Senator, because they don't want to find out who did it."

"Mrs. Laverty, forgive me, but that's a very serious accusation."

"It's a very serious situation. Someone wanted those people killed, my husband included. Andrew didn't tell you everything on the phone, Senator Janes. He had videotape of some people who had been massacred in Nicaragua, and one of the murderers left something behind—an ID card of some kind, a security pass for Ilopango Airport. Andrew was trying to get backing for another documentary in Nicaragua, and he was probably too free with that information."

"This is on tape?"

"Yes. He was going to show you . . ."

"But why didn't he tell me about that? About the security pass?" Kent asked.

"He and Sean—a reporter who was with him—decided to keep the name to themselves and try to find out who the man was. They figured if they publicized it the guy would vanish into thin air. Look, Senator, I can't bring my husband back, but I can try to prevent people from lying about his death. I'm carrying his child, and I owe it to that child as well as to Andrew."

"I'd like to see that tape, Mrs. Laverty. I'm going to be in California next month while the Senate is in recess. If you can let my secretary know how to reach you—"

"Fine," she'd said, standing up to leave and extending her hand. "Thank you for your time, Senator Janes."

As he watched her walk out, he felt a crack widening in his heart. He wondered who would be with her when her baby was born.

Kent got out of the car and walked tentatively up to the front door. He could feel the stillness inside as soon as he pushed the door open. Cecilia was probably asleep, or pretending to be. There were days when he walked into a hurricane of flying objects and angry words, but, fortunately, this was not one of those days.

He went upstairs, expecting to find her in bed, but he found only empty rooms.

"Jessica, where's my wife?" he called down the stairs.

"I don't know, sir. She left about an hour ago. She didn't say where she was going."

Kent went back outside and looked up and down the street. It was hard for him to believe that she had gone out on her own. A breeze lifted some of the heat from the air, and he looked up at the sunlight flickering out of the sky.

He thought of calling for her—yelling for her, actually—but he didn't want to attract that much attention. The best thing was to wait.

He returned to the house and poured himself a scotch. The bay window that faced the street afforded him a good view of both directions; he moved a chair over and sat down with his drink. Daylight was fading quickly now, as if it had been ordered to speed up its departure.

"Senator?" Jessica said softly. He hadn't even heard her come in. Everyone in this house was getting too quiet. "What shall I do about dinner?"

"I don't know. Why don't you just put it in the oven on low and call it a day."

"Yes, sir," Jessica said, and disappeared again. She was going to stay in the house with Cecilia while he was in California, and Kent wondered if she would spend those days in silence, tiptoeing across the floor and trying to remember the feel of her voice as it traveled through her throat.

Kent was about to get up and refill his drink when he saw a white Mercedes sedan pull up in front of the house.

She walked out of the house and bought a car? he thought.

He watched as Cecilia got out of the passenger side and a man he didn't recognize emerged from the driver's side. The man was short and slender, and as he moved around the front of the car, Kent noticed that he walked as if he were much taller.

The scotch was nibbling at the edges of his brain. All the signs were there for a very bad night. He went to the door and opened it before they could ring the bell.

"Hello, Senator Janes, I'm Martin S. Volish," the man said, extending his hand. Now that he was closer, Kent saw that the man's skin was much too taut and smooth; he found the tiny scars between his jaw and his earlobes and had to fight to suppress a smile. He estimated that Martin S. Volish's face-lift wasn't even a month old.

"Do I know you?" Kent said.

"No. We're neighbors, though—sort of. I live on the next

block. Your wife was in front of my house and she looked quite agitated. In fact, she almost got hit by a car."

Kent allowed himself to look at Cecilia, which he hadn't done since he opened the door. Her jaw was clenched and her eyes were wide and jumpy. "What makes you think she's agitated?" he wanted to say, but instead he said nothing. He reached out and took her arm, pulling her a little closer to the door. She was wearing a red wool skirt that looked ridiculous in the ninety-degree weather, and an orange blouse; the clash of colors hurt Kent's eyes.

Martin S. Volish looked too calm, almost as though he reveled in this role of good samaritan. He was shorter than Kent, five feet seven, maybe, and his cream-colored suit had been perfectly tailored. His white shirt was open at the collar, and a thin gold chain shone around his neck.

"Well, thank you for driving her home," Kent said finally.

"Oh, no problem," Volish answered, apparently not ready to leave yet. "She didn't seem like she was feeling too well, so I—"

"Yes, I know. Thank you."

"Let me give you my card, since we live so close. I'm an investment counselor. I work with a lot of people in the government, so if you ever need anything . . ."

"I'll be certain to call you, Mr. Volish," Kent said, and gently pulled Cecilia across the threshold.

He wondered, as he watched Martin S. Volish swagger back to his car, how he could so instantly dislike someone, but he didn't have time to ponder the accuracy of his first impression. Cecilia had swept past him like a tornado and was in the kitchen, slamming cupboards and opening the oven so violently it sounded like the door would come unhinged.

"Cecilia," he said, not loudly at all, when he got to the door of the kitchen.

"Where's Jessica? She just fixes dinner and leaves now? Is this a new arrangement I don't know about?"

"I told her she could go home early. Cecilia, what were you doing standing out in the middle of the street?"

Cecilia took the foil off the chicken casserole that Jessica had left and spooned some onto two plates.

"I wasn't standing around in the street. I was going somewhere."

"Where?"

"What does it matter? You're always after me to get out more. So I got out, and now you interrogate me about it."

Kent sighed. It was going to be a long night.

The truth was, Cecilia didn't remember where she had been going, or if she had ever had a destination in mind. She remembered the street, hot under her feet, and the houses, which had looked so unfamiliar. Had she ever been this far away from her home? Then this man came up to her and he wasn't like Kent. He wasn't trying to get inside of her head.

"Do you need some help?" he'd asked.

And she knew it didn't really matter whether she said yes or no. If she'd said no, he would have just left her there and never looked back. That's why she said yes.

Kent was always trying to bring her back into his world, where the lights were turned up too bright and people always wanted to *talk* to you. Like Dr. Easton. He always wanted her to *talk*; he didn't understand that her voice ripped through the veils of her secret world like a bolt of lightning and then she had to work so hard to get everything right again.

Just when she found a soft place in the shadows, where it was quiet and dark, Kent or the doctor would come along and start pulling her back into the lights. Martin hadn't done that. She had sat in his car without speaking, and he hadn't cared.

Kent was calling her name; it sounded like he was at the other end of a long tunnel.

"What?" she said when his voice got closer. Light tumbled in and made her head hurt.

"Cecilia, have you been taking your medication?"

"Jesus Christ! Will you get off my back? You're after me about everything—taking my medicine, getting out of the house. Don't you have anything better to do with your time?"

132

The light was white-hot now. She turned away from him and shut her eyes for a second, trying to put everything in place again. It was so hard when he kept rearranging her world. She opened the chrome bread box, carefully lowering her eyes so she wouldn't see her reflection, and got out a slice of bread. She thought of putting it in the toaster, but that was chrome too, so she took her plate into the living room and hoped that Kent wouldn't follow her.

Kent waited a few minutes and then walked out of the kitchen and into the dining room, going just far enough so he could see Cecilia sitting on the couch, the narrow light from a single lamp illuminating her small frame. She was hunched over her plate, the bones in her back and shoulders looking like the jagged rocks of a wind-stripped cliff.

There was something about her that was both rigid and vulnerable, but Kent had no idea who she was anymore. He turned quietly and left, going back through the kitchen to the back door, where he could sit on the steps and listen to the night sounds of crickets and cars driving past.

He thought about his daughter. It was fate's blackest stroke, the death of a child. But as the years had passed, the memory of her death had changed shape. He had begun to see it as something clear and pure, like a trickle of rainwater running back into the sea. Laura's time had been short and unencumbered by the sadnesses that weigh people down as their lives lumber into decades. Quick and bright as a firefly, she had flitted across the earth's face and returned to the safe folds of heaven, unscarred by her brief visit to a troubled planet. At times Kent imagined her spirit floating past him, like a cloud across a still blue sky. It made him feel that she hadn't really left, and that sometimes she wasn't even that far away.

Moths fluttered past his face, their wings silvery in the light. The liquor had turned sour in his stomach; a headache was starting at the base of his skull and was threatening to continue its conquest. He knew he should eat something, but he dreaded going back into the house while Cecilia was still awake.

133

Kent knew he would sit out there until he saw the reflection of the upstairs lights go off. He would listen to cars passing and imagine people going home to families that laughed and talked and had dreams and plans. And then, when the night grew quieter, he would walk softly upstairs and slip into bed beside someone he no longer knew.

16

*D*ARREN HAD TO SET THE ALARM NOW TO GET UP IN the mornings. She used to wake up automatically at five o'clock, which gave her just enough time to get dressed and get to the gym by five-thirty. But now she was so tired all the time and had so little enthusiasm, it was all she could do to force herself out of bed.

Sometimes Peanut would curl up in the spot where Darren had been sleeping, and Darren would know that she would be content to stay there, dreaming about whatever dogs dream about. But other times Peanut let it be known that, if Darren was foolish enough to leave without her, she would howl and whimper until she woke up everyone in the neighborhood. On those mornings Darren took her along to the gym and tied her up on the balcony that led to the glass front doors. She got attention from everyone who came and left, and she was happy to stand there and be fussed over while Darren worked out.

Cassie didn't push her as hard as she used to, and Darren wondered if it was because she was pregnant or because she was still encased in a thin layer of sadness, fragile as a sheet of ice. Maybe everyone was treating her differently; if she thought about it long enough, she would decide they were, so she put it out of her mind.

Outside the gym's floor-to-ceiling windows, Darren could watch morning roll across the sky in gentle shades of pink and gray. Ocean mist hung in the air at dawn, but within a few hours it would evaporate under the sun's flames. It was the hottest summer Darren ever remembered. Every morning she would glance at the sky, hoping to see a bank of clouds signaling the approach of a summer storm. But each day the air sizzled with heat and the sky remained blue and empty.

On this morning Darren was lying on her back doing leg presses, hoping that the churning in her stomach wouldn't turn to nausea until she was finished. Each time she pushed the platform up and eased it back down, her jaw clenched and she felt her face redden. She closed her eyes and imagined a wave cresting in her womb, splashing over her unformed child. She imagined that, at the exact moment she was straining to push up the weight, her child was giggling with pleasure at this unexpected change in the tides.

After her third set she stood up to walk the pain out of her legs. She went over to the window and looked down at Main Street. Traffic was thin, but there were people at the corner waiting for the bus. Every few seconds someone craned their neck to look down the street. A police car passed by and slowed as it approached a long-haired man in a ragged, soiled raincoat who was standing near the bus stop. Then it drove on; apparently there was no law against standing at a bus stop in the only clothing you owned.

Seeing the police car gave Darren an idea, but she wanted

Cassie to help her carry it out. She walked back to the leg-press machine just as Cassie was finishing her set.

"Want to help me out with something?" Darren said, squatting down so she was level with Cassie.

"Am I allowed a job description before I commit?"

"Sure. I want to go to the police station and talk to whoever it is that detectives report to. I'm going to complain that they're not really trying to find out who bombed the church."

Cassie massaged her knee and stared at the air in front of her.

"What do you think you'll accomplish?" she asked.

"I have no idea. You want to go with me or not?"

"Sounds like I'd better. Someone should be there to make sure you don't cause trouble."

That afternoon they drove out to the valley. As soon as they passed Mulholland Drive and started descending into the San Fernando Valley, the air turned thick and hot; smog hovered over them.

"Scenic, isn't it?" Cassie said.

"Yeah, healthy, too. I think I can feel the baby coughing."

When they pulled up to the police station, Darren experienced a moment of panic. She hadn't planned what she was going to say, and she wished she had talked to Sean before charging off on her own like this. But Sean was in Texas; he had managed to learn about a group of men who promoted themselves as patriotic mercenaries, dedicated to preserving democracy with as many bullets as it took. The fact that they were based in Texas made Sean think that they might be telling the truth. Both he and Andrew had been suspicious of the men they had heard talking in the bar after the village was massacred, and both had pegged them as Texans.

Darren told the uniformed woman at the desk that she wanted to talk to Detective Riley's superior. She tried to sound confident and self-assured, but she had to keep her hands out of sight because they were shaking so badly that anyone could have seen it.

137

"You want the detective's supervisor?" the woman said, looking at Darren quizzically. She said something to another officer, who went back and knocked on the door of a glass-walled office. There were a lot of glass walls in there, Darren noticed. Cassie must have noticed the same thing.

"Boy, it'd be hard to zip up your fly in here without everyone seeing you," she said.

The officer behind the desk glanced at her sharply but said nothing.

They were escorted back to the office, where a solemn, gray-haired man introduced himself as Lieutenant Dedrick. He had the kind of face that was made for poker games, but the lines in his forehead showed that he probably worried more than he let on.

"Lieutenant," Darren began, "my husband was killed in the bombing near here, the church . . ."

"Yes. And you are?"

"Darren Laverty."

"What can I do for you, Mrs. Laverty. As you've probably been told, we have no leads as to who might have been responsible."

"Yes, I have been told that, sir, by Detective Riley. But frankly, I just don't see how that can be possible. The widow of one of the other victims said her husband had received threats, yet Detective Riley said he had no information about any threats at all. She claims she told him." Darren remembered what Sean had said to her about keeping quiet, but she pushed it out of her mind.

"Mrs. Laverty," Lieutenant Dedrick said, "I can appreciate that you want to find out who did this. So do we. But often the victims' families get facts confused, probably because of the emotional toll their loss has taken on them. No one gave us any information about any threats, but frankly, even if someone did, it still might be a dead end. Unless the person gave some indication of who they were working for, or with, there would be nothing to go on. I've seen people identify the wrong person because they wanted so badly to feel that someone was in jail for the crime that turned them into victims."

"I just don't believe this woman was inventing things," Darren said, but she knew she was losing ground. Why did he have to sound so damn logical when she knew she was right and he was wrong?

"All I can tell you, Mrs. Laverty, is that we're doing everything we can. We're not going to close the book on this—"

"Well, that's exactly what it sounds like you're doing," Darren said abruptly. She could feel Cassie's eyes boring into her, telling her to cool down.

"I'm sure that's how it appears to you," the lieutenant said. "I hear it frequently. Nothing happens as quickly as we would like—at least not in my line of work."

They walked out of the police station into the heat-swollen air and squinted as the sunlight assaulted their eyes.

"Well, I'd consider that a complete waste of time," Cassie said. "How about you?"

"I wouldn't exactly say the trip was worth it. But at least he knows I'm not a complete idiot, that I'm smart enough to know when I'm being lied to."

"Uh-huh. I'm sure he's going to lose a lot of sleep over that, Darren."

"You did what?" Lawson said when they stopped at his house to pick up Peanut.

"Lawson, please don't lecture me," Darren said, but she could tell by the way his face was getting red that the lecture hadn't even started yet. Cassie slid out of the room, and Peanut—who put raised voices in the same category as firecrackers and earthquakes—followed her.

"What were you thinking of?" Lawson continued, pacing back and forth in front of the window. "You can't just blatantly accuse the police of not running a proper investigation."

"Why not? They're *not* running a proper investigation. They're concealing evidence."

"Just because they're not keeping you up to date on every new development does not mean they're concealing things, Darren. We keep butting heads on this, but I have to tell you that I am terribly worried about this crusade of yours. It's dangerous, the way you're proceeding here, and I honestly think your time would be better spent adjusting to the way your life is now, without Andrew, so your baby will not have to live through the residue of your grief."

"My baby is already living through it," Darren said softly.

When Darren got home she found the tape that Andrew had made in Nicaragua and locked it in a drawer in the desk. She had suddenly realized, when Lawson mentioned danger, that the tape was the most important piece of evidence she had. By the time she had dropped Cassie off, she had almost convinced herself that it had been stolen, that someone had broken into her house the same way they had broken into George's—just to steal evidence. When she raced through the door and found the tape right where she had left it, by the television set, she felt her breathing relax and her heart start to slow down.

This is not healthy, she told herself. This kind of paranoia is not good for me.

But she couldn't convince herself that her fears were unfounded. She called Danny and asked him if he could make a copy of a videotape for her.

"Sure," he said. "What tape?"

"It's the one Andrew brought back from his second trip to Nicaragua. And Danny, I'd like you to do something else for me. Will you keep the copy and put it in a safe place? Lock it up somewhere?"

"Darren, I don't like the sound of this. What does this tape have on it?"

"Well, let's just say it couldn't be used to get tourists into Nicaragua. Do you have to take it somewhere to get the copy made?"

"Well, I usually take it to the FBI—they do a good job," Danny said. "Would you prefer I took it somewhere else?"

"Ordinarily, that would be funny, Danny, but under the circumstances . . ."

"OK, sorry. Yes, I have to take it somewhere, but don't worry. I'll stop by tonight and pick it up from you."

As she was talking to Danny, she was watching Leland through the kitchen window. He wasn't chasing Peanut around the yard the way he used to, and even more unusual, he wasn't yelling. He was standing in one spot, tossing the tennis ball to Peanut and waiting for her to retrieve it.

Darren went out to the yard and sat on the grass.

"Hi, Leland."

"Hi."

"Want to talk?"

He threw the tennis ball to Peanut and sat down beside her. "Sure. Did you have something on your mind?"

"Actually, I did. You seem a little quiet these days. You miss Andrew, don't you?"

"I guess so," he said, pulling out a blade of grass and brushing it across his mouth. "It feels different without him here."

"I know. And it's never going to feel the same again. We're going to have to make a new life. But I think we can still be happy—just in a different way. I think Andrew would want us to try, anyway."

Leland turned and faced Darren, and suddenly his eyes looked older to her, as if he had aged years in the past two months.

"I wasn't really unhappy when my parents died," he said. "I was too young. I was just a baby, so I don't even really remember them."

"But now you have parents who love you just as much as your real parents did. You see, life gives you things, and sometimes it takes things away, too."

"Peanut's sad, too."

"She'll be happier if she sees that we're happy. Dogs are very sensitive to our feelings."

Leland studied Peanut as she lay staring at them, the tennis ball in her mouth, waiting patiently for the game to resume.

"Have they arrested anyone?" Leland asked.

"No, not yet."

"I bet I could catch 'em."

I bet you'd probably do a better job than the police, Darren thought. "Well, if it looks like they need your help, I'll give them your name," she said.

She wondered, as she walked back inside, why it seemed like this child was giving her more support than Lawson was. Maybe, in a strange sort of way, Leland understood her better.

17

*D*ARREN KNEW THE FEARS THAT KEPT BUBBLING TO THE surface of her thoughts were mostly irrational; it was part of being pregnant. But she felt like they were undermining her confidence just when she needed it the most.

At the gym she was afraid that she would drop a weight on her stomach or injure some muscle that would trigger a miscarriage. If she drove past a truck that was transporting tanks marked POISON, she would hold her breath until she was safely past it, fearing that toxic fumes might be leaking out and her baby would inherit a lifetime of suffering if she inhaled them. She took twice as long at the market, scrutinizing the labels on everything she bought, afraid that one of the ingredients with a name she couldn't pronounce would appear in the morning paper as the latest chemical found to cause birth defects . . . but only after five million women had already consumed it. And there were moments when the quiet inside her—the stillness—would make Darren afraid that the baby had died and was lying motionless inside her like a cold, round stone.

She didn't know what she was afraid of exactly when Senator Janes's office called to schedule a lunch appointment while he was in Los Angeles.

He would be staying at the Westwood Marquis, the secretary said; perhaps they could meet there. Darren said fine and that the following Wednesday would be all right. But then she stood in the kitchen listening to the sounds of the house—the hum of the refrigerator, the clothes tumbling around in the dryer—and wondered at this new anxiety that was moving in on her.

It was eight-thirty in the morning and a watered-milk sun was struggling through the mist. Darren filled the tea kettle and turned on one of the burners; the blue flame danced above the gas jets. She realized what it was; the reason for her fear formed in front of her as though someone were drawing it in the air. She might really discover who killed Andrew. If Kent Janes was willing to talk publicly about it and resurrect the incident in people's minds, she might eventually get the answer she thought she wanted. And it was that answer that was frightening her.

On the Wednesday she was supposed to meet Senator Janes, Darren spent an hour choosing what to wear. She wanted to find something that was comfortable, but that didn't make her look too fat. She was into her third month, but she didn't look pregnant yet; she just looked overweight.

She went through her closet and immediately ruled out half her wardrobe. The clothes either wouldn't fit or were designed to fall off one shoulder, which wouldn't work now because her breasts were so swollen she'd had to buy a bra. In fact, she'd ended up buying four, in different sizes so she wouldn't have to repeat the ordeal when she grew even larger.

When she walked into the lingerie department, Darren had realized that the last time she'd shopped for a bra was in high school, where it was socially important that a girl wear one whether she needed it or not.

"What size?" the saleswoman said, peering over wire-rimmed reading glasses at Darren's chest.

"I don't know," Darren answered self-consciously. "You see, I'm pregnant, and—"

"Well, what size do you normally wear?"

"I don't know that either. I don't normally wear a bra."

"Thirty-six B," the woman sniffed, obviously adept at determining breast sizes with just a glance. "You must have underwire or you'll sag. Of course, there's no guarantee you won't sag anyway. And you'll probably need a bigger size in a few months."

"Fine. I'll take two bras in thirty-six B and two the next size up . . . whatever that is."

She finally settled on a yellow gauze shirt, which she hadn't worn in years but which was billowy enough to conceal her new voluptuousness; and a white peasant skirt. She tied a bright scarf around her waist and studied her image in the mirror. She looked like she was on a holiday in Mexico, but after three changes she had run out of options.

By the time Darren dropped Peanut off at Lawson's, she knew she would be late. That, and the fact that she kept forgetting to get the air conditioner in her car fixed, made her so irritable she wished she could just go home and forget the whole thing—reschedule it for winter, when she would at least be able to drive in comfort without her clothes sticking to her.

Ordinarily she would have driven past the valet parking sign and found a spot on the street, but she was already fifteen minutes late, so she pulled up behind a gold Jaguar. One dusty Volvo among a fleet of expensive luxury cars.

The air-conditioning in the lobby almost made her gasp, but she felt her nerves settle as her skin started to dry. At the doorway to the dining room, Darren looked across a sea of white tablecloths set with crystal glasses and tiny silver flower vases. She saw Kent Janes immediately but allowed the maître d' to escort her through the room.

When the senator stood up and extended his hand, Darren wondered why she hadn't noticed before how attractive he was.

He'd obviously been in California long enough to replace his East Coast pallor with a tan that set off the blue-green of his eyes. They made Darren think of the sea, made her forget the sweltering day and the smell of melting asphalt.

"I'm sorry I'm late," she said. "I ran into traffic."

"That's all right. How are you?"

His look was so direct that she wanted to escape from it. She studied the vase and the silverware, but his eyes pulled her back.

"I'm doing OK," Darren said finally. "I wish I could tell you that I'm less bitter than when we talked before, but I'm afraid that still hasn't changed much."

"You have more reason to be bitter than most people I know."

She thought he was going to say something else, but the waiter came up and they allowed him to go through his memorized list of specials before ordering salads off the menu.

"Tell me about the men your husband said sabotaged his film," Senator Janes said after the waiter left.

"One of them was fired before the end of the filming . . . but Andrew told you about that. When everyone got back to L.A. the film was stolen and never recovered. I don't think any of us doubted they were working for the government—probably the CIA. I mean, who else would be interested. And it was pretty slick. Suddenly these two men dropped off the face of the earth. Their phone numbers were disconnected, the place where they supposedly worked had never heard of them. I'm sure their names were invented. So, they did their job and vanished."

"Darren—may I call you Darren?" She nodded. "And I'm Kent. Darren, after everything we learned about during the Iran-contra scandal, it's hard to be shocked anymore. But I have to tell you, I was shocked when you told me about the videotape your husband made and the security pass he found. Soldiers of fortune are one thing. If they're getting help from the government, that puts it in a whole different league."

"Sort of makes you proud to be an American, doesn't it? And people wonder why we're not as popular around the world anymore."

"Your husband did tell me about the child they found," he said.

"There are hundreds more like him." Darren's thoughts went for a moment to the schoolhouse, and Guadalupe climbing into the protection of Tica's arms.

The waiter came to the table with their salads, and Kent waited until he was gone to speak. "Children are the biggest tragedy of any war," he said.

"This isn't any war. In fact, it's not supposed to be our fight at all. So that makes those kids more than just tragedies. And we're responsible for what's happening to them."

"Darren, I'm not arguing with you," Kent said softly. "I'm on your side. I'd like to see the videotape that Andrew made. Would that be possible?"

Darren played with her salad for a few seconds before answering.

"I'll make a deal with you, Senator. I'll let you see the tape if you agree to do an interview with the reporter who was with Andrew on that trip. If it's public knowledge that you're concerned about what really happened that night—about who bombed that church—then maybe the police will stop dragging their heels."

Kent leaned back in his chair and smiled at her. "I didn't realize I was coming to the negotiating table today, Darren."

"Well, there you are. Life's full of surprises, isn't it?"

"All right. I'll agree to those terms."

After lunch Kent offered to walk Darren outside to get her car, but she managed to talk him out of it. For some reason she felt her face flush with embarrassment at the thought of him seeing her ancient, unwashed car.

When she got back to Lawson's house, she found him in the garden, tossing a tennis ball for Peanut.

"Well, I see she's got you where she wants you," Darren teased.

"I'm afraid so. I never should have started this. How was your lunch?"

"Fine." Darren wasn't sure how much to tell Lawson; she

didn't have the energy for another disagreement. "Senator Janes might do an interview with Sean while he's here in town," she added, hoping that would close the subject.

She sat down on one of the white wrought-iron chairs and felt like she could fall asleep right there. The day was warm and drowsy, and the trees were dead still, as though waiting for a breeze. Her energy in the mornings had gotten better, but she found she still needed to lie down for a while in the afternoons.

"Lawson, can I go upstairs and take a nap before I drive home?"

"Are you ill?" he said, coming over and feeling her forehead.

"No. Just pregnant."

She went into the same room she had slept in the night Andrew died. It had the kind of anonymous, genderless decor that guest rooms often have. The walls were a muted beige and the double bed was covered with a quilted maroon spread. There was an oak dresser and rocking chair, and the nightstands had matching brass lamps on them.

Darren lay down on the bed and closed her eyes. She tried to think of something she wanted to dream about. She often tried to program her dreams now, because too often her sleep was like a black tunnel, full of winds that had no place else to go.

Kent Janes's face surfaced in her mind, but she pushed it away, not at all sure that he should be anywhere near the slow waters of her sleep.

18

*D*ARREN WOKE UP LATE. THE SKY WAS ALREADY GET-
ting light and she knew that, by the time she got to
the gym, Cassie would be halfway through her workout.

Several days had passed since her lunch with Kent Janes, and
the heat wave had broken. It was gray and cool outside, and the
dampness was so thick that a fine mist was falling. Darren turned
on the windshield wipers and hoped that the rest of the day
would be like this. She would build a fire, lie on the couch, and
read, or take Peanut down to the beach and watch sea gulls circle
above the gray water.

"Overslept, huh?" Cassie said when Darren found her in the
gym.

"Yeah—sorry. I'll just finish working out with you and then
ride the Life-Cycle for a while."

She worked out for about twenty minutes, and when she

went over to the row of stationary bikes, she could see that there was still no sun cutting through the clouds. She might actually get her wish for a cool, misty day. She rode until her thighs ached and sweat was running into her ears, gluing her hair to her neck.

It was almost nine when Darren started driving home. Sean and Kent Janes would just be starting their interview. They were meeting for breakfast somewhere, but she was glad she hadn't asked where. She'd probably be tempted to drive by and peer through the window, so she could study their body language and determine whether or not they were hitting it off.

She had expected that Sean would probably call her when they were finished. What she wasn't expecting, when she picked up the phone a little after eleven, was Kent Janes's voice on the other end.

"I hope I'm not disturbing you," he said. He sounded tentative, almost awkward.

"No, I was just sitting around reading. How did the interview go?" Darren asked.

"Very well. Your friend Sean is an interesting young man. I almost felt as though we should switch places. He has much more firsthand knowledge about Nicaragua than I have. I did call for a specific reason, though, Darren—other than to arrange a time to see the tape. Sean mentioned that Andrew took some notes while he was there."

"Uh-huh." She pictured the brown envelope tucked away in the desk drawer she couldn't bring herself to open.

"Would it be possible for me to take a look at them?" Kent asked.

Darren took a deep breath and let it out in a long, slow stream. She could feel him waiting for her answer, could imagine his eyes studying the air in front of him while he tried to decipher her silence. She had brought herself up to this line, and now she had to cross it.

"Yes, I guess that would be OK," she said finally. "Should I drop them off at your hotel?"

"You don't have to go out of your way. I'd be happy to come get them."

"If you want. I'll be here all day, except I promised my dog I'd take her for a walk on the beach this afternoon."

Kent hesitated for a moment. "Would you like some company? I haven't walked on the beach in a very long time."

The mist had lifted, and Kent felt the sun moving across his face as he walked along the brick path to Darren's front door. He noticed the clay pots with bright impatiens spilling over the sides and the jasmine vine climbing up the wall toward the roof.

Peanut ran out of the door as soon as Darren opened it, and jumped on him.

"This your watchdog?" he asked, laughing and scratching Peanut's head.

"She used to be a little better at it. I'm hoping this is just a phase. Her name is Peanut. Since it looks like she's holding you in place there, I'll go in and grab the leash and we can go."

It was a ten-minute walk down to the beach. They had little chance for conversation, with the steady stream of traffic passing them, but in a strange way, Kent was grateful for that. For that brief time, he could be a spectator, observing Darren as she moved through the familiar structure of her world. When they passed the small, neighborhood gas station, they had to wait while Peanut wrestled with the dog who usually slept beside the gas pumps.

At the Coast Highway, Darren pointed to some steps that led down to the mouth of a tunnel.

"That goes under the highway, and we'll come out at the beach," she said, raising her voice to be heard above the traffic.

The tunnel was damp and smelled of urine and stale beer. Graffiti were scrawled on the cement walls.

"You walk through here by yourself?" Kent asked, his voice echoing and bouncing off the walls.

"I do a lot of things by myself now."

They walked up the steps at the other end and onto white sand. Peanut yelped and strained at the leash; when Darren freed her, she raced into a flock of sea gulls and sent them screeching into the air. Moments later she was back, with a stick in her mouth and her eyes on Kent.

"She knows a good throwing arm when she sees one," Darren said, laughing.

It was low tide, and the sky was reflected in the wet sand. Kent threw the stick out into the water and Peanut swam out and rode a wave back in, with the stick in her mouth. No matter how many waves came between her and the stick, she always managed to get it.

"Is there anywhere this dog won't go to retrieve this thing?" he asked.

"I don't think so."

Kent's eyes traveled across the water to a sailboat reduced to the size of a toy by the stretch of blue distance. He turned back to Darren and noticed how perfect she looked in this setting. It was like she had been born to stand on a white beach with waves breaking behind her and the salt-ripened wind rummaging through her hair. He imagined her leading a child out through mounds of sea foam, lifting the small body over the waves.

"How far along are you in your pregnancy?" he asked.

"Three months. Do you have children?"

"I did—I mean, we did—but she died. She was two years old." Kent was amazed at how easily the words came out. He couldn't remember if he had ever actually said it to anyone before.

Darren said nothing. She looked out across the water and then watched Peanut stalking a sea gull, waiting for just the right moment to charge it. The subject of children drifted away on the afternoon air.

"Can I ask why you want to see Andrew's notes?" she said after several minutes. "Was there something specific you thought you might find?"

"No, not really. I just thought he might have written something down that he neglected to tell you about, or that he did tell you about and you've forgotten. If it seems like an invasion—"

"No, it doesn't. Really—I was just curious. May I ask you something else?"

Kent nodded.

"You do believe that Andrew and the others in that church were murdered, don't you? You don't think they just happened to be in a church when someone happened to toss a bomb in?"

"My personal opinion is that they were murdered deliberately, but Darren . . . my personal opinion doesn't really matter. If nothing can be proved, then it's all speculation."

Darren looked back at the city. It sparkled in the orange, late-afternoon light. "I know—I just wanted to know what you thought."

They didn't speak for a long time; the breaking of the waves filled the space between them, and when they turned back the sun was already slipping from the sky.

By the time they got back to Darren's house, a half-moon was floating above them. Her house was shadowy and quiet, as if daylight had moved out hours before.

"Make yourself at home," Darren said. "I'll just feed Peanut and then I'll get those notes for you. If you have time, you can see the tape now . . . but I might not watch it with you."

She was surprised, when she stood in front of the desk with her hand on the drawer, how hard it was to make herself open it. It was almost as though she expected Andrew's ghost to float out and vanish on a gust of wind. She had never opened the envelope, never read the notes he had taken; seeing the tape had been difficult enough. And even as she opened the drawer, she thought she could smell smoke.

"I'll get these back to you very soon," Kent said when she handed them to him.

"That's all right—take your time. I hope you find something that will help."

Darren slid the tape into the VCR and started to leave the room, but she was stopped by the memory of her own reaction when Andrew had played it for her. She had been so grateful that he was there, that she wasn't alone watching the hideous aftermath of someone's uncontrolled hatred.

She came back and sat down on the couch beside Kent. As the twisted, blood-soaked shapes filled the screen, she could sense Kent's eyes filling with tears even before she turned to look at him.

"Are you sure you want to see this?" she asked, touching his arm lightly.

He nodded, and she knew there was no room in his throat for sound.

Darren saw things on the tape she hadn't noticed before: the trembling of the camera and the way it seemed at times to drop slightly. She could trace the progression of Andrew's emotions by the movement of the camera, and she understood why, when he had played it for her, he had watched with dry eyes. Nothing could equal the horror and pain of coming upon people massacred so brutally; after that, all that was left was numbness and the bitter realization that one human being had done this to another.

When Kent left, there was a moment of awkwardness as they stood at the front door. Neither of them knew what to say, and Darren found it difficult to look at him.

"I'll be talking to you soon," he said, and touched her hand quickly.

Darren watched him walk down the path, past the gardenia bushes that Andrew had planted when they first bought the house. There were times when she swore she saw Andrew's shadow fall across the path, moments when she would hold her breath, certain that she had heard his key turn in the lock. And now she was watching someone else walk down that same path, crossing through the shadows that always deceived her. She wanted to call out to Kent, tell him to be careful where he stepped; there were things he couldn't see there that had to be preserved.

When she went back into the house, night was curling through the rooms. The wind had come up; she listened to it sweep past the fence outside, heard leaves scratching across the ground. It was the sound of loneliness—hollow and rushing and going nowhere. She sat on the couch for a long time, looking out the window, remembering the sound of Andrew's footsteps. The memories were rising around her like deep water. She knew she couldn't stay in the house that night—a night that would not be gentle with her.

Lawson answered the phone on the second ring.

"Hi," Darren said. "Can Peanut and I come spend the night?"

"Of course," he said. "Are you all right? Do you want me to come get you?" And she knew he would have.

"No, I'm fine. It's just . . . one of those nights."

Kent ordered dinner in his room, and while he waited he dialed his home number. It was almost ten o'clock in Washington; Cecilia might be asleep already. But the strength of her voice when she answered the phone told him she was not only awake, she was in a surprisingly good mood.

"I've had a wonderful afternoon," she said. "Martin came to visit me and we had tea and talked."

"Martin S. Volish?" Kent asked dryly. "Did his car break down in front of our house or was one of our neighbors having a probate sale?"

"He left work early to come visit me because he knew I was alone. He's a very nice man."

"Uh-huh. Well, I'm glad you had a good time," Kent said, wishing she could have a good time with someone else. There was something about Volish he didn't trust, and he hated the idea that this man was having long, confidential conversations with Cecilia. It took only a minute of superficial dialogue with her to know there was something out of balance there. Washington was a small town—too small—and gossip traveled at lightning speed.

"You just don't want me to have any friends. That's it, isn't it?" Cecilia said.

"It's not that and you know it. But you just met this man, and—" It was useless. They were headed straight for an argument, and Kent felt too raw to add a shouting match to the evening's agenda.

"Cecilia, it's late. We'll talk about this another time. I'm really very happy you had a nice day."

The brown envelope containing Andrew's notes was beside him on the bed. After he hung up Kent slid them out and shuffled through the pages, hastily scrawled in pencil. Sean had told him about the men they heard talking in the bar of the Inter-Continental, and Kent wanted to see if Andrew had written

155

down his impressions. He found, among the pages, a cocktail napkin on which Andrew had written down the same things Sean had overheard—"get an eyeful," "peasant bastards"—but in the corner of the napkin Andrew had written "the Colonel?" Either he had heard something Sean hadn't, or Sean had forgotten, but Kent suspected Sean didn't forget too many things. He put the notes back into the envelope; he had to take his mind off Nicaragua for a while.

He took off his shoes and shook sand into the wastebasket. The smell of salt air was still on his clothes, and his skin remembered the feel of ocean mist blowing over him in gentle sheets.

Darren's laughter came back to him, bell-like and clear, as uncomplicated as the crashing of a wave. Then he tried to bring Cecilia's face into his mind—a memory of how she had looked in greener seasons. But the image was gone with his next breath. Hard as he tried, he couldn't hold on to it; it melted into a picture of Darren.

There was a part of him that knew he was feeling things he shouldn't. But the feelings had been stagnant for so long, he didn't want to quell them. He wished he could watch Darren's body ripen in the coming months as her belly swelled and her breasts filled with milk. She was proof that new life was born even after death seemed to rip away all hope. He had forgotten until that day how amazing it was to see a woman carry another life inside her. He had made himself forget, because that memory belonged to another time. But now it was in front of him—birth and death, as necessary to each other as the two sides of the moon.

19

*M*AYBE IT WAS THE RAIN STREAMING DOWN THE REAR windshield that made the headlights look closer than they really were, but when Darren looked in the side mirror, she could see the car was following her much too closely. It was five-thirty, and instead of staying in bed and listening to the sound of the rain on the roof, she was on her way to the gym . . . all because the night before she had studied her body in the mirror and decided that her legs were looking thick and fleshy.

The rain had started sometime during the night. She heard it as if in a dream—a slow, heavy pattering on the leaves and the swell of the storm as it gathered strength. Once she woke up, in the early hours after midnight, it seemed that she never really got back to sleep again. She lay in bed, with the smell of wet earth drifting through the partly open window and the warm gusts of the summer storm slapping the sides of the house, and argued with herself about going to the gym. By the time the clock read five, she was tired of the argument and decided just to go.

But now she was on a wet, empty street. with the rain making everything look wavy and distorted, and someone was following her. She decided to turn right and go around the block, as if she were going to one of the apartment buildings, but when she did the car stayed behind her. She got back on Ocean Avenue and it was still there, the headlights looking large and liquid through the glass.

Darren could hear her heart beating; it echoed in her head like thunder, and the blood in her veins felt as if it were crystaliz-ing. There were cars passing her the other way. She considered rolling down her window and yelling to one of them, pleading with them to help her. But the rain was coming down in sheets, and everyone probably had their windows up. What if she pulled over to the side and stopped? Would someone get out and shoot her? Pull her out of the car and leave her lying in the street with the rain washing over her?

She realized that, if she turned left and went up to Fourth Street, she could drive right to the police station. That was what you were supposed to do if you were being followed; she remem-bered her father telling her that when she first got her driver's license.

She turned so fast that the car almost skidded, and she heard the car behind her splashing through the water that was stream-ing into the gutters.

It seemed like forever before she reached the entrance to the police station. As soon as she saw the lights and the cars parked in the lot, she felt her breathing get a little slower. Suddenly her rearview mirror was dark; the car had sped away as soon as she made the turn. She drove in anyway and stopped when she saw a cop walking out to one of the cars. He had a yellow slicker on and he looked at her quizzically, as if he wasn't sure for a moment which category she fell into—victim or criminal.

"Excuse me," she called out, rolling down her window. Rain blew against her face.

He walked over and leaned down, scanning the inside of the car before focusing on Darren's face.

"I was being followed," she said. "I turned in here and they drove away, but they were definitely following me."

"Where you off to this time of the morning?" he said, glancing around the car again.

"The gym. Just off of Main Street up there." Jesus, what did he think? That she was a prostitute driving over to her pimp's house to pay him his percentage?

"Tell you what," he said, apparently satisfied that she was telling the truth. "I'll follow you to the gym, just to make sure you don't have any more trouble, OK?"

"OK, thanks."

The sky was getting light—a weak gray dawn struggling to be seen through the clouds. It was almost quarter to six. But it would even things up on one level; lately Cassie had been at least ten minutes late every day. When she pulled into the parking lot of the gym with the police car close behind her, she saw Cassie getting out of her car. Darren pulled into a parking space and waved to the cop, who then backed out of the lot and drove away.

"I know you don't like driving in the rain, but a police escort?" Cassie said, coming over to her. "Isn't that taking it a little far?"

"I was being followed, Cassie. All I could think of to do was pull into the police station. One of the cops offered to follow me. I think I'm still shaking," Darren said, holding out her hand.

Cassie's expression changed and she looked at Darren with narrow, concerned eyes. "Could you tell who it was?"

"No, it was too dark, and with the rain . . . Let's go in, Cassie. I'm getting soaked, and now I really need to work out."

She was almost finished doing calf raises when the first clap of thunder rumbled through the sky, rattling the windows and splitting open the clouds so that new torrents of rain were released. Darren thought about Peanut and knew she would no longer be sleeping peacefully on the bed. She had visions of angry neighbors leaving notes on her door informing her that her dog was making too much noise.

"Cassie, I'd better go. Peanut's going to wake up the neighborhood."

"You're going to be a great mother, Darren," Cassie said. "Be careful driving, and call me if you need anything."

When she pulled into her driveway, Darren got out and stood in the rain, listening, hoping the sound of barking would not be one of the instruments in the morning's orchestra of noise. She held her breath after the next roll of thunder and heard nothing but the gurgling of water in the gutters and the hollow, metallic plink of drops hitting the car.

She reached up to unlock the front door before she realized it was slightly ajar. She kicked it open and screamed, "Peanut! Peanut, are you here?" She heard nothing—no paws thundering across the floor, no dog tags jingling. When she got to the bedroom, Darren heard Peanut's tail thumping against the floor.

"Peanut?" she said, more softly now.

She looked behind the bed and then, following the noise, went to the closet. Peanut was cowering in the corner, behind her shoes.

It was only after she had checked Peanut thoroughly and decided that she wasn't hurt that Darren turned her attention to the house.

"I guess you're not much of a watchdog when it comes right down to it, are you, girl?" she said as she moved from room to room. She knew someone had been in her house. Darren never forgot to lock the door, and she could feel that a stranger had walked through the rooms even though, so far, nothing was disturbed.

Until she came to the shelf beside the television where all her videotapes were piled. They were no longer neatly stacked; someone had rummaged through them and tossed them back onto the shelf. Darren turned around slowly, taking in the rest of the room. Some of the books in the shelves were sticking out, but nothing else was disturbed. She unlocked the desk drawer where she had put Andrew's tape after showing it to Kent; it was still there.

Suddenly her legs felt weak and her heart sounded like it would burst through her chest wall. She sank onto the couch. "Come here, Peanut." And Peanut quickly scrambled into her lap and frantically licked her face.

The thunder was moving farther away and the rain was lighter—a chorus of tiny drummers playing on the roof. Darren looked at the drops trickling down the glass and held on to Peanut. The phone rang, but she didn't move to answer it. She had turned off her phone machine two days earlier, after Kent's interview came out and she was mentioned as Andrew Laverty's widow. It had prompted several calls from reporters, and she had decided to just stop answering the phone.

"Why did you have to mention me?" she had asked Sean.

"How could I not mention you? You do have a small part in this saga," he'd answered.

As she watched the path of raindrops on the window, the emptiness of the house started to close in on her. She had been followed in the dark hours of early morning, her house had been broken into by someone who knew exactly what to search for, and her phone was ringing with people she didn't want to talk to. She tried to push away the feeling of panic that was starting in her knees and creeping toward her throat. She lifted Peanut off her lap and went over to the phone. When it stopped ringing she looked up Danny's number in her book and picked up the receiver.

"Danny, it's Darren. Did you put that tape in a safe place?"

"Yeah, uh-huh." She could tell he'd been sleeping.

"Could you check and make sure it's still there?"

"Now? For Chrissakes, Darren, it's—I don't know what time it is, I can't find the clock. It's morning; why do I have to look now?"

"Because it's important. Someone broke into my house, Danny, and that's what they were looking for."

"Shit!" He suddenly sounded awake. "I'll come right over."

"No, Danny, you don't need to. I'm all right. Everything's all right. Just go make sure the tape's there, OK?"

"OK." She heard rummaging on the other end of the phone, something that sounded like a chair being scraped across the floor. In a few minutes he was back.

"Yeah, it's there. Are you sure you don't want me to come over?" he said.

"No, really, I'm fine."

But she wasn't fine. The panic was still there; it was a familiar feeling to her these days, descending on her too frequently. It was the man under the bed, the ghost lurking in the cellar, the wind that finds unlatched windows and hurls them open with an icy blast.

Sometimes it followed her out of the house, sneaking up on her at unexpected moments—in the market, going through the aisles under the ice-white glow of fluorescent lights. She would glance into other people's carts and see their lives reflected there. She could tell who had large families at home and would envision them crowded around a dinner table, laughing and talking. And she would suddenly feel exposed, as if everyone in the store knew she was alone.

It had happened before, but this time, standing in her kitchen with the taste of fear still sour in the back of her throat, it was worse.

"Come on, Peanut, let's go walk in the rain."

She drove down to the highway, the wet asphalt making a swishing sound under the tires. The streets were nearly empty and she imagined that most people were in bed with a cup of hot coffee and the newspaper.

Darren decided not to push her luck by walking through the tunnel. The parking lots were empty and the only other person on the beach was a surfer, who seemed oblivious to the fact that it was still raining. She walked along the storm-littered shore, watching the ocean mist rise and mingle with the rain. Soon the panic that had grabbed her loosened its hold and she felt her chest relax, as if it were willing to let her breathe again.

By the time she got home, the rain had gotten heavier again;

drops the size of marbles exploded against the windshield. As soon as she turned onto her street, she saw a beige Chrysler that looked too familiar. As she got closer she saw Kent Janes sitting behind the wheel.

He jumped out and ran across the street.

Darren got out of the car and stared at him. "Are you OK?" he said, the rain coming down between them like a waterfall.

"What do you mean?" Darren said slowly. She could taste the rain running into her mouth. Did Kent know that her house had been broken into?

"I tried to call you yesterday and again this morning. There was never an answer and I got worried," Kent said, wiping rain out of his eyes.

"Someone got into my house this morning. I think they were looking for the tape."

"Did you call the police?"

"No—they didn't take anything."

Kent grabbed her arm and pulled her toward the front door. "Come on, we're both getting soaked out here.

"Darren, this is very serious. Don't you have a security system or anything?" Kent asked once they were inside the house.

"No, I—this is a very safe neighborhood. Look, nothing was taken and they didn't find what they were looking for. I'll have more locks installed tomorrow. You know, you're making a puddle on my floor. Why don't you go into the bathroom and get out of those clothes. I'll give you something of Andrew's."

Kent looked down at his blue T-shirt and gray sweatpants, which were now sticking to him. "OK, sorry about the mess," he said, and walked into the bathroom, leaving a trail of water behind him.

"I haven't been answering my phone for a couple of days," Darren said when Kent came out to the kitchen wearing the clothes Andrew used to wear for running. For a moment it startled her, the sight of someone else wearing her husband's clothes, but, she told herself, they were just sweat clothes, the same thing thousands of people wore every day.

"Since I was mentioned in your interview with Sean," she

163

continued, filling a saucepan with water and pouring oatmeal into a measuring cup, "I've gotten messages from a few reporters, and I don't want to talk to them."

"Darren, I'm very concerned about what happened here this morning. Can't you stay somewhere else for a while?"

"I'm not going to be driven out of my house, Kent. This is my home and this is where I'm staying."

"All right. I don't want to meddle in your life, but since I've already started doing exactly that, I'd like to just suggest one more thing: you should use the publicity that's being offered to you. You said yourself that you thought my doing that interview might make the police be more aggressive in their investigation."

"But you're a prominent person."

Kent walked over to the stove and stood next to Darren. "That doesn't matter. Publicity is publicity."

"I'll think about it," Darren said, spooning oatmeal into two bowls. "I made you some cereal, too. I guess you must have looked hungry—I didn't even bother to ask if you wanted some."

Kent moved over to the window and looked outside. The rain was getting lighter; Darren knew that, by afternoon, the storm would be over.

"Darren, there's a very small person in a black slicker coming into your backyard," Kent said.

"That's Leland." She got two spoons out of the drawer. "Could you open the door before he knocks? My doors have dents in them from his fists."

"Hi, who're you?" Leland said, coming toe to toe with Kent.

"I'm Kent. And you're Leland, right?"

"Uh-huh. Darren, can Peanit and I play in the puddles?"

"Only if you hose the mud off her afterward."

Leland ran out to play, and Darren and Kent carried their oatmeal into the living room and sat on the couch.

"So, is Leland going to baby-sit for you when he's old enough?" Kent asked.

"Leland will never be old enough."

"Darren, I hate to bring up a serious subject over breakfast, but did Andrew ever mention overhearing those men in the bar talk about a colonel?"

"No, I don't think so. Why?"

"Just something I found in his notes. And my assistant found a Colonel Hadley mentioned frequently in some magazine articles about mercenaries. Supposedly, he lives in Miami. It could be nothing, but I thought I'd ask."

Darren listened to Leland and Peanut outside and the rain tapping on the roof. "I have a question for you," she said. "Why isn't your wife here with you?"

"You mean here in your living room? She hates oatmeal."

"I'm serious. Why are you in California without her?"

Kent put down his bowl and studied Darren. He wondered if the words would come easily again, as they had when he told her about his daughter. "My wife is not well," he began, and he felt each word form on his tongue like a smooth white pearl. "She is a manic-depressive. It started after our daughter died. She drowned in the swimming pool at our house, and Cecilia blames herself. I thought it would get better with time, but instead it's gotten worse. I frankly don't know where it will end."

"I wouldn't have asked if—"

"I know. But I'm glad you did in a way. Maybe it's something I need to talk about."

He told her about his memories of his daughter and about how he and Cecilia had met. He described Cecilia as she had been and tried to explain what their life was like now. As they talked, the light outside the window changed and the rain ended. Leland had let Peanut into the house without their noticing, and she was lying on the kitchen floor, dripping with muddy water.

"Do you feel like your daughter is with you sometimes?" Darren asked as sunlight sparkled through the raindrops that clung to the glass, making them look like diamonds.

"Sometimes, yes. I can't explain it, and I've never told anyone about it before, but a feeling comes over me once in a while. It's as if the wind has suddenly changed directions, and I think she must have done it to get my attention."

Darren didn't question it when Kent stayed and helped her wash the mud off Peanut, or when he carried the trash out and helped her clean up the kitchen. She didn't question it because, if she had, she'd have made him leave.

And she didn't question it that afternoon when thin white clouds scraped past the sun and Kent put his arms around her and pulled her in tightly against his body. She pulled back and saw a tear balanced on the rim of his eye as if it couldn't decide which way to go.

"What is it?" Darren asked softly.

"I don't know."

When their mouths met she tasted the tear; it slipped between their lips like it belonged there. And with it still stinging on her tongue she led him through the afternoon light into the bedroom.

His hands were warm and strong as they explored her, and Darren imagined they were leaving trails of heat across her body. She could smell the rain in his hair and on his skin, and when she tried to open her eyes, she couldn't. His kisses traveled over her face and down her neck and shoulders; when his tongue found her nipples and circled them gently, she no longer felt uncomfortable with the fullness of her breasts. She knew then what it would feel like to have her child drink from her, nourish itself from her body. When he entered her and their movements became slow and deep, she thought she felt another heartbeat—tiny and frail and new—pulsing between them. She wondered if her child, in some secret part of its soul, was aware that something wonderful was happening outside the boundaries of its watery world. Maybe, in the midst of its somersault dreams, it would smile at the realization that the world outside was not all cold, that people found ways to melt the arctic layers of their lives, if only for a moment.

A shiver of wind woke her up. Darren's eyes sifted through the evening shadows that swirled through the room like veils and found Kent standing by the window pulling his shirt over his head.

"You're leaving?" she said in a sleepy voice.

He came over and sat on the edge of the bed. "I think I should."

"Were you going to sneak out without waking me?"

"No, of course not. But . . . I just think I should go. Promise you'll be careful, and that you'll call me if anything happens."

He kissed her lightly on the mouth. She listened to his footsteps on the hardwood floor, heard the door close behind him and the start of the car engine. After a few minutes she got up, pulled a robe around her, and went out to the kitchen to feed Peanut. It was getting darker, and with the night came the realization that she had made love with Kent in the same bed she had shared with Andrew. She felt like she should apologize to Andrew, explain to him that she was lonely and it had felt so good to be touched, to have another body next to her.

She needed to talk to someone, and the only person she thought might understand was Cassie. Without bothering to call, Darren got dressed and called to Peanut that they were going for a ride. Cassie lived in a small guest house in Santa Monica, a five-minute drive from Darren. As she turned on San Vicente, she saw the moon above her and a cloud floating across its full, round face. There was a ring of light around it, like a halo. It was a Halloween moon, but Halloween was more than two months away; it was still August and the moon had no excuse to look so magical.

20

*W*HEN DARREN FINALLY DECIDED TO PLUG HER PHONE back in, the first call she got was from Sean.

"Where the hell have you been?" he said, apparently trusting she would recognize his voice.

"Hiding."

"Oh. Well, now that you're back, can I buy you dinner? I have some news that will interest you."

Darren hesitated, glancing around the room at the workmen, who had been there since late morning. "That would be great, Sean, but we might have to wait until they finish putting in this security system. They should be almost done."

Over dinner she told him why she now had a security alarm, and she watched his expression darken.

"Sean, I don't want to dwell on this, OK? I've had enough lectures." Although she deliberately didn't say who the lectures were from. "Tell me what your news was."

"Emerson Kyle turned up," he said between bites of pizza.

"The guy with the security pass? Where?"

"In an alley in Miami, with enough heroin in him to kill an elephant."

Darren pushed her plate away; fear tapped her on the shoulder again and she did what she usually did—tried to ignore it—but it wasn't working this time.

"Sean, I'm scared," she said.

"I know. Me, too. You know what? I'm going to sleep in your extra bedroom tonight, OK? It'll make both of us feel better."

Darren had to move her paintings aside and make up the single bed that alternately functioned as a couch and a place to throw things.

"I don't know how comfortable this is going to be," she told Sean.

"It's fine. Now, tell the truth—don't you feel better knowing I'm here to defend you?"

"Yes, Sean," Darren answered with a laugh. "I'm sure I'll sleep much better."

But as she crawled into bed and pulled the blankets up around her chin, she realized that she did feel better. Her fear was gone—for the moment—and sleep was quick and deep.

In her dream Darren was walking up the same road in Nicaragua where Tica had been killed. She was walking slowly, deliberately, as if she were being guided by a force that didn't care whether or not she wanted to go there. Brown leaves were drifting down from a hole in the sky; they blew around her and brushed her face with their sharp edges.

When she reached the spot where Tica died, she saw that white flowers had sprouted out of the cracked, dry dust. Darren bent down to look at them more closely. Their stems were red and slippery with blood. She stepped carefully around them and kept walking, the leaves still raining down on her.

She saw Tica up ahead, just off the road; she was sitting at the edge of the hill, looking down at a deep river, which rushed

169

in white-frothed fury, slapping the rocks that were in its way. Tica turned to her and smiled; the sun bounced off her hair in gold splinters.

Darren ran to her, leaving the storm of leaves behind, and suddenly she was in a calm bath of sunlight. She hugged Tica and smelled the earth and the sky in her hair. Then she followed the flight of one of her own tears as it fell through the air and landed where Tica's legs should have been . . . but weren't.

"It's all right," Tica said. "I don't need them."

A squirrel scampered past Darren and sat by Tica's arm, looking up at her with trusting eyes.

"Oh, you're hungry?" Tica cooed. "Here you are."

She held out her cupped hand to the tiny, eager animal, and Darren saw it was full of stars. The squirrel nibbled at the glittering jewels that had fallen from the sky into Tica's hand.

"I thought you were gone," Darren said, wiping a stream of tears from her face.

"Why did you think that? I've been here all the time waiting for you. You must have come a long way. Are you hungry?"

She held out her other hand and it was also full of stars. Some fell through her fingers and hung in the air, as if gravity did not apply to them.

"Help yourself," she said. "There's plenty."

Darren woke up and was surprised to find herself in bed; the dream was so real, she expected to find herself lying on dry, dusty earth, with fallen stars around her. It was still dark outside, but she couldn't go back to sleep. Her pillow was wet from her tears, and the sound of Peanut's breathing was the only interruption to the silence that hung like a net in the room.

She got up, made herself a cup of tea, and went out to the garden to watch the sunrise. It was Saturday; she didn't have to go to the gym. She didn't *have* to do anything . . . but she did. And she knew now what that was.

She waited until eight-thirty to wake Sean up. "Sorry," she whispered, sitting down on the floor by the bed, "but this is important."

"Are you OK? Is something wrong?" He was immediately awake.

"I'm fine. How would you like to take a trip with me back to Nicaragua? Can you get some time off, convince your editors to let you go back?"

Sean cleared his throat and sat up. "Darren, are you sure this isn't hormonal or something? I mean, I've heard that women get a little strange sometimes when they're pregnant."

"It has nothing to do with that. I want to go back, but I don't think I should go alone."

"Uh-huh. Well, I don't think you should go at all, but for the purposes of discussion, could you tell me what caused this brainstorm?"

"Maybe we'll see those men again. I don't think at this point that there are too many Americans in Nicaragua, not with what's happening to the economy there. So a group like the one you and Andrew saw should be easy to find."

"Gee, why didn't I think of that?" Sean said. "They're probably just sitting around in the same bar waiting for us to show up. Maybe they'd let us watch them slaughter some campesinos."

"Sean, I'm serious about this."

"I know you are. That's what's worrying me."

"Come on, Sean, you're a reporter. I thought you were supposed to leave no stone unturned."

Sean wadded his pillow into a ball and held it against his chest. "The problem here is that I don't see any stones marked 'turn me over.' If I say no, what will you do?"

"Go by myself."

"That's exactly what I was afraid of," Sean said, lying back and putting the pillow over his face.

PART FOUR

21

*I*T WAS RAINING WHEN THEY LANDED IN MANAGUA. THEY waited outside the airport for almost thirty minutes for a cab to take them to the Inter-Continental. Darren felt memories tugging at her. Despite the rain, she could taste the heat and the dust that had blown over her the first time she and Andrew were there. She closed her eyes for a second and saw Andrew's face in her mind; it made her feel like he was with her now, encouraging her.

"I asked for two rooms close to each other," Sean said once they were in the cab. "So we'll hope for the best. I didn't want to give you too much free rein, you know. I'm not sure I can trust you these days."

"Well, it may surprise you, but I do have a plan," Darren said. The taxi was warm and steamy from the rain, and she had to take deep breaths just to get enough oxygen.

"Does this mean you're going to let me in on it?" Sean asked.

"Uh-huh. I'm here looking for my boyfriend. The bastard got me pregnant and the last time I heard from him he said he was going to Nicaragua to do his duty as an American, whatever the hell that means."

"And you expect what?" Sean asked. "That someone will point you in the direction of a heavily armed group of commandos, and you can walk up and ask if they've killed any civilians lately?"

Darren saw the Inter-Continental looming up ahead. As the driver slowed down she said, "Sean, I know you're trying to play devil's advocate, and I can appreciate your reasons, but could you be a little less vehement?"

For the next two days they either walked or drove around Managua. The skies were unpredictable, sometimes billowing with storm clouds that would drench them with rain, sometimes opening to miles of blue. They walked through the *mercados* and listened to the rumors and the news of the day. A busload of workers had been attacked near León, and all but a few had been killed. The Sandinistas claimed it was a contra ambush; the contras blamed Sandinista soldiers. Children wearing almost nothing played in the mud; they had heard this kind of news for years.

It was obvious to Darren that Nicaragua was dying under the weight of war and poverty. Children looked at her with eyes haunted by hunger; they didn't even bother to beg. They probably didn't have the strength. It seemed to her that there were fewer people on the streets. She had read that thousands had fled and she knew that thousands more had died. They saw a few Americans, but Darren didn't bother to talk to them. She was beginning to think Sean was right—she was wasting her time and energy—but she was glad she had at least tried.

She thought about Lawson frequently. When she had left Peanut with him, he got so upset with her he had almost shouted at her. "How can you be so irresponsible?" he'd said. "It would be bad enough if you weren't pregnant, but since you are, that means you're endangering your child's life as well as your own."

"Lawson, I don't know what you expect of me. Should I just accept Andrew's murder as something that will never be solved, never be vindicated? I can't do that." She had tried to keep her words calm, but her eyes burned and her jaw was clenched so tight it ached.

"Sean, you do understand why I had to come back here, don't you?" Darren asked on their third night in Nicaragua. They were sitting in Sean's room, and outside a dark rain was falling.

"Yeah, sure I do. . . . I feel like I have to watch out for you, though. Sometimes I'm tempted to tie a little bell around your neck, so I'll be able to find you if you go wandering off on your own."

They decided to go to Los Antojos for dinner; Sean had been telling her about the parrots since they arrived, and Darren knew she was going to go home soon.

She noticed them as soon as they walked into the restaurant—four men, sitting at a corner table, leaning toward each other as if they were having a business meeting. They were middle-aged and looked like they could be salesmen or farmers or anything American and wholesome. Not gunrunners. Certainly not killers.

"I recognize one of those guys," Sean whispered after they sat down.

"You do?"

"He was one of the guys we saw that night at the hotel bar. I've never seen the others, though. And before you jump up and make a fool of yourself, Darren, could we please discuss this rationally and unemotionally?"

"Sean, give me a little credit, OK? I'm not going to go ask them why they're here."

"Good. What are you going to ask them, since you're already moving your chair back from the table. I know that getting-ready-to-pounce look, Darren, and it makes me very nervous."

"I'm going to tell them that I came down here looking for my boyfriend. He's a helicopter pilot and he said he was doing a job in Nicaragua. I have no idea if he was telling me the truth, but I had to come down here because I'm pregnant, and if he thinks he's going to run out on me he's wrong. So, since they obviously speak English and I don't speak Spanish, I thought I'd ask them."

Sean thought for a minute. "Does this phantom boyfriend have a name, I hope?"

"Brian . . . uh . . . Leavitt."

"Oh, that's good. Some nice Jewish boy is flying choppers into Nicaragua while his pregnant girlfriend is wondering if she'll ever see him again. I bet you read a lot of Nancy Drew books when you were younger, didn't you?"

"As a matter of fact, I preferred the Hardy Boys," Darren said, getting up from the table. "And by the way, you're my brother."

She could feel her nerves shiver as she walked over to their table.

"Hi," she said, casually, she hoped.

The four men pulled back in unison, like a flower opening, and Darren suddenly felt as if she was the prey, flying straight into something she couldn't get out of. For the first time since she had arrived in Managua, she was frightened. She tried to summon the anger that had taken her this far, fueling her with the steadiness of its flames, but she found that even that was shaky.

"What can we do for you, little lady?" one of them asked.

He was about twenty pounds overweight, with a receding hairline and glasses. Darren noticed a gold wedding band on his finger. They all looked like husbands and fathers. Some were probably grandfathers . . . she had to be wrong.

"I thought maybe you gentlemen could help me," she said, moving closer to the table. She might as well finish what she had started. "I came to Managua a few days ago, and I haven't seen too many Americans here. I don't speak Spanish, so it's been hard for me to communicate—"

"What do you need—a tour guide?" one of the others said, ignoring laughter at the table.

"Actually, I'm looking for my boyfriend. He said he was going to do a job in Nicaragua. See, the thing is, I'm pregnant, and I think he's planning on running out on me. I don't have much money, so I'm not going to let him off that easy, you know what I mean? The guy's got an obligation."

"What's your boyfriend's name?"

"Brian Leavitt. He's a pilot—flies helicopters mostly. I don't know why he'd be flying to Nicaragua, but that's what he said. So I followed him, but I haven't been able to ask anyone. Then I saw you guys, and I thought . . . well, I thought you might know something."

She felt their eyes on her, studying her. The man who had first spoken to her shook his head.

"I know some pilots, but I never heard that name," he said.

"Well, I know there was a chance he was lying to me. I mean, I couldn't really figure out why he would be working here. I mean, things have sort of died down around here, haven't they?"

"There's enough goin' on for a good pilot to make a few bucks, but like I said, we never heard of this one." The man's eyes traveled up and down her body, and Darren was aware that she still didn't look pregnant. She wondered if he believed her.

"You men seem to know what's going on around here," she said. "And you think if he was telling me the truth, you'd have heard his name?"

Two of the men nodded. "It's not a big country," one of them said.

"Right. Well, thanks for your help. If I ever do find him, I'm going to beat the shit out of him," Darren said. She started to walk away and then, as if it were an afterthought, turned back and said, "Say, would you mind if my brother took a picture of all of us together? You know, so I'll have a memento of my trip—even though it was sort of a waste."

"Sure, we'll even autograph it to your boyfriend," said a wiry, dark-haired man, who had been silent up to that point.

She went back and got her purse; she'd been carrying the camera with her since she arrived.

"Come on, brother dear," she whispered to Sean. "I want to get a picture with my new friends."

She sat on the overweight one's lap and smiled at the camera, just another tourist. Inside, however, her nerves were still on edge, and she didn't want to speculate on what might have happened if they hadn't believed her.

"Where you staying?" the man said, his breath hot and sour against her face.

"Oh, we're leaving tomorrow," Darren said, sliding off his lap. "I really want to thank you for being so nice to me, though. Bye!"

She said nothing until they were back in the hotel, in the hallway outside her room.

"Why would they know pilots, Sean? Unless they were into things they shouldn't be into. I didn't get the impression they were talking about airline pilots."

"No, they probably weren't. But I'll tell you something, Darren. If you weren't serious about leaving tomorrow, you should have been. I think we should get out of this city. I've been here too many times, and if they checked around, they could probably find out who I am. And the Inter-Continental is not exactly an out-of-the-way place."

22

*T*HEIR FLIGHT WAS MORE THAN FORTY MINUTES LATE, which might not have been too unbearable except that they had already been waiting at the airport for two and a half hours. Sean had insisted they get there early; he had learned that a Senator Betts was arriving by private plane sometime in the late morning.

"That's about as specific as they get here," he told Darren. " 'Late morning'—I call it Nicaraguan Standard Time."

They had waited in lines, gone through customs, and looked around the souvenir shops in the small terminal. Now the sun was blazing its way toward noon, and Darren didn't care anymore if Sean got a statement from the senator or not. She was getting more and more edgy as the minutes ticked by; she wanted to be up with the clouds, high above Nicaragua and heading for home. She hadn't slept well the night before. She kept imagining men with guns beating down her door, demanding to know why she'd lied to them and threatening to kill her unless she told them why she was really there. The restlessness deep in her body had kept her awake, too. She thought it was her baby, turning fitfully inside her, complaining about the added adrenaline in her blood.

Sean was sitting near the window, reading a newspaper. Occasionally, he would glance out at the sky to see if he could spot a private plane coming in. Darren wondered if he even knew how late their flight was. If he did, he apparently didn't care.

"Do you think they'll call our flight before the next century?" she asked, although he obviously would have no way of knowing.

He tossed the paper aside and got up. "I'll go find out," he said. She knew her nervousness was driving him crazy.

She wandered over to the window and looked out at the runway. Antiaircraft guns lined it on both sides, and a few military planes were parked on the tarmac. There were clouds at the edges of the sky, and she knew it would be raining by afternoon.

"Shouldn't be too much longer," Sean said, coming up behind her. "I hope the senator gets here first. Did Kent Janes mention anything to you about someone coming down here?"

Darren felt her throat tighten, the same way it had when she told him that Kent had contacted her about getting Andrew's notes. It was as if she expected Sean to look through her skull to the thoughts inside her mind.

"No, why would he tell me?" she said, not looking at him.

"I just thought that when he got those notes from you— God, Darren, you're a little touchy today."

"I'm sorry. I didn't sleep very well last night and . . . I really want to get out of here. So, why do you think he's coming here?"

"I would assume it's some kind of fact-finding trip. It could be a good sign. Then again, it could be bullshit."

Darren paced up and down in front of the window. A baby was crying about ten feet away, and she saw the mother trying to quiet her child with no results. The noise was starting to grate on her, and she hoped that what she'd heard was right: it's different when it's your own, you don't mind so much.

"Sean, this might be the senator's plane," she said.

A blue-and-white plane was approaching the runway, soaring down from the sky like a large, metallic bird. She wished she had the nerve to run out and tell the arriving party that more was going on in this country than they could ever imagine. But she knew she would stay right where she was, behind the glass, keeping her wishes to herself. She realized that it could just as easily be Kent coming to Nicaragua to search out the facts on his own, and she wondered why it wasn't him, why he hadn't mentioned it as a possibility.

When the plane stopped, several men in dark suits descended the portable steps onto the tarmac. One was older than the others; Darren assumed he was the senator and the other two were aides. Sean was looking through his bag for a notepad and pen, and Darren was about to turn away from the window when she saw the older man slump down and fall to the pavement.

"Sean! Something happened—he had a heart attack or something!"

The men beside him were yelling; Darren could see their mouths moving and their arms waving frantically, but at that distance, from behind the glass, it was like watching a movie with the sound turned off.

Sean was standing beside her, and Darren studied his face, trying to read something on it that would indicate she had been wrong. Maybe the man just fainted, or tripped. Sean's breath was clouding the glass and his eyes were tense and serious. When Darren looked out at the tarmac again, she could see the blood, like an emblem, on the man's chest. Other people were running across the tarmac and then an ambulance pulled up, blocking her view. She reached over and took Sean's hand, squeezing it as hard as she could. She wanted to feel life, wanted to feel the warmth of his body travel into hers . . . because she knew the man they were putting into the ambulance was dead.

*　　*　　*

183

Their flight was being called, and Sean took her arm, pulling her away from the window.

"Sean, are you crazy? We can't leave now!" Darren said.

"Wrong. We're getting out of this country while we still can—before all hell breaks loose," he said. He was pulling her toward the line that was already forming. The rest of the people had moved away from the window; another death held no more interest for them than the departure of another plane.

"I can't believe you're even thinking of leaving," Darren said. "You're right here—you saw it. There's probably not another reporter anywhere near the airport right now. This is your story, and you're just going to get on a plane and leave?"

Sean turned her around to face him. His expression was hard and unyielding. "Darren, I came down here with you because you wanted to come back. If I were here by myself, I'd have been down on that tarmac ten minutes ago. But I'm not by myself. And I'm not taking any chances with you. We're leaving on this flight, no more arguments."

As they hurried out to the plane, Darren looked across the tarmac at the cluster of men who were still talking in loud voices. One was pointing to the terminal.

"The shot probably came from the terminal," Sean said. "A high-powered rifle."

A pool of blood stained the cement at the men's feet; she wondered if anyone would come to clean it up.

The plane took them high above the volcanoes and lakes, high above the tiny pool of blood drying on the tarmac. Darren could see, below her, the Camino Real, where wealthy people would hear the distressing news over lunch and discuss how tragic it was as their glasses were being refilled with wine.

"I'm scared, Sean."

"I don't blame you. My prediction is that troops will be on their way to Nicaragua before we walk in our front doors."

Darren leaned her head against the window and closed her eyes. She wished she could sleep, but her heart was beating too fast and her breathing felt heavy and sad. She remembered the first time her parents had taken her on a plane. She was twelve, and they took her to Minnesota to visit her grandmother. The plane had taken them up through the clouds into clear, blue skies, and Darren had looked down at a landscape of white billows. She thought of diving into them and, when the sound of the engines put her to sleep, her dreams were soft and white as the clouds.

She opened her eyes and looked down at terrain she didn't recognize, and her heart beat a little slower. Nicaragua was behind them, and before nightfall she would be back in California, where wars were something people only read about.

It was midnight before Darren got home from Lawson's with Peanut. The anger he had expressed when she left had been replaced with fear; she found him on the edge of desperation, certain that she was lying dead somewhere in the jungle. Maybe it wasn't just a senator—maybe they were killing all Americans. Darren could see that, as the day dragged on, rational thought had eluded him and the worst scenarios began to look like certainties.

She was both hungry and tired, but tiredness won out over the rumbling in her stomach. As she climbed into bed and turned off the light, the phone rang. She was tempted to pull the pillow over her head and let it ring, but she could think of several other people who would probably like to hear that she wasn't dead, and one of them answered her when she picked up the phone.

"Darren, thank God! I was really worried," Kent said.

"I just got back. I was at the airport waiting to leave when it happened. Did you know him?"

"Yes, we'd clashed many times over the issue of contra aid. I'm just glad you're out of there. I was going to contact the embassy if I didn't hear from you by tomorrow. Troops are already on their way to Nicaragua, so this is definitely not the time to be there."

"You sound like Sean."

"Yes, well, someone got their wish. Military intervention is inevitable now."

"Do you think it was the Sandinistas?" Darren said.

"I don't think they're that stupid, personally. But I think someone wanted it to look like Senator Betts was murdered by Sandinista soldiers. Darren, I'm going back to Washington soon, and I'd like to see you before I leave."

When she hung up the phone, Darren let her head sink into the pillows. The night was still as ice. Silence crawled over her and slid between the covers, filling the bed and reminding her that she was alone.

23

*C*ECILIA THOUGHT THAT IF THE PHONE RANG ONE MORE
time she would slice the cord in two. In fact, when
Martin got there, she had manicure scissors in her hand and was
trying to remember if you could electrocute yourself that way.
The only unattractive part of that possibility was that she might
live through it. She didn't know how the press had gotten their
home number, or why they would be so anxious to get Kent's
statement on something that had happened in Nicaragua, and she
didn't care. She just wanted the noise to stop. She wanted the
silence that always seemed so fragile, that was continually shattered by someone or something.

What drew her to Martin was that, whenever he arrived, he
seemed to usher in a new wave of silence. Noise fell away and
she could crawl back inside the borders of her dark world and

not be disturbed. Even his voice helped her return there. She could grab on to its soft tones and glide back to where it was safe and dim.

He had answered the phone twice since he had been there, calmly telling whoever was on the other end that Senator Janes was out of town and, no, he didn't know where he could be reached. Then he led her upstairs to the bedroom and pulled the drapes. He didn't mind being inside her dark spaces—not like Kent, who was always allowing the sunlight to crash down on her.

"Cecilia, do you know where your husband is?" he asked quietly. Her eyes hadn't adjusted to the dark, and it was as if the air were speaking to her.

"He's in Los Angeles. I can't remember where," she said. "Why?"

"Oh, I just wondered. It would be interesting to know what he thinks of these recent developments. He's been so outspoken about his opposition to contra aid. I would imagine you've gotten tired of the subject—I'm assuming, of course, that he discusses it at home, too."

The outline of his body was taking shape in the black, sunless room. Cecilia liked it that he was small, probably because she seemed to grow smaller every week.

"Not really," she said.

Just as she was drifting back into the deepest regions of darkness, the phone rang. Martin picked it up quickly, saving her from the invasion of more noise.

"Hello, Senator, this is Martin Volish. Yes, she's right here."

He handed the phone to Cecilia, and as she took it, she wished she had gone ahead and cut the wire into shreds.

"Cecilia, what the hell is Volish doing there? How much time are you spending with this guy?" Kent's voice roared over the line, filling her head with sound and making her skull ache.

"He's my friend. He helps me," she answered. Even her own voice hurt her now.

"I think that's Dr. Easton's job. Have you been keeping your appointments with him?"

"He doesn't understand anything. Martin understands." She could see, in the dark room, a flash of white teeth when Martin smiled at her.

"I don't think we should continue this conversation now," Kent said. "I wanted to tell you that I might be coming back sooner than I'd originally planned, depending on what happens with Nicaragua. I guess I'll just call you when I know for sure."

Kent took a long run through the streets of Westwood, trying to clear his head and relax his nerves, but nothing seemed to help.

When afternoon deepened the color of the sky, he drove to Darren's house. Along the center strip of San Vicente, joggers were passing people walking dogs and the shade of coral trees made patterns on the grass. Kent had been thinking of Darren all day—of the strength of her arms when they were wrapped around him and the smell of her hair as it fell across her face. And all day he had known, although he didn't admit it until he turned onto her street, that he would be seeing her for the last time.

She was in the front yard sweeping leaves off the path when he pulled up. She was wearing loose white shorts and an over-size green shirt the color of the grass. As soon as he got out of the car, Peanut ran up and jumped on him.

"Sorry," Darren said, pulling Peanut away, "I can't seem to break her of that."

Kent tried to memorize everything—the sound of the wind chimes, the clouds floating overhead, the traffic far below on the highway, so faint that if he closed his eyes he could imagine it was rushing water.

"I'm sorry you were worried," she said as he followed her into the house. "But maybe it was worth it. I took some pictures down there."

She handed him an envelope and he pulled out the photographs of Darren sitting on a strange man's lap with several other grinning men around her.

"They seemed to be pretty plugged in to who was flying in

and out of Nicaragua. Maybe someone on your staff can find out who they are."

Kent looked past Darren at the beams of sunlight dancing on the floor. "Darren, please promise me you won't do anything like this again. You know what the risks are. Emerson Kyle drops a security pass in Nicaragua and months later he's found dead, a needle stuck in his arm. You won't talk to the press in this country, but you go flying off to Nicaragua."

"But that wasn't what you came here today to say to me, was it?"

"No . . . I wish I could stay here with you, Darren. It seems as though I wish a lot of things these days that just can't come to pass. I was wishing all day that this wouldn't be the last time I saw you, but I know it has to be."

"I know. It's funny, but the way my life is now is the way I always thought it would be before I fell in love with Andrew. I always assumed I'd be alone, and that was all right. Then, when we started living together, I still thought it probably wouldn't work out and I'd go back to being alone. But then we got married, and I decided I'd been wrong. I told myself I was meant to be in this relationship and share my life. I guess I was right the first time."

"Darren, don't say that. You can't know whether or not you'll fall in love again."

"Yes, I can know. And I do. It's all right, I'll have my child, and my friends, and I'll have a nice memory of this time with you."

Their footsteps were soft and hesitant as they slipped between the afternoon shadows and went through the hallway to the bedroom, where they lay down with the sun peeking through the window like a curious neighbor. They were more familiar with each other, and their lovemaking was slower, as though both of them wanted it to last as long as possible.

Darren stayed curled next to Kent for a long time afterward, feeling the rhythm of his breathing and the heat of his skin. The sun had moved behind a white cloud, and the light in the room had turned golden.

"The light in here shouldn't be this beautiful," Kent said sleepily. "Nature should be more sympathetic."

"You'd feel better if there was a thunderstorm, or maybe a hurricane?"

"Well, it would be more appropriate."

She knew he was going to leave soon, and she felt a small ache begin deep in her chest. But she knew it would fade; she had, after all, become adept at healing her own wounds.

"I want to ask you some things," Darren said, sitting up and pulling the sheet up over her breasts, which still embarrassed her because they had gotten so large. "About Nicaragua. About what you think will happen."

"I think more troops will be sent," Kent said, turning over on his side and propping his head up on his elbow. "I think we're seeing the beginning of what some of us have feared for a long time."

"They're never going to catch whoever shot Senator Betts, are they?" Darren said.

"I doubt it. So, we're going to assume it was a Sandinista soldier—or at least a supporter of the government—and we are already acting on that assumption. Darren, I mentioned to you before that maybe you shouldn't shy away from the press. And I feel I should say it again, particularly in light of what's happened. People who never gave Central America a moment's thought before are going to be thinking a lot about it now, because their sons and their husbands or boyfriends are going to be sent over there. You could make a big impact right now. Will you just think about it?"

"Okay, I'll think about it. But I'm not making any promises."

Darren walked down the path with Kent and waited as his car disappeared around the corner. Fog was moving in from the ocean, and she watched as it curled around the trees and enveloped the house with its long white arms.

When she went back inside, she sat in the living room with the doors and windows open, letting the mist blow into the room and settle on the furniture. When she looked out the window, she could no longer see the mountains or the neighboring houses. It was as if she had carved herself a hole inside this soft, white cocoon, and that was her protection against any more pain. She wanted to pull the fog around her like a shawl and huddle there until she was ready to come out.

She stayed and watched the room fill with fog until night moved in and she had to close the windows against the chill.

24

*I*T HAD BEEN TWO WEEKS SINCE KENT HAD LEFT, AND DARREN was still debating whether or not she should gamble on the mercy of the media. In that time, more troops had been sent to Nicaragua, but so far no one had fired a shot. It was as though everyone was waiting to see who would be the first to raise their weapon.

Also in that time, Darren had found a baby squirrel, shivering under a mound of pine needles out in front of her house. She waited an hour, and when no mother squirrel came back for it, she took it up to the tree house that Andrew had started to build but never completed and made a nest for it using an old sweatshirt and the pine needles that it kept crawling back to. She got a tiny nursing bottle from the veterinarian and, every couple of hours, held the tiny animal in her hand and fed it a mixture of evaporated milk and water.

The weather had turned warm and steamy, with thick gray clouds hovering in the sky, threatening a summer storm but never quite getting around to it. In the mornings at the gym, people talked about how strong the smell of the ocean was; it drifted inland and made the air smell salty and thick. It was as if the sea were announcing some inexplicable change deep beneath its surface.

As Darren fed her squirrel, she would smell the sea and think about the smells of Nicaragua—the dust and car exhaust, and the sweet, sickly smell that had hung in the air when Tica died. She would feel the squirrel's tiny heartbeat in her hand and watch its mouth hungrily reach for the nipple of the bottle, and she would wish that her child was already born and could share this with her. Maybe it was the squirrel that helped her make up her mind; maybe it was cradling the small creature in the palm of her hand that made her remember the little one-armed girl in Tica's schoolhouse and the faces of the children in the *mercado* who didn't have enough to eat. Suddenly, Darren felt selfish sitting up in her tree house, nursing a baby squirrel while children far away in a country she had come to care about cried and bled and died with no one to hold them.

The storm finally came the night before Darren was scheduled to appear on one of the morning talk shows. She was spending the night at Lawson's because they were sending a limousine for her at four A.M., and she knew Peanut would feel better staying with him.

She heard the rain start a little before midnight, just after she had listened to Lawson tiptoe down the hall in order to see if the light had disappeared from under her door. She closed her eyes and tried to sleep, but she couldn't slow her thoughts. She slid her hand across her stomach and thought she felt the baby unfurling like a new leaf. She wondered what it would have been like going through this pregnancy with Andrew; she had gotten so used to it as a private, solitary thing, it was hard to imagine it any other way.

Finally, the steadiness of the rain lulled her to sleep. In her dreams she found herself fighting through a crowd of people.

They all seemed to know her—everyone was calling her name—but no one had a face. It was like an unfinished painting, as if the artist had given up and walked away before defining the faces. She was searching for something, but she didn't know what. Helpless, she was pushed along by the throngs of shouting people, and somehow she knew she was heading in the wrong direction. But she couldn't turn around, and the feeling of panic was tightening inside her like a wire. . . .

The alarm clock shattered the picture. Darren lay still for several minutes, staring at the clock and thinking about her dream. She finally forced herself out of bed and groped through the dark to the bathroom. In the cruelty of the bright light, she studied her face in the mirror; there were dark, puffy circles under her eyes and her skin looked pale and lifeless.

"Rembrandt would have trouble fixing this face," she said aloud to her reflection as she dumped her bag of makeup out on the counter. She had chosen a loose blue Moroccan dress, which she used to wear with a belt, and boots. When she was dressed she stood back from the mirror and was glad that she finally looked pregnant instead of just overweight.

She crept downstairs, hoping not to wake Lawson, but when she got to the kitchen, he was standing at the stove waiting for the kettle to boil.

"Lawson, what are you doing up?"

"I didn't want you to have to get up by yourself at this ungodly hour."

"So you thought you'd suffer along with me, huh?" Darren said, kissing him on the cheek. "Does this mean you no longer think I'm wrong in what I'm doing? You haven't voiced any protest in a long time."

"No, I haven't changed my opinion. I just got tired of arguing with you." Through his robe, his shoulders looked thin and frail.

He took out two bags of peppermint tea and poured steaming water into the cups. "I'm making you an English muffin, too. Remember when you used to stay over when you were little and we'd have breakfast together?"

"I do remember. You'd let me use as much jam as I wanted. It was great."

The toaster popped open and the smell of warm bread drifted through the kitchen.

"I had a very strange dream last night," Darren said. "A crowd of people was calling my name and pushing me, but no one had a face."

"Ah yes, the old faceless crowd dream."

"Do you know what it means?"

"Haven't a clue," Lawson said, and winked at her.

They sat at the kitchen table with warm smells around them, sipping tea and eating English muffins smothered in jam until the buzzer rang and a voice said that the limo was there.

Darren walked out into a gentle rain and rode down from the hills in the light-studded blackness. The limo sped past closed shops and streetlights, heading into the depths of Hollywood. It glided elegantly past people huddled in doorways, covered with newspaper, shivering in the dampness. Darren put down the window and a light wash of rain blew against her face.

"You'll catch cold like that," the driver said, peering into the rearview mirror.

"No, I won't." She wondered if he gave any thought to the people he'd just passed, who probably had pneumonia.

A pile of newspapers had blown free and pages were dancing across the street—the day's headlines fluttering uselessly in the wet dawn.

Sean had agreed to meet her there, and he was waiting when she walked into the studio. She wasn't sure what she'd expected the studio to look like, but this wasn't it. It was a large, empty building that looked more like a warehouse than a TV studio. Crew members were milling around, smoking and drinking coffee out of foam cups.

"Welcome to show biz," Sean said. "That's the hot seat over there. It's satellite, so you'll be talking to a red light."

He pointed to a small platform with one chair that faced in the direction of the cameras.

"It looks like the electric chair," Darren said.

"Well, I wouldn't go that far, but it does look threatening. Appropriately so—they're not exactly going to ask about your favorite recipe for chicken pot pie."

She was led over to the chair and hooked up to an earpiece and a microphone. A makeup girl came by and dabbed some powder on her forehead. "You're shiny," she said.

"I wish that's all I was," Darren said to Sean. "I don't think I want to be here."

"You'll do fine," he answered, squeezing her shoulder.

A middle-aged man with an overgrown mustache came up to her and said, "We'll be checking the sound in a few minutes. You comfortable?" He hurried off without waiting for an answer.

"Is he kidding?" Darren said in a low voice.

A woman's voice came through the earpiece. "Can you hear me all right, Ms. Laverty?"

"Yes."

Darren fought back a feeling of light-headedness as they checked the sound levels and told her to watch the red light.

"Darren Laverty lost her husband several months ago," the disembodied voice said, "in a bomb blast that destroyed a church and took several other lives as well, including some members of the group Safe Haven, which is dedicated to harboring Salvadoran refugees. Now, with a senator murdered in Nicaragua and American troops there and waiting, she has revealed that she has reason to believe her husband's death was not a random act of violence, as the police concluded. Ms. Laverty, the first question that comes to mind is, why now? Why didn't you speak out sooner?"

"For one thing, I was trying to cope with the loss of my husband," Darren answered, feeling her jaw start to clench. She already hated this woman, and the interview had just started.

"Yes, of course. But as I understand it, you're saying that your husband was targeted because of several trips he made to Nicaragua in which he saw things he shouldn't have. Is that correct?"

"Yes. He not only saw evidence that weapons were being shipped to the contras at a time when that was forbidden, he was

197

told by a survivor of a brutal massacre that Americans were among the killers. And at that village he found a security pass for Ilopango, the Salvadoran air force base. The man whose name was on that pass has since been killed."

"Well, I am familiar with what you're referring to. There has been speculation that a man named Emerson Kyle, who was a known mercenary, was murdered. But the facts are, he was found dead of a drug overdose. Now, Ms. Laverty, you're not actually suggesting that the government is sponsoring mercenaries in Nicaragua at this time, are you?"

Darren paused. "That's exactly what I'm suggesting. I don't think, if you look at the history of American aggression in other countries, that this should be surprising. It's happened before, and I believe it's happening again."

"Unfortunately, we're out of time, Ms. Laverty, but I'm sure we'll be hearing much more about this in the future. We're going to take a break and be back with our next guest, who will tell us about a revolutionary new method of exercising your facial muscles to avoid the pain and expense of plastic surgery."

In a split second, Darren was unwired, escorted to the door, and thanked perfunctorily.

Outside, Darren took a deep breath and looked up at the sky. The clouds had broken up and the last stars were fading.

"I knew it would be tough, but I didn't think it would be like that," she said to Sean. "I've seen convicted killers get treated better than that."

"Yeah . . . well, people have their biases. That lady probably wears her panty hose to bed."

"I don't know if I can go through something like that again, Sean."

"You probably won't have to. Not everyone thinks like her."

"Well, why don't you do an interview with me?" Darren asked.

Sean looked down at his feet and kicked a piece of broken glass across the asphalt. "First of all, Darren, I already did a piece on the bombing right after it happened. Second, it wouldn't exactly be an unbiased interview, would it? I mean, I have to maintain some objectivity in the pieces I do."

"OK, I understand. But I think I might prefer having a root canal to doing another interview like this."

Darren was in the kitchen the next evening, fixing dinner and only half listening to the news on the television in the living room, when she heard Nicaragua mentioned. She dropped a partially peeled carrot into the sink and ran to the set. She had to switch to three different stations before she got the whole story: a military jeep with four soldiers in it was parked in downtown Managua when it was sprayed with gunfire. All four men were killed. Darren turned off the television and sank down on the couch. No one would believe her now. Four Americans had been killed; it gave the U.S., according to most people, a perfectly valid reason to bomb the whole damn country. She could shout from the rooftops that the killings might have been set up to look like a Sandinista attack, but no one would listen. She would be talking to the wind, and even that would blow past her as though she wasn't there.

She took some carrots and almonds up to the tree house; the squirrel was crawling around and chirped at her when she came up the ladder. For a week he hadn't ventured out of his tunnel of pine needles, but now he was starting to think about climbing. Darren could tell; she would watch him tilt his head up toward the branches, as if to measure the distance. He scampered over to her and took an almond from her hand.

"It's almost time, isn't it, little fellow," Darren said softly as she watched him chew on the almond. "You've outgrown your milk bottle, and you're not afraid of open spaces anymore. One day soon I'll come up here and you'll be gone."

He stopped chewing and looked at her, blinking his gray eyes, and no one could have convinced her that he didn't understand everything she'd said.

25

*I*T WASN'T OCTOBER YET, BUT THE GEORGETOWN MORN-
ings had turned cold enough that Kent had to wear
sweat clothes for his run. As he ran through the gray morning, he
saw lights blink on in some upstairs windows and imagined
children being woken to get ready for school.

As he neared his own house, his footsteps sounding hollow
and loud in the quiet air and his breath forming white clouds in
front of him, he saw that the kitchen light was on. Cecilia was
up, and he felt the familiar feeling of apprehension; he never
knew what to expect anymore when he came through the door.

She was standing by the refrigerator, stirring milk into a cup
of coffee.

"Good morning," Kent said tentatively. "You're up early."

"I've been up for a long time," she answered, staring into
her cup. "You kept me awake, tossing around in your sleep."

Her voice was brittle as dry wood, and Kent did not want to wait around to see if things were going to get worse.

"I have to shower and get to the office," he said, trying to exit the kitchen as quickly as possible.

He crept around the house like a thief, wincing each time a noise interrupted the stillness, afraid it would push Cecilia over the slippery edge that she seemed poised on this morning. He had a hazy recollection of tossing around restlessly in his sleep; his dreams had been harsh and violent, but he couldn't remember them exactly. He suspected, though, that they had something to do with the four soldiers torn open by bullets as they sat on an empty Managua street.

By the time he got to the office, Kent had decided that he wanted to make a statement to the press about the assumptions that were leading the U.S. into war. There was no proof that the Sandinistas were responsible for Senator Betts's death—in fact, they had issued a denial and an apology that such a thing had happened in their country. And there was also no proof that the four young men in the jeep were killed by Sandinista soldiers. Wars shouldn't be started on the basis of unfounded judgments, he wanted to say.

It wasn't quite eight-thirty when he sat down at his desk and looked out the window at the gray, overcast day. He wished he was a child again, with nothing more on his mind than a new school year. He picked up the phone and dialed his press secretary's home number, bracing himself for an unpleasant conversation. Pat Morley didn't always like it when Kent chose his moments to appear before the press, and he particularly didn't like it if he got the information before nine o'clock in the morning.

"Good morning, Pat. I hope I didn't get you in the middle of breakfast," Kent said, sounding more amiable than he felt.

"Just finishing up, Senator."

"I'd like to go to the Press Gallery sometime today and make a statement. Could you set that up for me?"

"Certainly, but don't you think we should discuss what you're going to say first?" Pat said, a note of irritation creeping into his voice. "I assume it's about the most recent development in Nicaragua."

"You assume correctly."

"Well, maybe we could just do a fifteen- or twenty-second sound bite."

"I have more to say than that, Pat. Everything in the world can't be reduced to sound bites, you know."

"All right, I'm leaving now for your office. We can talk about it as soon as I get there," Pat said.

Kent leaned back in his chair. A dull light fell across his desk and rested on the stack of papers that he had to go through that morning. He felt unfocused and edgy, and he wondered if all public relations people were as irritating as his own press secretary.

When Pat walked into Kent's office, it was obvious that he had been thinking about their conversation the whole way over. He walked in with the authoritative air of someone who was about to conquer Wall Street, except that he always made Kent think of a child prodigy who went straight from diapers to neckties. Pat was wearing a dark blue pin-striped suit and a maroon tie, and his blond hair was slicked back with so much gel that not one hair would dare go askew.

"I know you feel strongly about this, Senator," he said, sitting down without bothering to say good morning, "but I don't want to get into another situation like we had after the bombing of Tripoli, where I had to do a lot of damage control because of your statements."

"Pat, you should know me well enough by now to know that I express my opinions, even if they may be unpopular at the moment. And I felt very strongly that we were wrong to fly over a city at night and drop a bomb on sleeping civilians. I thought that our real intention was wrong as well; I can't applaud an attempt to assassinate another world leader, regardless of what I might think of him."

"Yes sir, but the majority of the American people did applaud it. They didn't care if the whole country was wiped out."

"Well, that's their problem," Kent said.

"And yours, if they don't vote for you again. Now, as far as your comments today go, can we keep them on the tame side?"

"I doubt it. There has been no proof that the Sandinistas have committed an act of aggression against any Americans, and I have been getting too much information that weapons are still being shipped to the contras, probably privately, but undoubtedly with the knowledge of someone in our government."

Pat shook his head. "But the point is that Americans have died there and most people blame the Sandinistas and are fully supportive of the sending of troops."

"Pat, I'm not supportive of it, and I'm going to say so. Now, would you please arrange for me to go to the Press Gallery today?"

He was supposed to be at the Press Gallery at four o'clock; Kent left his office at three and said nothing about where he was going first.

His visits to the Vietnam Memorial had usually taken place at night or early in the morning, when the first light of dawn was a gray line on the horizon.

But on this day he stood in front of it with the low sky reflected in the black granite and leaves crunching beneath his feet. He stared at the names that fit into his own reflection—lives that were now just letters etched on a wall. He found his brother's name; he had to stretch his arm up to touch it, and as he reached toward the sky, he realized how appropriate the movement was. He remembered his daughter, standing on tiptoe, stretching her tiny arms up to touch the trail of a shooting star. She must have felt so small and overpowered by the huge dome of sky, just as he felt overpowered by the wall.

At exactly four Kent walked into the Press Gallery. It always reminded him of a classroom; small, uncomfortable chairs were set in rows facing the front, where the podiums stood before a backdrop of the Capitol framed by blue curtains.

Kent stood in front of the backdrop and looked out at the reporters, who, he guessed, had not stopped to eat all day. On hot news days these people lived on caffeine, cigarettes, and the blood of world events. He waited until the room was quiet.

"I want to try to inject some rationality into what looks like a war fever in this country. When Senator Betts was assassinated at the Managua airport, troops were immediately sent into Nicaragua, although there was no—and still is no—proof that the assassin had any connection to the Sandinista government. And now we have to add four more deaths to that list—deaths that wouldn't have occurred if the troops hadn't been sent there. For some reason we seem to conveniently forget that the justice system in this country is based on innocence until there is proof of guilt. I have yet to see incontrovertible proof that the Sandinistas have murdered American citizens. In fact, it's looking more and more to me like a plot to get us into Nicaragua, a plot that seems to have succeeded so far."

"So you think the contras may have killed Senator Betts?" one reporter asked.

"I'm saying that it can't be ruled out. My office has received information from a couple of sources that weapons are being flown into Nicaragua through El Salvador, which means someone in our government has to know about it. I've brought this up to CIA Director Braden, but so far he has not seen fit to investigate it. Things may not be as they appear, and we can't rule anything out at this point."

"Can you tell us more about the information you received?"

"Not at this time, no."

On the drive back to Georgetown, Kent rolled down the window and let the wind blow across his face. The sky had cleared earlier in the evening, and the night was cold and sharp as glass.

As he pulled into his driveway, he noticed Martin Volish's car parked at the curb.

Volish and Cecilia were sitting on the couch in the living room, eating dinner in front of the television. The first thing Kent noticed was that Cecilia was actually eating, a phenomenon he rarely witnessed when he shared a meal with her. Volish looked up at him as if there were nothing at all unusual about the situation.

"What are you doing here, Volish?" Kent said. He felt his self-control splintering into a thousand matchstick pieces.

Before Volish could answer, Cecilia fixed Kent with a look that would have chilled him on any other occasion. But tonight nothing could faze him.

"We're having dinner and watching the news," Cecilia said calmly. Too calmly.

"We were watching you a few minutes ago, as a matter of fact," Volish said. "I can't say I particularly agree with you, but I guess one has to respect you for speaking your mind."

The bastard was lecturing him in his own house, as if Kent were the visitor and Martin S. Volish belonged there.

"I think it's time for you to leave," Kent said. His voice felt like sandpaper in his throat.

Volish didn't move a muscle. "Cecilia invited me," he said.

Kent walked over and loomed above the other man. In an instant he saw everything—Volish's pale blue shirt with the sleeves carefully rolled up, his hands that looked too manicured, too soft. He could even smell his cologne, applied generously enough that his presence in a room would be remembered long after he left. . . . Kent picked up a drumstick from the plate and shoved it into Volish's shirt pocket.

"I wouldn't want you to miss out on a free meal," Kent said, hoping that his face radiated as much hatred as he felt. "Now get out of my house."

"It's your wife's house, too, Senator," Volish said, ignoring the drumstick in his pocket, which was now making a wide grease stain on his shirt.

"Volish, let me tell you something. I pay the mortgage here, I pay for the food you've been stuffing into your face, and I paid for that couch you're sitting on. And I don't want you around any of it. I don't know what you're up to, or what you want from my wife, but you're going to have to run your game somewhere else. This house is now off limits to you."

Martin S. Volish pushed the tray back and rose to his full height, which still left him shorter than Kent.

"If I could just express an opinion, Senator—"

"No, you can't," Kent roared, the words exploding out of him with volcanic force. "This is not a debating class, and I'm not interested in your goddamn opinion. I've heard enough of them and all the other twisted ideas you've been feeding my wife. You have definitely made your presence felt, but it is not going to be felt here any longer."

Kent stood at the front door and watched Volish walk to his car; he felt Cecilia's eyes burning into his back and knew her rage was white-hot. For a moment, standing at the open door with a glittering design of stars above him, he was tempted to walk away into the darkness. But instead he turned back and closed the door behind him, bracing himself for another endless night.

26

*D*ARREN HAD ANSWERED SOME QUESTIONS FROM *NEWS-week* and *Time* and had done a few interviews for smaller, local papers. On the gray, sullen day before Halloween, she was scheduled to do an interview for a new women's magazine, which was only three issues old.

They wanted to come to her home, but she had refused, compromising by meeting them at Lawson's house. She didn't want anyone from the press invading her home, particularly since she had started painting again and her work was all over the house. She was working in oils and was doing a series of nude self-portraits of the progressive stages of her pregnancy. In each room she would run into pictures of herself, her belly swollen and round, her breasts heavy.

Lawson's house was always presentable, due to a diligent staff, and it was large enough that anything personal or revealing could be hidden away. Self-conscious about the opulence of his estate, Darren had made it clear to the man who set up the interview that it was a friend's house, not her own.

"Bet you ten bucks that when the piece is printed they'll have you living in the lavish estate you once shared with your husband," Sean said, and she wasn't sure whether or not he was joking.

The interviewer arrived at precisely the appointed time. She looked more like a model than a journalist. Corinne Shearson was tall, slender and fit-looking—probably an aerobics junkie, Darren decided. Her short, dark hair was layered and blow-dried, and her forest green skirt and silk blouse were a perfect match. Even her suede boots picked up the brown in her tweed jacket, which was cinched at the waist with a leather belt. Darren looked at Corinne's waistline enviously, wondering if she would ever again be able to belt her clothes like that. At the moment it felt like she would be pregnant forever.

"What do you expect to happen from the interviews you've been doing?" Corinne asked, and Darren was taken aback by the sharpness of her tone.

"Well . . . I suppose I would like to see people question what the government is telling them. We did this once before, didn't we? The government said we needed to be in Vietnam, and a lot of people believed them—and a lot of people died as a result."

They were sitting in Lawson's living room, a room rarely used except to entertain visitors. It was large and spacious, with plate-glass windows that offered a panoramic view of the city. The lamplight that cascaded into the room was a contrast to the sunless day outside. Darren sat on the couch with her shoes off and her feet tucked under her; behind her, the mural of the city was shrouded in fog. She looked out the window and decided this would be her last interview.

"I assume," Corinne said, checking her cassette recorder, "that you believe, as some people do, that this has all been orchestrated to get us into a war with Nicaragua."

"I certainly do."

"Senator Janes has expressed his thoughts about that, and

you've had some help from him, I understand. Do you know him well?" Corinne said in the same lacquered voice.

Darren tried to see beneath this woman's polished manner; maybe she knew something. Maybe this was the "don't you want to confide in me" part of the interview.

"Andrew, my husband, spoke with Senator Janes shortly before he died," Darren said, keeping her tone even and noncommittal. "I felt that he was the one person in the government who might be able to shed some light on what's really going on."

Darren answered the rest of Corinne's questions by rote—how she was coping after Andrew's death, how she felt about raising a child alone. She'd answered them all before. But she kept watching Corinne, trying to determine if her question about Kent Janes was just part of the interview, or an indication that she was a better investigator than Darren wanted her to be.

"Well, I think I have enough here," she said finally, clicking off the cassette recorder and zipping it into her Louis Vuitton bag. "Thank you for your time. I can show myself out."

When the front door closed, Darren unfolded herself from the couch and padded across the floor in her socks—a soft, muffled sound in the large stillness of the house. She walked out into the hall, feeling like a child again as she wandered past paintings that stared down at her. She remembered how, the first time she stayed at Lawson's when she was a child, she had gotten lost. She couldn't find Lawson or any of the servants, and in her six-year-old mind, the world had ended and she was the only survivor.

As she approached the study she noticed that Lawson had replaced the painting that used to hang outside the door with one of her early ones. It was one of her first experiments with encaustic; she had made a thick, wavy texture of deep blue—the color of the sea—and into it she had stuck pieces of wood, some old tin cans, a milk carton. Man's abuse of the sea was what she had had in mind, although she never got around to giving the piece a title.

Lawson was sitting at his desk going through some papers.

"You hung my painting up," Darren said, sitting down on

the couch. "I haven't seen that one in years. I'd forgotten all about it."

"I was going through some things in the attic and I came across it. Amazing the things we forget about, isn't it? So, how did your interview go?"

"I don't know if I hate that woman or envy her."

"That's an interesting dilemma."

"She was so put together, so perfect, that I found myself wishing I could be like that. She was in complete control, but she was so impenetrable that part of me despised her."

Lawson leaned back in his chair and laughed. "That's probably part of the training program for being a good journalist. They learn how to enamel their personalities so nothing shows through. All you see is the high-gloss finish."

"Sean's not like that," Darren said.

"An exception to the rule, probably."

Darren stayed at Lawson's that night. Before she went to bed, she took Peanut for a walk around the grounds of the estate, under dense trees where there was only a narrow path, illuminated by the beam of her flashlight. She heard rustling in the branches and wondered if it was a squirrel; her own squirrel had grown big enough to climb out of the tree house on his own and explore the highest branches. She saw him sometimes, scampering around the trunk with a new friend, but even though he would come up to her and cock his head, he would never be hers again. She turned off the flashlight and stood in the dark, a cold wind wrapping around her and the glow from the city reflected on the clouds. It used to wrench her apart when she had to say good-bye to an animal or a person she cared about, but that seemed like a lifetime ago. Now she looked at it as something inevitable, just as she looked at death as something that was always there—the ripple of sound that breaks the stillness of a summer day or the shadow that the eye almost catches as it passes across a field of sunlight. She turned the flashlight on again and walked back to the house with the songs of crickets rising around her.

*　　*　　*

The next morning Darren got out of bed before dawn. Peanut was curled up on the pillows and the house was hushed and still.

She had been staying at Lawson's so frequently that she made a point of leaving some workout clothes there, and in the dim glow of the closet light she dressed quietly, trying not to wake Peanut.

When she opened the front door, she was slapped by a wind that smelled like rain. As she got an umbrella from the brass stand in the entryway, she thought about all the children who would be disappointed if the rain prevented them from going trick-or-treating, and she knew that that never would have occurred to her before she was pregnant.

Mulholland was dark and eerie-looking; it was after six, but the clouds refused to let dawn peek through. The warm air from the heater filled the car, and Darren could see the city lights glistening below. She liked it that, on this cold, black morning, she was the only traveler on the road, and when she saw headlights behind her, she was annoyed that her solitude had been invaded. She considered pulling over and letting the car pass, but she was almost at the freeway, where she would certainly not be the only traveler.

As she got nearer to the on ramp, she glanced in the rearview mirror again and saw what she had failed to notice before: the car behind her was a police car. The fact that she wasn't breaking any laws was irrelevant; it was nerve-racking having a police car behind you. She decided to go past the on ramp and turn onto Sepulveda, which paralleled the freeway all the way to Sunset. She assumed the police would take the faster route and she'd be free of them.

But when she stopped at the light, she saw that they didn't pull into the left-turn lane, which would have taken them to the freeway; they were still behind her. When she saw the lights flash at her, she thought there must be something wrong with her taillights, and she pulled over.

Darren watched in the mirror as a cop got out of the passenger side and walked toward her car.

"Morning, Mrs. Laverty."

"How do you know my name?" A familiar fear curled around her neck.

"Well, we've been waiting for a chance to talk to you," he said, leaning down so his face was almost touching the half-open window.

"Who's we? The entire police department? This is an odd way of looking me up, isn't it?"

"My partner and I do some private work for an individual who would like to speak to you. He has some information about your husband's death, which he thought might interest you."

"Yeah? Well, it seems to me he could have called me on the phone or written me a letter. And if he has information, why doesn't he give it to you? You're the police—aren't you? Or did you buy your shield at a costume store?"

He handed her a laminated identification card. "See for yourself," he said.

Darren looked at the picture on the card, then at the man standing by her car, then back to the name on the card.

"Myron Hrabowecki? What kind of name is that?"

"Mrs. Laverty, the person I mentioned lives nearby, and I think you would benefit from speaking to him. If I could ride with you so I could give you directions, my partner will follow us."

"Why don't you just give me the directions and you can both follow me—in your own car."

He looked exasperated. "Traffic is starting to build. If you make a wrong turn, we'll lose you. This won't take long," he said, sounding as if what he was saying was the most logical thing in the world.

Darren knew she was letting curiosity win out over common sense, but she unlocked the passenger door and let him in.

They turned right toward the valley, heading into the traffic that was starting to back up with people going to work. Darren noticed that the police car was following so close that, if she had slammed on the brakes, it would have driven right through her.

The first raindrops splattered against the windshield and a

flash of lightning set fire to the sky for a quick second, followed by a rumble of thunder that was almost deafening.

"Gonna be a bitch of a storm," Myron Hrabowecki said, clicking his tongue as if he were scolding the sky.

"Uh-huh."

"Turn right at that street up there and stop at the third driveway," he said.

"These were pretty complicated directions, Mr. Hrabowecki," Darren said, no longer intimidated by his uniform. "I couldn't possibly have managed this on my own."

There was a tall hedge bordering the driveway and a wrought-iron gate with two men standing guard. From the street it looked like the type of protection one would have for a large mansion. But when the men opened the gates and she started down the driveway, Darren saw up ahead of her a modest, beige stucco house that couldn't have more than three bedrooms.

"So who's your boss? Donald Trump?" she said, trying not to laugh.

"No, ma'am. His name's Colonel Hadley."

"Hadley?" Darren's foot slammed down on the brake, forcing the police car behind her to do the same. She felt the thud against the back bumper and knew he had dented it, but at that moment she didn't care.

"What the hell are you doing?" Myron said, grabbing onto the dashboard. "You trying to send us both through the windshield or something?"

"Sorry, I—I mean, I—Hadley. I know who Hadley is. He's supposed to live in Florida."

"Well, he has a house here too. I don't see why that should be cause for a car wreck. Now, you wanna pull up to the front door or were you planning on driving around in reverse for a while?"

27

*D*ARREN WAS TAKEN INTO THE LIVING ROOM AND DE-
posited there while Myron went to get Colonel Hadley. She looked around the room, trying to assess Hadley's personality by what she saw there, and decided that if he was
anything like his home he was a very confused man. An expensive Persian rug lay on top of rust-colored shag carpeting, and a
Formica end table supported a Tiffany lamp and some hotel
ashtrays, stolen no doubt. The gaudiest piece of furniture was a
chest that had been carved and curlicued to death. Darren knew
it was a replica, but she wouldn't have paid a dime for the
original. There was no artwork on the walls, just framed photographs of Hadley with what she assumed were contras, Hadley
with CIA Director Braden, Hadley with a fur-draped woman,
some old military pictures. . . .

She stopped before she could finish the pictorial history of his life because footsteps were coming toward the door.

Following Myron Hrabowecki was a thin, gray-haired man in a maroon silk robe and slippers. It had to be Hadley, but Darren had been expecting someone more physically imposing. She stood up when he walked in and realized that he was actually taller than he appeared. It was just that age had tugged on him mercilessly.

"Please sit, Mrs. Laverty," he said, a request that came as no surprise; he looked so frail that walking down the hall must have exhausted him. "Would you like something? Tea or coffee?"

"No."

Darren watched him squirm into a beige corduroy armchair—another black mark on his decorating instincts—and wondered how this man had ever made it through military school. She was sure no one would have voted him "most likely to become a colonel."

"Well, I'm sure you're wondering why we asked you to come here," he said. His voice was gravelly and thin—an old man's voice—but she heard in it the strident tone of someone who was used to barking out orders.

"I wouldn't exactly say I was asked. *Coerced* might be the word I'd choose," Darren said.

Rain was pelting the windows and she could see that the sky was dark and vengeful-looking.

"So, what is this information you have about my husband?" Darren glanced at her watch to emphasize that this was not a social visit and she wanted to be on her way.

"It's funny how death can be such a surprise guest, isn't it?" Hadley said.

"Excuse me?" she said. Myron Hrabowecki moved quietly out of the room, and Darren wondered if this was some sort of standard speech that he'd heard a thousand times before.

"Have you ever considered how often we tempt death?" Hadley asked in an even, calm voice. "We walk into crosswalks in front of cars, fully confident that they'll stop for us. We plug

215

in electrical gadgets with no thought that we could be electrocuted, or we use kitchen knives without considering that with one wrong swipe we could open up our veins. The evening news constantly runs stories about people being mutilated in their homes for a few trinkets or some spare change, yet we go to sleep at night utterly sure that we'll wake up in the morning. Have you ever thought about this, Mrs. Laverty?"

"No, I can't say I have," Darren said. What was this man talking about?

"Well, you should think about it. You see, every action has a reaction. Your late husband went someplace where he shouldn't have been, and he ran right smack into death. Now, if he'd gone bowling that night, or taken you out to a nice restaurant, his destiny would have been different. Of course, I'm not suggesting that we have complete control over our destinies, but we can certainly influence them. Action and reaction, Mrs. Laverty."

"Uh-huh. And all the thousands of Nicaraguans who have been murdered by people you call freedom fighters—what about them, Colonel Hadley? Were they just too uneducated to comprehend your philosophy about action and reaction? I mean, if they'd just chosen that time to take a holiday in the Bahamas, why, they'd all be alive today, wouldn't they?"

"Casualties of war, Mrs. Laverty. Every war has its casualties."

"Funny, I don't remember any formal declaration of war. I must not have read the paper that day."

"Young lady, I'm discussing your late husband, not a bunch of peasants who can't even write their names. It might be of benefit to you to understand his particular blunder. And, after all, we never know when a blunder will prove fatal, do we?"

Darren looked at this pale man in front of her and a horrible realization bloomed in her mind. He'd had Andrew killed. She wanted to leap across the room and strangle the son of a bitch, but she wasn't sure what he had in mind for her. Had he already decided to kill her too, or was this a warning so he wouldn't have to bother?

"So this is the information you had for me?" she said in a tightly controlled voice.

"Yes," Hadley said, smiling at her. "I'm giving you a lesson in how to fool death. You have a tremendous responsibility now, don't you?" He waved a green-veined hand at her stomach. "I think of death as a henchman standing in one spot, swinging his ax. It's our steps that determine whether his blade slices us into little bits. We can walk right into it, or step around."

His eyes had taken on a strange look; they were almost gleaming. If she had been watching him without hearing his words, she would think he was recalling a fabulous meal he'd had, or an expensive wine.

"Let me make sure I'm getting this, Colonel Hadley. This is really just the old "watch your step or I'll kill you" speech, isn't it?"

"Mrs. Laverty"—he dragged out the syllables of her name in a slow, melancholy tone—"I asked you here to help you, not threaten you. I've lived a lot longer than you, because I know how to dance away from death. Obviously, your husband didn't have that particular talent. I'm wondering if you do. It would be a shame if you didn't."

Darren stood up. "So, are you going to let me leave after this invaluable lesson, or chain me in your basement until you're sure I've absorbed its significance?"

"I'm not a big fan of sarcasm, Mrs. Laverty," Hadley said. His eyes had lost their gleam and were like slivers of blue steel. She imagined that this was how he looked at his soldiers—with a diamond-hard glare that bored holes in anyone's plea for sympathy.

"Actually, Colonel Hadley, I have learned a lot this morning. I finally learned who killed my husband. And even though you and I both know I can't prove a damn thing, there is a certain sense of satisfaction in finally having a focus for all my hatred. Someday, sir, the tables will turn. There may not be justice in this city, or even in this country, but I still believe that, ultimately, there is justice in the universe. And when the whole goddamn universe turns against you, I hope I'm around to watch it, because it'll be the best laugh I've had in a long time."

She strode out of the room, through the hallway, and out the front door, closing it behind her. She half expected someone to

217

stop her. Maybe they would radio the men at the gate to hold her there. She noticed, with some amusement, that the dent in the front of the police car was much worse than the dent in her bumper. She drove up to the gate and the men opened it without a second of hesitation.

It was still raining. Darren remembered that Cassie was probably waiting for her at the gym, but she was too distracted and angry to think about working out.

She pulled into a gas station and called the gym from a pay phone.

"Yeah, hold on," an out-of-breath voice said when she asked for Cassie.

"Cassie! Phone!" It was loud enough on Darren's end; she could only imagine what it sounded like in the gym.

When Cassie came to the phone, Darren told her she'd had some car trouble and she wouldn't be coming in.

"OK. You got everything under control? Need any help?"

"No, I'm fine. It's just the battery, I think."

Darren felt a twinge of guilt about lying to Cassie, but she wasn't sure yet whom to tell about what had happened to her, or if she should tell anyone.

She went back to Lawson's, picked up Peanut, and managed to get out without having to lie to him, too . . . but only because he was busy and didn't have a chance to ask her how her workout went. On the way home she decided she had to tell Sean.

After leaving three messages on his machine, he finally called back.

"Darren, what's wrong? You don't need to go to the hospital, do you?"

"Sean, that's a few months away. I just have to talk to you. It's important. Can you come over?"

She realized when she hung up that she had just invited him to come into a house that was full of portraits of a nude pregnant woman. She wouldn't have minded as much if they weren't of her, and for a moment she wished she had used a model.

When Sean drove up, Darren ran outside with two jackets, a towel, and Peanut.

218

"Let's go to the beach. It's not raining right now and I need a walk."

"Darren, the wind's blowing at about thirty miles an hour and the clouds look like they're going to fall on us. Did something happen, or are you getting weird on me again? You're not going to ask me to go back to Nicaragua with you again, are you?"

"No. Come on, it'll be fun."

The sea was slate gray and churning with whitecaps. Darren looked at it with a painter's eye and decided the only thing missing from the picture was a shipwreck. An icy wind whistled past them and puffs of white foam skipped across the sand.

"So, don't keep me in suspense. What's all this about?" Sean yelled over the din of the wind and the sea.

"I met Colonel Hadley this morning."

Sean stopped and faced her. A sea gull swooped past them, screaming at the cold, gray skies. "Don't tell me, you met by the melon bin at Von's and he helped you pick out a ripe cantaloupe."

Darren told him the whole story, from the moment Myron Hrabowecki approached her car to the moment when she drove off Hadley's property and the gates closed behind her.

"You know what this means, don't you?" Sean said, the wind howling violently around them. "The police are in on this, which explains why they wrapped up the investigation into Andrew's death so quickly. I don't know where to go with it, Darren. He was pretty clever. I mean, we know what he was talking about, but he didn't really say anything. The guy really sounds like a lunatic, though. Like a character out of *Heart of Darkness*."

"The thing is, I can't do a damn thing about this. He'll deny I was ever there, and no one else on the property will confirm that I was. People would think I'd cracked up."

Rain was starting to lash at them from a black cloud that had blown in from the sea.

"Kent Janes would believe you," Sean said as they turned and ran back toward the car, the rain stinging their faces.

* * *

She couldn't send Sean home shivering in his wet clothes. So this would be it—the first person to view her latest creations.

"Jesus, Darren," he said, stopping in front of one canvas after he had practically collided with it coming through the front door. "This is incredible!" It was a full-length portrait of her in profile, her hair falling across her bare breasts and her hands resting on her stomach. Her head was tilted down, as if she were talking to the child inside her.

"Sean, the word *incredible* can be interpreted different ways."

"It's beautiful! I had no idea this is what you were doing. Don't you know how good it is?"

"No. I have a tremendous talent for insecurity."

They built a fire and sat huddled in front of it with mugs of hot tea. The sound of rain and crackling logs filled the room.

"You know what the strangest part of my visit to Hadley's was?" Darren said. "I had the strongest feeling that I'd met him before. But I know I've never seen a picture of him. I can't figure it out."

PART FIVE

28

*A*N ICY RAIN HAD PASSED THROUGH WASHINGTON THAT afternoon, but by nightfall only its wet, fertile smell remained. Kent turned up the collar of his wool overcoat as the cold air shivered across the nape of his neck. His Georgetown neighborhood was quiet; most people were inside warm, firelit homes having dinner with their families. His shoes made a hard, clicking sound on the wet sidewalk, and rain dripped from the trees.

His days now seemed to begin and end in darkness, and he was starting to understand Cecilia's addiction to its soft folds. His morning runs started earlier and lasted longer these days; he would get home just as dawn was washing down through the bare branches of the trees onto lawns that were starting to yellow from the cold. He liked to witness the soft beginning of light, but the harsher reality of day was something he barely endured until evening, when he would once again walk through the dark neighborhood streets.

Cecilia was never there now when Kent got home. Since he had thrown Martin S. Volish out of their house, she spent her time at his house, and short of physically restraining her, there was nothing Kent could do. She was calmer these days, but it was a smug calmness, like an animal who had just devoured its prey.

Soon it would be Thanksgiving and then Christmas—the time of year that made Kent ache inside. He would have to run past houses strung with Christmas lights, and the cheerful colors blinking in the darkness would seem to laugh at his pain.

After Laura died he had thought they had weathered the worst. Somehow they would get through the pain, patching up the wounds with happier things like Christmases and vacations . . . maybe another child. But time had made a fool of him. Kent felt as though he must be doing penance for sins buried in the fathoms of lives he couldn't remember. And the worst part was, he was starting not to care. The filaments of his soul were shriveling, one by one. He thought this must be how death comes—in whispers. One day you search the map of who you thought you were and find nothing but pale, bleached bones and a fine layer of dust.

Kent turned the corner and realized he was heading toward Volish's house. For a quick second he contemplated ringing the bell and demanding that his wife come home with him. But he didn't have the energy for that sort of confrontation. He turned around and retraced his steps back to his own house.

Mute shadows and the single lamp he had left on earlier were all that greeted him when he unlocked the door. He felt like an intruder in a secret, noiseless world. Pouring some scotch into a large tumbler, he went upstairs, leaving the light on for Cecilia.

He undressed in the dark and opened the drapes. Sliding between the sheets, he lay in the dark, staring out the window at the cold night. He had opened the window just enough to let a trail of wind into the room; it drifted across his face and brushed his arm as he reached for the glass. He tried to savor the sensations of heat and cold, of the chilly stream of wind and the flame of the liquor sliding down his throat. But even these were dull and vague. He felt old. He wondered where it went—the white heat of what now seemed like another lifetime that had made everything look possible.

The front door closed downstairs and he heard Cecilia's footsteps on the stairs. He pulled the covers up around his shoulders and pretended to be asleep; it had become a reliable escape for both of them.

He heard the sliding shut of the drapes, the click of the bathroom light, and the sounds of rushing water and drawers opening and closing. Kent remained motionless through all of it, like an animal feigning death to avoid being ripped apart.

Kent was summoned to Braden's office at ten the next morning. He knew he was about to be reprimanded for his comments to the press, and he also knew that, in another time, he would have approached the meeting with indignation and an angry resolution to speak his mind. But now the fact that he would soon be sitting in Braden's office being chastised like an errant schoolboy rattled through his brain like a useless pebble.

He arrived precisely on time. Probably, if he had still had the same fire, the same eagerness to do battle for what he believed was right, he would have gotten there early. He smiled blandly at Braden's secretary, and her pinched face looked back at him with nothing that remotely resembled a smile. After several minutes she ushered him in.

Braden didn't look up when Kent entered the office; he kept his eyes focused on whatever he was writing, as though it were important enough that any interruption might deprive the world of a work of immeasurable genius.

Kent sat down and waited, wondering if Braden was really immersed in what he was doing or if he was just practicing intimidation tactics. His money was on the latter.

"Good morning, Senator Janes," Braden said finally, putting down his pen. "I'm glad you could fit this meeting into your busy schedule. No press conferences this morning?"

"Sir, I am aware that my statements to the press are the

reason for this meeting, and I have to say that I have held off sharing the information I've been getting for a long time. But now, with American boys being sent over to die—"

"They're being sent over because this country doesn't take it lightly when a United States senator is murdered. They're being sent over in response to what most of us perceive as an act of war. They are not being sent over to die, Senator."

"Tell that to the families of the four men who were shot into unrecognizable pieces, sir."

Director Braden took off his glasses and glared at Kent. "You know, I'm goddamn tired of you liberal bastards thinking that America has to keep turning the other cheek instead of defending herself. If it were up to you, you'd probably have us sending flowers."

"Not true, sir. As a matter of fact, I have no problem with the United States defending itself. What I do have a problem with is people who would invent a reason for war. Need I remind you, Director Braden, that you have no idea who shot Senator Betts? It could just as easily have been a contra soldier as a Sandinista. And for that matter, you have no idea who shot those four servicemen."

"Well, logical reasoning would suggest—"

"Logical reasoning doesn't hold up in a court of law; why should it be substituted for proof in international affairs?" Kent said, feeling his old anger return, like an elixir.

"Senator Janes," Braden said slowly, and Kent was sure he saw his face redden, "there are things this agency knows that you do not know. We have a very sophisticated organization here, and our knowledge of what is going on internationally far surpasses yours."

Kent pulled out the photographs of Darren and the group of Americans she had encountered on her last trip to Nicaragua. "Do you have any idea who these men are?" he asked, handing the pictures to Braden.

The director shuffled through them quickly and tossed them onto the desk. "No, but I seem to recognize the young woman.

226

Isn't that the widow of the man you insist was murdered? She certainly succeeded in eliciting your help, didn't she?"

Kent felt like he'd been hit from behind, but he forced his expression to reveal nothing. "I think she deserves some help, sir. And, yes, I am certain her husband was murdered."

"Senator Janes, I think this has become an obsession with you. Why don't you spend some time at home instead of chasing down someone else's suspicions. I've heard your wife is not well."

Kent stood up and said good-bye coolly. When he walked out of the Old Executive Office Building, the sun was struggling through the clouds. He felt sick, as though he had lost control of everything in his life. There were rumors, he knew, about Cecilia's health. Some said she had cancer or some other terminal illness that prevented her from attending social functions. But maybe Braden knew more—maybe he knew everything. Kent thought about Volish and how little he really knew about this man who had invaded their lives. He needed someone to blame; he was like a drowning man, grabbing at anything that looked different from the water rushing around his head.

29

THE ACCESS TO LAWSON'S ATTIC WAS THROUGH THE CEILING
of one of the upstairs bedrooms. Darren had to stand
on a chair to pull down the trap door. Before climbing the
ladder, she studied the size of the opening and compared it to the
size of her stomach in order to determine which way she should
turn so that she wouldn't get stuck.

Ever since Lawson had dug out one of her old paintings, she
had been wondering how many others were up in his attic,
forgotten under layers of dust. In the back of her mind, she
thought she might try showing her work again, particularly since
Sean had been so enthusiastic about her most recent efforts.

The attic was cool and dark, and the smell of dust hung in
the air. She waited until her eyes adjusted to the darkness and
then maneuvered her way past boxes and old furniture to the pull
chain that dangled from a single naked bulb. Even with the light

on, the room was dim, and Darren squinted into the corners, trying to find where Lawson had stacked her paintings. She finally saw them behind the bicycle he'd given her for her tenth birthday.

As she looked through the paintings, she tried to decide if any of them were worth the effort it would take to bring them down from the attic. They were dark and somber—her existentialist period—and they held little appeal for her now.

She moved away from the paintings and sat down in an old rocking chair; a fine cloud of dust rose up as she leaned back and heard it creak on the floor.

As a child she had loved to come up to the attic and go through the mementos of Lawson's past. There were scrapbooks with faded snapshots of people who looked like they had stepped out of history books, wearing clothes that looked, to Darren, as if they had been borrowed from a museum. And there were boxes filled with old curtains and clothes. She found Lawson's military uniform, the fabric creased and limp, but she also found a picture of him as a young man, smiling at the camera in the same uniform when it was still starched and crisp and new.

She remembered, as she rocked back and forth, all the afternoons she had spent up there, foraging through someone else's history like a spy. And she remembered the day she had listened to Lawson and her father arguing down in the hallway. From the vantage point of her shadowy hiding place, she could hear everything.

Her father was chastising Lawson for spending so much money on gifts for Darren; he was spoiling her, her father said. Lawson insisted that Darren showed no evidence of being spoiled. In fact, she gave many of her toys away to her friends. But her father wouldn't relent, and Darren knew he was just jealous that he couldn't afford to give her what Lawson could.

She sat up in the attic that day, listening to their raised voices and hoping they wouldn't remember she was up there. Gray shadows rested on the floor beside her and dust balls floated past her feet. Spiders spun their soft webs in the corners; she could almost hear them weaving silvery death traps for any creature foolish enough to fly that way. She had no idea what time it was, or if the afternoon sun had already left the sky, but she wanted to stay there forever, nestled in the shadows with spiders and velvet-winged moths moving quietly around her.

Darren lifted herself out of the rocking chair—she had to use her arms—and went over to the box that she knew held Lawson's scrapbooks. The most recent ones were on top, and as she turned the pages her childhood moved before her.

There were photographs of summer days, of herself diving into Lawson's swimming pool—a small, sun-browned body with blond hair made slightly green from the chlorine in the pool. And some were of the parties Lawson used to give; he always made a point of inviting her parents, and they sometimes brought her. "Grown-up parties," she used to call them, and she usually managed to sneak out and go play in the trees.

A photograph of one of those parties answered the question Darren hadn't been able to answer for herself. A small group of men were posed in front of Lawson's fireplace, smiling and holding drinks. And one of them was Colonel Hadley. Despite his youth and the boldness of his posture, the face was unmistakable. Darren stared at the picture until her eyes watered from not blinking. She squeezed them shut and opened them again, praying that the face in the picture would be different but knowing it would be the same. She hadn't told Lawson about her meeting with Hadley, but she had told him, weeks before, about Kent Janes's suspicions. And Lawson had said nothing; there hadn't even been a shift of his eyes or a tightening around his mouth.

She closed the scrapbook and held on to it, watching her knuckles turn white, as if they belonged on someone else's hands and the pain that was starting to travel up her arms wasn't hers. She wanted to cry but she couldn't; she felt hollow, as if someone had scooped out her insides and left just the outer shell of flesh.

She climbed down the ladder with the scrapbook wedged under her arm. It seemed to her that it was as heavy as lead, much heavier than the child in her belly or the wooden trap door that she closed behind her. Sunlight was resting on the window ledge, and she imagined holding a magnifying glass over the picture of Hadley and letting the sun burn a hole through it until there was nothing left of his image, just charred paper. But it wouldn't matter; nothing could burn away what she had seen and what she now knew.

Her footsteps sounded loud and slow as she walked down the hallway to Lawson's room. She had seen him in there when she passed his door on the way to the attic, a journey she wished she had never taken.

He was sitting in an armchair reading the *Wall Street Journal*.

"Hello, my dear. What do you have there?" He took off his reading glasses and looked from her face to the book under her arm.

There was nothing unusual in his voice or his manner. Maybe he really didn't remember knowing Hadley, Darren thought. But Lawson's memory was impeccable. He had told her stories of his boyhood and remembered the names of his fifth-grade arithmetic teacher and the school bully he had finally had to fight.

"Why didn't you tell me you knew Colonel Hadley?" Darren said. Her voice felt thick in her throat, and her arm ached as she lifted the book and turned the pages until she found the picture. She walked across the room to Lawson; the soft blue carpet suddenly looked like a frozen river that she had to cross. She handed the book to him and her arm felt lighter, as if her balance had been regained.

"I should have," he said softly. Darren forced herself to look at his face. The corners of his eyes were red and wet, and she stared as a tear followed a straight path along the side of his nose, falling into the crease at the edge of his mouth. She should feel something, should respond to his pain.

"I didn't say anything at first," Lawson murmured, "and it got harder after that to even think of how to approach it, how to explain my silence when you first mentioned him. I suppose I was afraid you would think I was sympathetic to what he was doing."

"Are you?" Darren said. "I don't know what to believe anymore."

"No, of course not. And I don't know for certain that the

rumors about him are true, but I know he's changed. He became addicted to war; it was his only reality."

"The rumors are true, all right, Lawson. I met him."

Lawson looked up at her, still standing in front of him like a mother disciplining a child. He looked drawn and tired; Darren saw the curve of his shoulders and the veins on his hands.

"I wasn't going to tell you because the meeting was so bizarre. The man's a lunatic. He had cops bring me to his house. He's a fucking madman, Lawson. And he killed Andrew."

"Darren, you don't know that—"

"Yes, I do know that. He told me, albeit in a vague sort of way, but he made himself clear enough." Her legs were getting heavy; she went over to the bed and sat down on the corner. "Jesus Christ, Lawson, are you against me too? I thought I could trust you." Darren didn't realize she was crying until she tasted salt. The air in the room was dead-still. She wanted to open the window, but she couldn't move to lift herself off the bed.

Lawson stared at her with the dull, watery eyes of an old man. He had never looked so old to her.

"I had no idea . . . ," he said, and his voice cracked. "I only knew he might be involved in illegal activities in Nicaragua. Darren, I didn't want you to get hurt. I love you—you're like my own daughter. And you were pursuing this with such vengeance, I was frightened for you. Every time I considered telling you that I knew Hadley, I wondered if you'd do something rash."

"Like what? Bomb his house? I should have."

Lawson opened his mouth to say something, but no words came out. The only sound in the room was the sound of their breathing; it filled the room like another presence.

"I just don't know how you could keep quiet about that," Darren said softly, almost in a whisper. "I don't understand."

"I was frightened for you. Maybe you'll never understand that. You've always been such a strong girl, even when you were a child. I've wondered if anything ever frightens you."

"A lot of things frighten me," Darren said, her voice getting louder. "I've been frightened ever since Andrew died. But I wasn't going to let anyone tell me it was a coincidence that he was killed! And you could have helped me. But instead all you did was discourage me!"

Lawson nodded, slowly, his face leaning toward the floor, toward the frozen river that lay, blue and slippery, between them.

"I think I'm going to need some time, Lawson," Darren said. "You know, you're all I have now. You're my family except for my baby. And now to find out that you kept this from me . . . I just need some time to figure out how to deal with it."

"I'm sorry," Lawson said weakly, and his eyes pleaded with her.

Darren stood up and started to walk over to him, but stopped halfway, unable to go the rest of the distance. "I know," she said. "It'll be all right. I just need some time alone, I think."

That night she took Peanut for a walk through the quiet streets around her house. Ocean mist hung in the glow of the streetlights and the air smelled like pine. She thought of how Lawson had looked that afternoon—bent over like a man broken by life, his face streaked with tears—and she knew she had to forgive him. Maybe she would have done the same thing to protect someone she loved.

She looked up at the sky and found the Big Dipper. So many nights she and Andrew had walked through these streets talking about their dreams for the future. Maybe they would leave Los Angeles someday, they'd said, buy some land where the air was clean and the pace was slower. Andrew had talked about moving to Seattle and buying a house on the sound, where they could sit for hours and watch the water.

It was almost ten when she got home. She knew Cassie would probably be asleep, but she dialed her number anyway.

"Cass? Hi, it's me. Sorry if I woke you up."

"That's OK. I wasn't really asleep yet—just almost. Is something wrong?"

"No, I just wanted to tell you I'm not going to come into the gym tomorrow. I'm going to go away for a few days."

"Darren, are you sure you're OK? You're the original homebody, and now you decide at ten o'clock at night that you're going to leave town?"

"I know it's kind of sudden. I'm going to go to Seattle for a few days. Andrew and I used to talk about moving there someday and . . . well, I'm just going to go check it out. I've been thinking it might not be a bad idea. Probably be a better place to raise a child."

"I guess. If you ever want to tell me the real reason, I'd be more than happy to listen."

The night outside her window was black and moonless, but in her sleep Darren traveled to a world of deep snow and pale, gray skies.

There were tracks in the snow and she knew they were the footprints of wolves. In her dream she was not pregnant; she was holding a small child—her son—against her, wrapped in a thick wool blanket. She could feel his breath like a tiny warm cloud filling the space between her clothes and her skin. Bare trees, stripped by winter, groaned under the weight of the snow. They were tall and old and had seen many winters come and go.

She followed the tracks until suddenly she was standing in front of Andrew. She knew it was him even though her eyes only saw a column of light. From behind the trees wolves watched her with soft yellow eyes.

"I had to go," Andrew said, and his words flew out like sparks, quick and bright in the cold air. They fell to the ground and melted the snow they touched.

"Why?" Darren asked.

"This is so much better, don't you think? It's where I knew I belonged. I always had my eyes on the sky, Darren, you know that."

"I was afraid to be alone at first," she said as her child moved against her, his mouth searching. Milk leaked out of her breasts in answer to his hunger.

Andrew laughed and snow fell from a branch above them, floating down like white feathers.

"You were never alone," he said.

234

"It's so quiet here."

"Yes, it's always quiet here. I knew it would be. But now you have to go."

Darren turned and followed the tracks again, past a tree that had been split by lightning. Half of it lay in the snow like a collapsed bridge. It got colder, the more she walked, and drops of her milk turned to icicles on her breasts.

She turned around only once and saw snow falling behind her, filling in the tracks that had guided her. There was nothing but a slope of white snow, soft and smooth as sifted flour.

30

*A*T THE SEATTLE AIRPORT, DARREN WENT UP TO THE NA-
tional Car Rental counter and asked for the biggest,
safest car they had; it turned out to be a bright red Cadillac with
matching interior.

"Sort of looks like a pimp-mobile, huh?" she said to the man
who handed her the keys; he didn't seem amused.

"It's just a red car," he said. "What you do in it is your business."

Sean had suggested that she stay in a small hotel called The
Inn at the Market. It was uphill from the open marketplace that
bordered the water, and it shared a courtyard with a clothes
store, a French restaurant, and a health-food snack bar.

The lobby of the inn looked like a living room, with couches
placed around a coffee table and two armchairs on either side of
a blazing fire. It was raining when Darren arrived, and she spent

the afternoon curled up in one of the armchairs, reading by the fire. She didn't have to do anything or go anywhere, and it was exactly the situation she needed.

Over the next few days, whenever rain washed down on the city, she would take refuge by the fire, reading or just staring into the flames. She would think about Lawson, about the way he had looked at her, his face so full of pain he had seemed like a stranger. And about how, when she dropped Peanut off on her way to the airport, his eyes had asked her for things his voice couldn't. Forgiveness. It was the question she couldn't answer yet, and she had left quickly, telling him she'd be back in a few days.

When the skies cleared, she would bundle herself in winter clothes and walk through the public market. There were stalls of vegetables and fruits and, on the other end, people displaying silver jewelry, pottery, and hand-painted T-shirts. Across the brick-paved street, the homeless begged for money. Some played music or did juggling acts, but some just sat in doorways with cups and scrawled signs that were as direct as "I need money" or "Help me—I'm hungry."

She passed a white-haired woman strumming a guitar and singing Spanish songs in a warbly, off-key voice. It took a few minutes before Darren realized that the woman's pale blue eyes, which stared intently at the sky, saw nothing but their own darkness. Darren dumped all her change into the shoebox at the woman's feet, grateful for the unmistakable jingling of falling silver that made the woman break into a gap-toothed smile.

She drove her rented Cadillac in whatever direction looked interesting, not caring if she got lost; she had nothing but time on her hands. When she found an area that she liked, she would mark it on the map with notations like "trees," or "view of the sound." Her map became a tool to tell her where she had ended up; she never used it to steer her in a particular direction.

She tried to imagine herself living in Seattle, taking the ferry home to an island or driving across the floating bridge. She looked for signs that would tell her, "Yes, you can belong here," but she found nothing but uncertainty.

On her fourth day there she decided, despite the thick clouds, to take the ferry to Bainbridge Island. It was the one area on her map that was not covered with notations, and it was a place Andrew had mentioned frequently.

After a thirty-minute ferry ride, she found herself in a tiny, homespun community where people seemed to be tucked into the simplicity of their corner-store, two-lane-road life. There was one movie theater, one gym, and a realtor's office in a small rustic cabin, where a kindly woman extolled the virtues of their uncluttered island life. Darren decided that it was a little too uncluttered for her; after a week there she'd probably be ready to move to Manhattan.

As the ferry took her back across Puget Sound to the city, she stood out on the deck, with snow-capped mountains in the distance and an icy wind numbing her face, and wondered about her real reasons for thinking about moving. She knew she was trying to run away—from her memories, from the parts of her life that seemed too difficult to deal with—and as the wind stung her eyes and dark blue water churned below her, she had to admit that that was a terrible reason to leave California.

She got back to the hotel just as the sky was starting to darken into an ominous color. As she pushed the glass revolving door, she noticed a familiar figure sitting by the fire. At first her mind argued with what her eyes were seeing. But as she stepped into the lobby, Sean grinned at her like a kid on Christmas morning.

"And how long have you been planning this surprise, Mr. Trudell?"

"Spur-of-the-moment thing," he said. "I thought you might like some company."

He was still wearing his jacket, and his face was flushed and shiny in the firelight. Darren sat down in the other chair.

"Yesterday, you might have been wrong about that. I was still trying to forget things like company and talking. In fact, I might not have remembered the English language yesterday. But today company sounds like a good idea, yours especially."

"Timing's always been my strong point," Sean said, winking at her. "And yours isn't bad either. Take a look outside."

A light snow had started to fall; frail, perfect flakes slanted past the window. Darren watched, enraptured, and after a few minutes the flakes got larger. Gray clouds leaned toward the earth.

"Let's take a walk," Sean said. "Perfect California response to snow, right? People who see it all the time stay indoors; we run out and take a bath in it."

They walked up to First Avenue and turned left, pushing against the wind that carried on it the rich smell of espresso from an outdoor stand, one of many that could be found on Seattle's street corners.

"These stands drive me crazy," Darren said. "It's like they're playing a cruel joke on pregnant women, exposing them to this smell."

They went into an antique-clothing store with price tags that made her wince, but the atmosphere was comfortable and elegant, so Darren looked around as if she were really considering spending that kind of money.

Sean insisted that she try on a jacket she'd admired, but she couldn't button it over her stomach and they left the store giggling at how ridiculous it had looked on her.

Next door was a shop, Bazaar des Bears, that sold stuffed bears and old lace. Inside it smelled like soap, and the lace and linens were so white that Darren felt like she was in a rich woman's boudoir where specks of dust were forbidden.

"Here, I want to buy this bear for your baby," Sean said, handing her the soft, brown animal. "See, this is a very adaptable bear. It has no lace or satin, no necktie. It can go either way, depending on what the baby is and what the baby wants the bear to be."

The saleslady obviously thought they were married and was delighted that they were buying a toy for their new baby.

Snow flurries teased them on their way back to the hotel. As they passed people hurrying through the cold, Darren felt like taking her time; she felt better than she had in days, and she wanted it to last. She could have spent the rest of the evening walking around Seattle with Sean, the snowflakes catching in her hair. But it was getting dark, and they turned into the courtyard.

"Did you book a room?" Darren asked.

"I was going to talk to you about that."

"Sean—"

"No, wait a minute. Don't jump to conclusions, OK? I'm just a little broke right now, and I pushed my credit card almost to the limit buying my plane tickets."

Darren pulled him under the awning of the clothes store and out of the snow, which was falling faster now.

"So, you either want me to loan you the money for a room or share mine with you, right?"

"Darren, I'd never ask you for money. I would ask you if I could sleep on your floor, though. I don't snore."

"Are you sure there's nothing here that we should talk about?"

"No. If I wanted to come on to you, I think I could come up with a better way than this."

"OK. My room happens to have two beds, so you don't have to sleep on the floor. But if you snore, you'll be sleeping in the bathtub. And, since you don't have any money, I'd like to take you to dinner. There's a French restaurant in the courtyard— it's called Campagne—that I've been wanting to go to, but I didn't want to eat by myself."

Over dinner, Darren told Sean about discovering that Lawson knew Colonel Hadley.

"But maybe he didn't know what Hadley was doing in his spare time," Sean said.

"He'd heard the rumors. And I think he knew they were true." The candlelight flickered between them, and behind Sean the window gave Darren a view of the sound and the lights of the ferry as it moved slowly across the dark water. "You know what's worse than the feeling that he betrayed me?" she continued. "It's that, if he had said something, maybe it would have helped. I could have passed the information along to Kent Janes or . . . I don't know. All I know is that now it's too late. Hadley's sitting back and letting the United States military take over for him. He doesn't have to raise a finger."

"Darren, I think you're being unrealistic. First of all, your uncle didn't betray you. He just held something back from you—for your own good, he thought. I'm sure if he'd known Hadley was responsible for Andrew's death, he would have acted differently. Can you honestly say that you've never taken the wrong course of action out of concern for someone you loved? And secondly, what the hell do you think you could have done? Kent Janes already had information about Hadley. More might have strengthened the case, but it wouldn't have proved anything. What I'm getting at is that maybe the lesson here is to not damage a relationship because of a mistake. Your uncle is getting old. My understanding is that he doesn't really have anyone but you. So, perhaps you should be a little less judgmental. Just some advice from a friend—take it or leave it. But while you're deciding, eat your salmon before I take it from you. It happens to be the most perfectly cooked fish I've ever eaten."

Darren thought about what Sean had said as she lay in the dark, with a thin wedge of night between their beds. She heard the sound of the ferry docking and the faint noise of voices in the courtyard below. The heater rattled when it came on and Sean shifted in his bed, but she assumed he was asleep until she looked over and saw him propped up on one elbow.

"You OK?" she said.

"Yeah. I wanted to ask you something. How long did your affair with Kent Janes last?"

Her stomach tightened and, as if in response, the baby kicked her—hard.

"How did you know?"

"Darren, I'm a reporter—I'm trained to see things that people would prefer I didn't see. I don't even know when I was sure of it, but your reaction every time his name came up confirmed my suspicions."

"Not very long. Not even long enough to really call it an affair. It's just something that happened. We were both vulnerable and we needed someone to hold on to, for just that instant. I really don't know if I can explain it."

"You don't have to explain it," Sean said. "I just wondered. Good night."

He lay back on the pillows and tugged the blankets up around his face, and Darren stared at the ceiling, wondering if he had purposely waited for a dark room before asking her about Kent.

31

*C*ECILIA TURNED ON THE LIGHT IN VOLISH'S BLACK-TILED bathroom. The pattern on the imitation zebra rug made her dizzy, but looking into the mirror at her own reflection was worse. For years now she had made a point of avoiding mirrors. They were a cruel reminder that she was still chained to her own flesh—this thing that made demands on her: feed me, wash me, clothe me. She didn't want to be bothered. In defiance of her body's wishes, she had started avoiding food the same way she avoided mirrors, ignoring the sounds her stomach made. They didn't matter. She was in control, and she could ignore any signals her body tried to send to her.

All she wanted was to float, light and aimless as a feather. If she could have willed it she would be invisible, just a wisp of something, an ash drifting on the wind.

She had thought Martin understood that. She thought that,

by some stroke of magic, their friendship had been anointed. So when he came at her with his shirt off and his flesh the color of an uncooked turkey, she felt her stomach shudder. She backed up until she fell onto the couch, pulling her knees up to her chest and screaming at him to get away. Such a loud sound had come out of her; she didn't know her voice could sound like that. For a minute she wanted to look around the room and see if someone else had come in and it was really that person's voice she was hearing. And he just stood there, beads of sweat collecting between the hairs on his chest.

She should have run out the front door, but she went for the stairs instead. And now she was trapped in this black room with too many mirrors and a fake animal skin on the floor.

She slid open the door to the medicine cabinet—a tube of Colgate, Excedrin, Tums, a box of Trojans. Then her eyes scanned the top shelf, the prescription shelf apparently. Small brown bottles were lined up, the labels neatly typed. One was for constipation; one was for pain, although it didn't specify what kind of pain. She stopped at a bottle of bright pink capsules. Seconal. Even the name sounded soothing. Seconal . . . she rolled the syllables around in her mouth. It sounded like water, like floating. And the color, so bright and beckoning. She wouldn't have to think about flesh and bones anymore, wouldn't have to drag them around. And she wouldn't have to go back downstairs where Volish's pale damp skin was waiting to press against her.

She opened the bottle and poured some out in her hand. How many should she take? Ten? Twenty? She decided on twenty. She poured water into the cut-glass tumbler that sat on the sink and swallowed the smooth pink capsules two by two.

It took so long to get them all down; she wasn't used to swallowing so much. Even that made her tired. She curled up on the floor with her body on the rug and her cheek resting on the cool tiles. Soon she would be far away, floating weightlessly, out of reach of everyone who wanted things from her—things she didn't even have anymore.

She thought of the pink color of the pills. That was the color that would take her where she wanted to go. She could almost see herself spinning into it, and beyond it was a darkness from which no one could call her back again.

Kent was watching the evening news when the phone rang. For some reason that he didn't understand, he thought it would be Cecilia on the other end although she never called him anymore.

"Senator, it's Martin Volish." He sounded frantic and out of breath.

"Volish, what do you want? Are you calling to tell me my wife's decided to move in with you? I suppose you'd like me to have her clothes sent over."

"Senator, I . . . uh, I don't know how to tell you this. I had to call the paramedics. She found some sleeping pills in my medicine cabinet—in my bathroom. I don't know how many she swallowed—"

Kent slammed down the receiver before Volish could get another word out. He was so panicked, it didn't occur to him to take the car; he simply bolted out the door and started running down the street. The houses and lights blurred past him as if he were on some high-speed carnival ride.

The ambulance was already there when he got to Volish's house. Kent raced through the open front door and saw them carrying a stretcher down the stairs. Cecilia's face was so pale it was almost blue, and there was a tube down her throat. Volish was standing at the foot of the stairs, red-faced and sweating. His shirt was untucked and buttoned incorrectly, and he had no shoes on.

"What the hell was going on here, Volish?" Kent said.

"Who're you?" one of the paramedics asked.

"I'm her husband. I'm going to ride in the ambulance with her."

"I thought he was her—well, whatever. You two work it out. But we gotta get her there fast."

Kent started to follow them out the door, then stopped and wheeled around. With all the strength he could pump into his arms, he shoved Volish backward into a plant stand. The Boston fern tipped over on Volish's head, spilling soil and broken fronds over his face.

"Nothing like this was supposed to happen," Volish said, his face crumbling into tears. "I was just supposed to get something on you."

"What?" Kent glared at the weeping man sitting on the floor, covered with dirt; sweat ran down Volish's chest, making dark stains on his shirt.

"Just something to embarrass you," Volish sobbed. "No one was supposed to get hurt or anything."

Kent heard the doors of the ambulance close. "You son of a bitch," he said to Volish as he ran out the door.

Riding inside the speeding ambulance, with the siren screaming in his ears, Kent felt his panic increasing. He was aware of the seconds ticking by, of the ambulance decelerating as they went through intersections. He watched the oxygen mask, praying that it would keep showing him the rhythm of Cecilia's breathing. He watched the IV dripping into her veins and wondered if he had a right to thwart her obvious intention to die. He knew, as he looked down at her pale, blue-veined eyelids, closed so gently that she probably thought she had finally escaped, that she had wanted this for years. She had been moving, slowly and deliberately, toward death for a long time; he just hadn't wanted to see it.

"What's that stuff going into her?" Kent asked the young man at his side.

"Narcan. It's commonly used in overdoses of this kind. And glucose. Just standard stuff."

Kent guessed the paramedic to be in his late twenties; he wondered how many suicide attempts he'd battled with his arsenal of tubes and bottles of dripping liquid.

Looking down at Cecilia again, Kent saw her chin had collapsed onto her collarbone and she was making a strange gurgling sound. The paramedic reached over and tilted her chin up, magically making the sound disappear.

"Does she have to have that tube down her throat?"

"Afraid so. We had to intubate her, particularly since we don't know how many pills she swallowed. You don't happen to know, do you?"

"How the hell could I? I wasn't there," Kent snapped, instantly regretting the acidity of his outburst but too tired to dilute it with an apology.

They screeched up to the emergency entrance, and Cecilia was pulled out of the ambulance and rushed through the doors. Kent followed as closely as he could, not wanting to lose her in the white, fluorescent cavern of noise and rushing people. Seconds, minutes . . . all passing too quickly. Was she still breathing? He couldn't see her anymore; she was disappearing into the maze. Someone was telling him to go up to the desk.

Name of patient? Relationship? Nature of injury? The nurse's questions were as crisp as her uniform. But Kent saw the moment when it dawned on her who she was talking to, and suddenly her manner softened. She became more sympathetic, even managing to smile at him, and he could almost hear the conversation she would have over her next coffee break. A senator's wife rushed into the emergency room after a suicide attempt—that information would tempt even the most reluctant gossip to chatter away.

"The doctor will be out to talk to you shortly," she said after she had finished her interrogation.

Kent went over to a green leather couch and slid down until his head rested against the back. A teenage girl was sitting in a wheelchair across from him, holding an ice pack on her leg. She was dressed in a ballet costume, and she was sobbing as if her heart were breaking. He assumed it was her mother beside her, patting her arm and trying to tell her it would be all right. There would be another chance to perform. He smiled weakly at them and then closed his eyes against the cold, rigid light. He wished he could sleep, even if just for a minute.

"Senator Janes, I'm Dr. Rossner." Kent opened his eyes on a serious-looking man with a pencil-thin mustache and smooth unlined skin, an argument to the gray streaks in his hair.

"The nurse tells me your wife was not at home when she took the pills."

"No," Kent said. "She was . . . at a neighbor's."

"So this was not her own prescription?"

"No. The only thing prescribed for her is lithium, but she won't take it. I don't think she's taken any for months."

"Uh-huh. Well, we pumped her stomach. You can see her in a little while. She'll be fine, physically. This is always a delicate matter, Senator, and I can appreciate that it's even more delicate in your situation. But there is a certain procedure we have to follow in suicide attempts. We're probably going to keep her here for medical observation for about twenty-four hours. There will be someone with her at all times—I'm sure I don't have to tell you the reason for that. After the twenty-four hours, if we think she's recovered enough, she'll be transferred to another part of the hospital for psychiatric evaluation. That could last anywhere from a few days to two weeks. You said she'd been prescribed lithium, so I assume she was seeing a psychiatrist. Is she still under his care?"

Kent shook his head. "She, uh, won't do that either." He realized how pathetic he must sound. "I'm sorry, Dr. Rossner, I'm not being much help. My wife and I don't talk too much anymore."

"No apologies necessary, Senator," Rossner said, standing up. "I'll let you know when you can see her."

Kent found a vending machine and punched the button for black coffee. There was a part of him that wanted to leave without seeing Cecilia. What would he say to her? "Now, I'd like you to tell me why you tried to kill yourself, dear. I realize we've only spoken about two words to each other in the past several months, but I thought maybe you'd confide in me now since we're here together in this sterile hospital room and the doctors have successfully condemned you to life, despite your impressive attempt to die"?

Kent felt his heartbeat quicken as the caffeine took effect. He should call Phillip and have him come to the hospital and drive him home. And Pat Morley. Someone should call him before the media started running toward the finish line with this story.

He went to the pay phone and punched in Phillip's number, saying a silent prayer that he would answer. When he did Kent went quickly through the details, leaving Phillip no room to inject questions or expressions of sympathy.

"I need you to pick me up at the hospital, Phillip," he was saying as he saw Dr. Rossner walking toward him. "And get hold of Pat. Tell him to meet us at the house. We have to deal with this situation tonight. It can't wait until tomorrow."

"You can see your wife now, Senator," Dr. Rossner said. "She's still groggy, but don't let that worry you."

Cecilia's half-lidded eyes were staring at the ceiling; she made no attempt to turn them in Kent's direction. The nurse who was sitting in the room, as insurance that Cecilia wouldn't make a noose out of her bed sheets, tiptoed past him and whispered, "I'll be right outside."

"Hi, Cecilia," Kent said, leaning over the railing of the bed, trying to interfere with her study of the ceiling. "How do you feel?"

"Sleepy," she said, still not meeting his eyes. Her voice was hoarse and raw.

"Yes, well . . . I guess that's to be expected."

"Martin didn't do anything."

"Cecilia, I may think the man is reprehensible, but I really didn't assume he poured sleeping pills down your throat."

She turned her face just enough to look at him with one eye. "That's not what I meant," she said.

Kent rested his hand on hers; the bones looked so tiny. He could almost feel the blood in her veins, so close to the surface of her skin which had become delicate as chiffon.

"Cecilia, I just don't know what I did. I know you've been trying to punish me for something, but I don't know what it is. If I knew, maybe we could fix it. I've tried to figure out how we got to be such strangers, how we managed to move so far away from each other while we were living under the same roof, and I don't have any answers. I need you to help me figure that out."

She was looking at him now, her face turned to him and her eyes wide and direct. But there was no expression. Some part of her was already dead—he saw that now—and she had just tried to follow.

He bent down and pressed his face against her shoulder. His tears formed tiny puddles in the hollows between her bones. He stayed like that until the last tears fell, and when he stood up he felt he might never have to cry again. There would be no point. He had been a fool, trying to make his life continue as it always had; it would never be the same again.

When he pulled away from Cecilia and looked down at her, her eyes were closed.

"Maybe you had the best solution all along," he whispered. "I just didn't see it."

Phillip was waiting in the hall when he came out. The nurse slid past him and went back into the room to continue her vigil.

"How is she?" Phillip asked.

Kent shrugged. How was someone supposed to be after she had just tried to die and probably still had that slotted in on her list of things to do?

"I called Pat—he'll be waiting for us at your house. I just . . . I don't know what to say in a situation like this."

"You don't really need to say anything."

A business-suited man was walking toward them, and Phillip said, "There are some reporters outside, Senator. He's going to show us another way out."

Kent was hurried through corridors like a mouse being escorted through a maze. He wondered who had claimed the honor of alerting the media. A nurse? The paramedics? Not that it mattered; he knew now what he was going to do.

Pat was waiting when they pulled up to the house. It was obvious from his expression that Phillip had told him the reason for this after-hours meeting.

250

"I'm so sorry, Senator," he said when they got out of the car.

"Thank you," Kent said, almost laughing at the absurdity of thanking anyone for anything after your wife just tried to kill herself. He walked into the house, across the living room to the sideboard, and got a bottle of scotch and three glasses.

"Here. We all need a drink," he said, setting the bottle and glasses on the coffee table.

"I don't drink, Senator," Pat said.

"After tonight you will." Kent swallowed some of the scotch and looked from Pat to Phillip and back to Pat again. "I'm going to quit, gentlemen. I want you to draft a statement saying that, due to personal difficulties, I am giving up my seat in the Senate."

An uncomfortable moment of silence followed this announcement. Finally, Pat said, "I don't think this is the time for you to make a decision like this. You've been through something very traumatic. It's going to take some time to sort things out. Look, I think we can do some quick damage control and minimize things a little."

"No, Pat, you don't understand. My wife locked herself in some schmuck's bathroom and downed a bottle of sleeping pills. I have no idea what was going on there before that point. In fact, I have no idea what was going on there any other night, since she was there about six nights a week. It's unfortunate that she didn't find the pills she's *supposed* to take as attractive as the sleeping pills. If she had this might not have happened. You see, she was supposed to be taking lithium, the commonly prescribed medication for manic-depressives. Does this shock you, Pat? You look shocked. And that's just a hint of what everyone else in this country is going to feel when they read about this in the papers. I was elected to look out for the needs of California; the people of that state trusted me to do that job. I can't do it anymore—not with my life falling apart around me."

Phillip put his head in his hands and massaged his temples. "Senator, I don't know if you can do this. I mean, I've never heard of someone quitting in the middle of their term."

"Ever hear of Nixon?" Kent said, pouring himself some

more scotch. "If a president can resign, a senator can. Pat, what happens if someone dies while they're in office?"

"That—"

"Well, I may as well be dead, because I am at this point incapable of doing the job I was elected to do."

Pat stood up to leave. "All right, Senator. I'll go home and draft a statement. My suggestion is to call a press conference so you can handle it all at one time. But I hope my phone rings sometime tonight and you're on the other end telling me you've changed your mind."

"Don't hold your breath," Kent said softly.

Pat closed the front door behind him, leaving Phillip and Kent staring at each other across a half-empty bottle of Johnnie Walker.

"So what are you going to do, Senator?"

"You mean with the rest of my life? I don't know. Move out of Washington, I would guess. Maybe I'll buy a boat and sail around for a few years."

The idea sounded appealing to him when he heard himself say it—measuring hours by the ebb and flow of the water beneath him, and days by the passage of the sun as it traveled across the sky.

"And where does Cecilia fit in?" Phillip asked.

"Good question. I don't know, really. I suppose I'll have to figure that out, won't I?"

It was midnight when Kent walked upstairs to the bedroom. His footsteps echoed in the house, bouncing off the walls and rattling the silence.

He got into the side of the bed he always slept in, just as he would if Cecilia were there. But the thin sound of his own breath rising and falling in the darkness testified to her absence.

He slid his leg across the bed; the sheets on the other side were cold as frost. He knew he was alone, but he didn't feel alone. He held his breath for a moment and listened. Nothing but silence answered him. But he knew there were ghosts in the bed and ghosts huddled along the edges of the ceiling. They were tricking him by holding their breath when he held his. As soon as he slept, they would drift over him, their white filmy arms brushing his face.

The clock read two fifty-eight—an hour that should cradle only the sleeping. But he couldn't close his eyes. They were waiting for him to do just that so they could swim out from their hiding places and encircle him, their ashen breath blowing over him like snow flurries and their laughter scratching his skin like splinters.

32

*D*ARREN WAS IN LAWSON'S KITCHEN COOKING DINNER
for them. She had convinced him to give his cook an
extra night off so she could have the kitchen all to herself. She
poured tomato sauce over spinach fettuccine and stirred in slivers
of tofu, which she hoped Lawson would mistake for cheese.

It was six-thirty and she could hear the news blaring from
the television in the den. Lawson's hearing had gotten worse
lately, and he was constantly turning up the volume on everything. She tried to ignore the news that was filtering through the
house. The war in Nicaragua was escalating and she had little
doubt that, before long, it would be a declared war. But her baby
was due soon, and she had become aware of how the child's
movements changed whenever she got upset or angry. So she had
made an effort lately to remove herself from news that she knew
would be upsetting.

She had started to redecorate the spare bedroom for the baby. The walls had been painted a pale shade of lavender—like the sky just before dawn—and she was planning to have faint white clouds airbrushed on the ceiling. The color of the room was soothing; it made her think of early-winter mornings and soft, pink suns. The clouds would give the illusion that there was no ceiling there, just sky. Children had a right to see horizons laced with gentle, muted colors even though the world outside would quickly instruct them that reality is rarely so sweet.

It was hard for her to sleep now. The pressure of the child filling up her body and the frequent kicking that she'd never quite got used to made her nights restless. Often she would wander through the house, wading through the shadows that bathed the floor. She would end up in the baby's room. There was a crib, which Lawson had insisted on buying for her, and she knew if she hadn't let him he would have interpreted it as a sign that she hadn't forgiven him. The only other furniture was a rocking chair and a small white chest of drawers on which Darren had painted some rabbits and cows. The rocking chair was a tight squeeze for her now, so she would sit on the floor and watch night move through the room. Peanut would wake up, notice her absence, and walk sleepily down the hall and into the room where she would curl up, perfectly content to sleep there if that's where Darren wanted to be.

She was stirring fresh basil leaves into the pasta when she heard Lawson yelling for her. As she ran out of the kitchen, she heard the wooden spoon clatter to the floor. If Lawson had fallen and was hurt, she didn't know if she'd be able to move him. But when she got to the den, he was sitting on the couch, leaning forward toward the television.

"Senator Janes's wife—" he said, and then stopped to listen to the newscaster.

Darren sat down beside him and listened to the rest of the report. Cecilia Janes was in stable condition after her attempted suicide late last night. She had been ill for quite a while, but it was unknown if that was the reason she had tried to take her own life.

Darren slipped her arm through Lawson's and slid closer to him.

"There has been no comment as yet from Senator Janes," the newscaster continued, "but there is speculation that he will resign his Senate seat."

Darren shook her head slowly. "They got all of us, didn't they?" she said in a soft voice. "We all walked into the same trap from different directions and for different reasons. But we've all ended up wounded."

"Maybe you should call him," Lawson said.

She had told him, finally, about Kent, mostly because it made Lawson feel better that she, too, had kept something from him.

"I don't think so. I'd have to go through secretaries and that might cause more problems for him."

She wondered if Cecilia's thwarted suicide had been a real attempt to die or just a play for attention. When Darren was in grade school, one of her classmates was the daughter of a famous actress who was as well known for her suicide attempts as she was for her movie roles. Finally, the girl had caught on to the real design behind her mother's botched attempts to die and suggested that, if she truly wanted to die, she might try slicing the vein lengthwise rather than across.

As she went back into the kitchen, Darren thought that Kent might well be the most wounded of all of them, the one who had suffered the most by trying to expose what he knew to be the truth.

33

*K*ENT STARED OUT THE WINDOW AT THE ICE-BLUE SKY. THE sun was doing nothing to thaw the below-freezing temperatures. The ground was hard and covered with frost, and the trees looked like dark, skeletal arms reaching for a sky that had forgotten them.

He had gone upstairs to the bedroom to see if Cecilia was awake but, not surprisingly, she was asleep. She slept almost all the time now—a poor substitute for death but, for the moment, the only alternative she had. She never complained anymore about daylight streaming in through the window; she didn't even seem to notice it. She had managed to remain in a world far away from her surroundings, a world that was nothing more than a shadow play of faint memories and whitewashed thoughts.

Kent did little with his time. He took long walks through the bitter cold days, and at night he sank into the darkness as though

257

he were falling to the bottom of a deep river. The phone almost never rang, and if it did it was usually one of Cecilia's doctors. That was the way it always was, he thought. The world goes on without you, as though you were never even there.

Occasionally, he and Cecilia spoke to each other, but the words that passed between them were quick and barely audible, like the muffled greetings of strangers who scrape by each other on a busy street.

He sat on the edge of the bed watching his wife. He thought of waking her and asking if she'd like some dinner. It was late afternoon, and the dark came quickly these days. He had let Jessica go; there was no point in having her around. He had nothing else to do with his time but sweep the floor and cook an occasional meal.

The light started to change outside the window, and Kent saw a shadow slide across the pillow, lingering on Cecilia's face for a second before it moved on. He decided to let her sleep. Why bring her back to a world she had grown to hate? He looked outside again and saw a bird sailing through the still air. He thought of all the small, winged creatures who have no place to go when the sky turns against them . . . and he thought of Cecilia.

The president was due to make a televised announcement in a few minutes and Kent planned to watch it, although he already knew what he would hear. He went back downstairs and fixed a cup of instant coffee. The breakfast dishes were still in the sink and he had forgotten to put the butter back in the refrigerator. It had softened into a shapeless yellow lump.

By the time he fixed his coffee and turned on the television, the president's speech had already started. His face filled the screen, and it looked somber and drawn; Kent thought he saw his hands trembling as they held the pages of the prepared text, but he wasn't sure.

". . . and this is a very grave situation," the president was saying. "No president can or should make these decisions lightly, and I can assure you that I have not done so. There has not been a night that I have not lost sleep weighing the seriousness of my decision. But the fact is that Americans have been killed in Nicaragua by a regime that is openly hostile to us and has made no effort to conceal that hostility. And the fact is, also, that the Sandinistas are a threat to all freedom-loving people in this hemisphere. Therefore, I know I will have the support of you, the American people, in asking Congress for a declaration of war."

Kent turned off the television; he'd heard enough. It was inevitable, he knew that. It was a plan that had been waiting in the wings for years, and plans like that do not just go away.

The room was almost dark now, but he didn't bother to close the drapes or turn on any lights. Cecilia had been right all along—the night was a much better place than daylight.

He walked slowly upstairs; some of the stairs creaked under the weight of his feet. He leaned over Cecilia to see if she was still breathing, always expecting to come in sometime and find that she'd willed her breath to stop. When he undressed and got into bed beside her, he moved closer to her than he had in years. He wished he could tell her that he finally understood. He finally knew how it felt to want to spin out into darkness, away from life and light and time.

Kent could hear, gathering in the blackness, the echoes of all the people he had failed. They were the ghosts who would come for him, but he wasn't frightened anymore. The sound swelled and filled his head, and he could feel them opening the walls, letting cold, snowy wind into the room.

He shivered and pulled the darkness over him like a blanket . . . and waited.

34

"*D*ID I TELL YOU I CALLED KENT JANES AFTER HIS AN-nouncement?" Sean asked as he carried one of Darren's paintings out to her car. A gallery in Venice was going to display her series of self-portraits, and she had to have them there that day.

"No, you must have conveniently forgotten to mention it." She leaned against the car and felt the sun seep through her sweater and press against her skin. It was a winter sun, so she didn't mind; its heat felt easy and light.

"I just thought he'd like to hear a kind word from some-body, Darren. I said I was calling for both of us." He opened the doors of his van and slid one of her paintings in. "Your car's full. I'll take the rest and follow you there."

As she drove toward Venice, keeping Sean in her rearview mirror, Darren wondered if she should have contacted Kent. Sean was probably right; he needed kind words.

After they dropped her paintings off, Darren coaxed Sean into going on a hike with her. They drove up to Will Rogers Park, the clear winter air shimmering around them and a cold breeze hurrying through the eucalyptus.

Because Darren sometimes had trouble catching her breath, they stayed on the main trail and avoided the narrow, steep paths that threaded through the mountains. With Peanut leaving a trail of dust ahead of them and Sean's footsteps falling softly beside her, Darren realized how comfortable his presence had become. It was as easy being quiet with him as it was exchanging words.

The trail ended at the top of the hill, Inspiration Point, with a cleared area with a bench in the middle for hikers to sit and look out across Santa Monica to the sea. They had the hilltop to themselves today, and it was clear enough to see Catalina in the distance. A single cloud floated above the horizon.

"Darren," Sean began, and she knew he was about to ask something that had been on his mind for a while, "you haven't taken any childbirth classes, have you? You've never mentioned anything about it."

"No, I think that's something you're supposed to do as a couple. I might feel a little out of place."

He stared at her, running his response through his mind before committing it to words. Darren could always tell when he was doing that; a tiny wrinkle would form between his eyebrows.

"I'll go with you," he said finally. "When I get back."

"Sean, that's really sweet, but you don't have to. I've read some books. I'll be fine. Back from where? You sort of snuck that in there, didn't you?"

"Nicaragua."

"I guess I should have been expecting that."

"But I won't be gone very long, not this time, anyway. I'll be back in a few days and I could go to some classes with you."

"Sean, why do you want to do this?"

"You really make things difficult sometimes, Darren. Because I care about you and because I don't want you driving yourself to the hospital while you're in labor, which, knowing you, is exactly what you'd do. And because"—he paused and stared at the ground for a few seconds—"because if I share that experience with you, I've shared something really special in your life. It's like a bond, you know?"

Darren let her eyes wander from the scrub-covered hills to the distance, where white buildings were catching the last rays of afternoon sun. She couldn't look at Sean. She had spent months becoming accustomed to living alone, and now she had discovered that she liked the idea of raising her child by herself. Sean was telling her he wanted to share a corner of the world she had designed to include only herself, her child, and her dog.

After scanning the entire skyline several times, she turned back to him.

"I don't know if I want to be any more bonded than we already are. It always turns out badly. You get close to someone and they leave, or die, or disappoint you."

"So, what are you doing to do about your child?" Sean said. "Keep things at arm's distance?"

"That's a cheap shot, Trudell. Of course not. That's a different situation."

"OK, I apologize. But you can't play it safe all your life, Darren. I won't bring it up again, but just think about it once in a while. And please, promise me you won't drive yourself to the hospital."

Daylight was leaving the hills when they walked back down. A deer bounded across the road in front of them and Peanut stopped and stared as if she had just seen a vision. Far away, the sun was dripping gold into the sea and, above them, the edges of the sky were tinged with purple.

Darren thought of all the sunsets she had watched with Andrew, and from behind her, a ribbon of wind touched her cheek and slipped across her mouth.

262